six feet over it

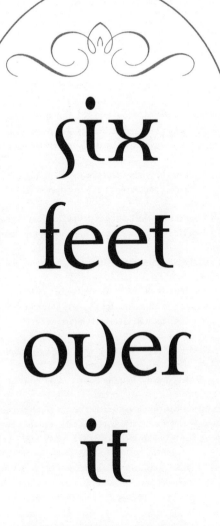

six feet over it

Jennifer Longo

RANDOM HOUSE  NEW YORK

Text copyright © 2014 by Jennifer Longo
Jacket photograph by Cusp/SuperStock

All rights reserved. Published in the United States by Random House Children's Books, a division of Random House LLC, a Penguin Random House Company, New York.

Random House and the colophon are registered trademarks of Random House LLC.

Visit us on the Web! randomhouse.com/teens
Educators and librarians, for a variety of teaching tools,
visit us at RHTeachersLibrarians.com

Library of Congress Cataloging-in-Publication Data
Longo, Jennifer.
Six feet over it / Jennifer Longo.—First edition.
p. cm.
Summary: When fifteen-year-old Leigh's father buys a graveyard and insists she work there after school, she learns much about life, death, and the power of friendship.
ISBN 978-0-449-81871-8 (trade)—ISBN 978-0-449-81872-5 (lib. bdg.)—
ISBN 978-0-449-81873-2 (ebook)
[1. Cemeteries—Fiction. 2. Family life—California—Fiction. 3. Friendship—Fiction.
4. Death—Fiction. 5. California—Fiction.] I. Title.
PZ7.L8634Six 2014 [Fic]—dc23 2013026249

Printed in the United States of America

10 9 8 7 6 5 4 3 2 1

First Edition

Random House Children's Books supports the First Amendment
and celebrates the right to read.

For Cordelia,
all in the world

There is a land of the living and a land of the dead and the bridge is love, the only survival, the only meaning.

—THORNTON WILDER, *The Bridge of San Luis Rey*

six
feet
over
it

prologue

FOR THE BODY you go to the mortuary. A lot of people don't know this. Kids at school don't know this. They think bodies come to us. They also think we're out here at dusk with a pickax and a kerosene lantern, digging graves with a shovel, rotting, moonlit hands reaching from the upturned earth to pull us down with them. So dumb. Digging a grave really requires a backhoe, not just a shovel, and also we never see bodies, dead or undead. By the time we get them they're drained and dressed or burned, in a box and ready to be buried. It's just a cemetery. We're not living in the "Thriller" video.

What's worse is when actual customers don't get that bodies aren't our thing. It's so bad. Awful. Why doesn't anyone tell them how to do it? The logistics? All we do is graves. That's it. Well, and headstones. But they're pretty much part and parcel, so same diff.

Now the Pre-Needs, they know what's up. They bought their graves a long time ago, before they needed them. But everyone else—I can't blame them for not knowing because months ago I had no idea either. I have to remember to be patient, because for crying out loud they're here on sometimes the worst day of their lives. But then what do I know? I'm just a fourteen-year-old girl in jeans and a T-shirt trying to sell some graves, which—it's just stupid. It looks stupid. I know this, Wade knows this, everyone knows this. It's a really classy way to run a business, making your teenaged daughter sell graves because you're too lazy to look farther than across the dinner table when searching for employees, but that's Wade. No corner is too sacred to cut.

We all pretend it's okay I'm shoving my algebra homework aside to make room for the headstone brochures, the maps showing where to find the best grave sites . . . away from the road, something with a view, maybe near a tree? People and their trees.

A few months and it feels like forever. A few months since we left the ocean, and sitting here with all these dead people has made me a world-weary curmudgeon; everything bugs the crap out of me. I'm turning into Wade. Tall, dark, and probably twice as ridiculous.

"Ever think you'd get to live in a *park*?" Wade sighs dreamily every ten minutes or so.

A park. Drop that qualifying *memorial* and it's more than just a creepy euphemism. It is Wade's loving tribute to his greatest real estate conquest ever, his golden ticket away from the drudgery of years in a cramped Re/Max office cubicle. Here he has his very own sovereignty, a million tiny little plots of land to sell. Buying this thing has given him an enviable joie de vivre that in virtually any other situation (i.e., one not involving hundreds of dead bodies) might have been infectious. He is King of the Hill. Sierrawood Hill(s).

I only have to hold down the office fort three days a week, a blessing owing more to Wade's lack of scheduling prowess than to any actual parental concern, even with my begging him to take it down closer to zero. When enlisting my heretofore-untapped grave-selling skills, he got me for a bargain: five dollars an hour, cash under the table of course, me being underage and super underenthused. Before I had a chance to turn him down, Wade let me know it wasn't so much an *offer* as it was a *requirement* that I wasn't *allowed* to turn down.

"An after-school job builds character!" he declared. "Any kid would be lucky to have this chance! Couple hours after school in your very own office"—says the guy who hated being in an office so much he's making his family live in a *graveyard*—"*and* you're getting *paid*? It's icing on the cake!"

"I don't want cake," I whispered.

"Leigh. *Leigh*. We need you. I need your help."

A Sasquatch sighting of his actual sincerity and desperation. Unfair.

"Please?" I begged. "*Please*."

He gave me maybe half a second.

"No one's asking you to wrestle a bobcat in a phone booth; just sell a few graves and call it a day, jeez! Don't be so dramatic. You love it!" No one loves real-time revisionist history more than Wade.

3

I love it.

Done.

My job training three months ago was twenty minutes of Wade giving me the lowdown on his way to lunch one afternoon. The whole operation basically involves binders. Two three-ring binders: one holds the maps of each section's graves, decades of names written in corresponding representative rectangles, and the other features general section maps of the entire park: *Harmony Haven, Memory Meadow, Vaunted Valley.* Seven sections in all, each one titled like a Lifetime original movie. Standard burials can be single-spaced, double-spaced (side by side, popular with spouses and siblings), or single or double depth (just what it sounds like). Cremains go in small drawers or in containers in the ground.

The mausoleum is a hulking white building made of drawers of caskets, each with a bronze plaque and a bud vase. People come to visit these drawers and tape notes to them, photographs, haiku about loneliness and circling birds.

Headstone orders are easy, just checking boxes, filling in forms. There are plenty of brochures and catalogs featuring lots of styles of granite and marble and bronze and examples of engraving details for people to browse through. Flowers. Birds. Tractors.

Beneath the pile of catalogs, Howard the County Coroner's business card is taped eerily to the desk. "Just in case," Wade likes to say.

In case *what?* Cripes.

Howard and his secretary, Terry, are both middle-aged and very patient on the phone, the only kind of contact I've had with them. I also only phone-know Dave, the go-to Baskerville Headstone guy in North Carolina (who keeps calling me *Lay* no matter how many times I tell him my name is pronounced *Lee* and if he doesn't knock it off I'm going to start calling him *Deev*), and Jason, the super matter-of-fact mortician over at Chapel of the Pines who is only twenty-eight years old and according to Wade wears a ton of hair gel and became a mortician on purpose just to piss off his orthodontist father. All these guys, like the grave-buying clientele so far, clearly couldn't care less about my probably illegal plot selling. Apparently this backwoods inland Northern California town ("Hangtown," a sentimental homage to all the gold rush vigilante hangings committed here) has retained its devil-may-care-but-we-sure-as-hell-don't attitude regarding things like adherence to child labor laws. Maybe I'll report myself.

I am allowed to clock out (read: write my hours on a Post-it) and lock the office door at six p.m., which sucks now that it's autumn and the sun's gone so early. Because, three months to get used to it notwithstanding, who wants to go traipsing through a bunch of graves in the dark? *A park, a park, just a park.* I whisper this mantra as I wend my anxious way around and over the people beneath my feet in the damp green hills, down into Peaceful Glen and onto the narrow dirt road that goes beyond the mausoleum and past the tin toolshed. Past stacks of cement grave liners perched precariously atop one another in lopsided piles. Past a silver single-wide trailer reflecting the very last, low sunlight through black silhouettes of pine branches.

Until I reach a line of flat headstones. Headstones with mistakes etched into them: misspelled names, wrong birth or death date. Wade, never one to waste good granite (or miss an opportunity to be regarded as clever), has taken all these "mistake stones" and laid them in a snaking path through our yard, straight to the front door of *our house*. He has demonstrated rare restraint in turning them text-side down. They gleam, cool and sleekly polished, beside more grave liners, filled not with people but with soil and sprouting geraniums and marigolds, hearty annuals and perennials that don't mind blooming in boxes normally found down in a grave with a casket nestled inside, one more barrier between the body and the earth to which it is supposedly returning.

The headstone path, the caskets in the garden—over the past five months Wade has continued to muddy the line between the graveyard and the house a little more every day. Because he thinks it is funny. Because death is hilarious. And *I love it.*

part one

PRE-NEED

one

I WAS BORN DEAD. Or died shortly after—Meredith's story changes depending on her audience and her mood. "The first thing Leigh did after she was born was *die!*" she loves bragging to people, working her well-worn "tragedy + more tragedy = comedy" routine. And yes, I was born nearly three months early—a two-and-a-half-pound "micro preemie"— but I have since learned from watching medical dramas that premature babies flatline all the time, and these days reviving them is really no big whup. Wade says it's just bravado masking Meredith's injured maternal pride over how I subsequently lived—*thrived*—without the protection of her womb, but most parents wouldn't drag that chestnut out for laughs. Makes me cringe.

"Oh, *Leigh*," she and Wade constantly moan. "Don't be so dramatic, my God!"

If my eyes so much as mist up, get a little dewy over *any*thing—epic Wade and Meredith eye rolling. Sighs are heaved. A person lucky enough to be brought back from a birth/death and go on to enjoy freakishly perfect health has nothing to cry about.

They buy graveyards on the sly and perform stand-up comedy routines about their kid's near death and *I'm* dramatic?

I don't remember when I started calling them Wade and Meredith.

So here we are. I am. Non-selling days I walk home as fast as I can from school, step on every crack I see. No, living here is not technically Meredith's fault; Wade bought the grave-yard without even telling her, saw a classified ad—*Graveyard for Sale*—and signed mortgage papers she never even saw. But still—come *on*.

I keep my eyes down all the way to Sierrawood, through our out-of-control Gothic black wrought-iron entrance gates, yet another genius Wade idea. They're just stupid. Every single time I look at them, I think, "Last night I dreamt I went to Manderley again . . ." and I'm in a Daphne du Maurier novel, alone behind the gates of a creepy estate coincidentally also presided over by a ridiculous man. Huh.

Just inside the Manderley gates, ducks paddle in a pond, beside which is a wooden sign, small and low to the ground, that reads: THIS IS A NON-ENDOWMENT CARE FACILITY. *Non-endowment*, according to Wade, means the families don't pay extra into funds to maintain the graves; therefore everyone should be grateful he even gases up the mower and runs it at all. A little farther past the pond, another very small, care-fully hand-printed sign reads: ALL FLOWERS, ARTIFICIAL AND

REAL, WILL BE REMOVED ON TUESDAYS TO FACILITATE MOWING. Which everyone knows is a big joke—people are figuring out pretty quickly that most of the signage around Sierrawood, like Wade himself, is all talk, no action. GATES CLOSED AT DUSK? If we remember. NO MUSIC ALLOWED? Tell that to Mrs. Irvin, who hauls a boom box over to J 72 in Peaceful Glen so she can blast the sound track of the Broadway show *Carousel* for her sister week after week. Even with Wade's mower running and my headphones on, every Wednesday I can hear Shirley Jones hollering about having "a real nice clambake."

With all my attention concentrated on the gravel road beneath my feet, I pretend the graves away. Most of the headstones are flat, so if I squint it's *just a house, just a nice house near a nice park, just a park.* But on digging days the pretense dissolves as I run to the house, my heavy backpack beating me senseless, away from the backhoe and the pile of soil beside it, Jimmy the contracted grave digger leaning casually on his shovel.

Today is an office day, Wednesday, so I do not run. I trudge from school, moving especially slowly so that I miss Real Nice Clambake. She honks and waves on her way out as we pass through the Manderleys. In the office, I toss my backpack beneath the desk and shove the dusty stack of back issues of *Mortuary Monthly* magazine to the floor. (Why do we continue to get this thing? We're not a mortuary! I've called them twice to cancel already.) This stupid brown cave. Tiny building beside the pond, the hills of graves rising all around it. There are windows on every wall, large and well positioned for crow's-nest-type spying, but the dark wood paneling, matted brown shag rug, and black vinyl wingback chairs seem to suck the light right out. Like the clientele aren't depressed enough. The shag and walls are gummy with residual pipe smoke from the previous owner, who sat in here puffing for fifty-three years before selling Sierrawood to Wade and packing his pipe off to Maui. Who in the world who isn't a British detective smokes a pipe? People who own graveyards, apparently. I bet he wore a monocle, too. The smell makes my head hurt.

I prop the door open and heave the ginormous English lit book we've been assigned onto the funeral-scheduling desk calendar.

The heartsick Ceres seeks her daughter / She searches every land, all waves and waters.

Okay. Here's the thing about Ovid, about *Metamorphoses*: I do *get* it—Troy falls, Rome rises. The universal principle, nothing is permanent, everything changes, anything, any*one* you may have to hold on to, take comfort or care from, will leave. Die. Which is awesome. But then really, Ovid? You need fifteen books of narrative poetry to present this worn-out thesis? *That* I don't get. Beauty for beauty's sake, Mrs. McKinstry says, and we're not reading all fifteen books, just the greatest hits, so count your blessings. Keep reading. She keeps quizzing.

Through the open windows I hear the sound of tires on the drive. My hands go damp—*Not today, just let me sit here with Ovid, please oh please*—and thank God it's not a customer, just the flower van. *Rivendell Nursery.* They seem to be

Sierrawood's number one provider of beauty-queen-contestant-sashed wreaths. *Mother. In Memoriam. Miss Sierrawood Hills.* A lady brings them, and she also does weekly and monthly bouquets for out-of-town relatives and infirm or lazy local family members. Birthdays, holidays. Paying a stranger to visit your dearly departed seems sort of beside the point, but whatever.

The van passes the pond, and halfway up Poppy Hill the lady hops out wearing denim overalls; her hair is tied in a knot on top of her head and she lugs heavy baskets of uninspired calla lilies across the grass. But then someone else climbs out the back of the van.

Emily.

My only friend, left behind at the ocean. Months since I've seen her and I thought she was gone forever, but now here she is.

Emily?

No. My brain loves to turn every small, dark-haired girl I see into Emily, but no. This girl is maybe a little taller, and she's out there wearing a dress—a *dress*, for crying out loud—and tall black boots. She runs to help with the lilies. She heaves armloads of arrangements and potted plants, refers to a list, searches for headstones, places blossoms and baskets. That dress is going to get filthy.

Just some girl.

Not Emily.

I salt the wound, pick up the phone receiver. Dial Emily's Mendocino house.

The number you have reached . . .

Same as the last hundred times I tried. Why do I do it to myself?

Back to Ovid.

Chill October air moves through the window and the open door, swings the dust and stale pipe residue around my head full of Ceres searching for her daughter and a sound track of ducks quacking beneath the willows.

"Hello?"

I slam my hand into hardback Ovid, startled. In the doorway, Dress and Boots Girl winces.

"Oh God, sorry! Sorry!"

I rub my red knuckles and she steps in.

"Are you okay? Can I . . ."

"No, it's fine, it's . . . okay." I squeeze my pink fingers, push Ovid aside.

Not Emily. Younger than me. Small. The knots of her dark hair are braided, wound and pinned above each ear. Her dress is cotton, pale blue stripes, and she has a white soil-stained apron tied around her waist. The black boots are leather, tall as her knobby knees. She should be herding Alpine goats. Instead, she's just standing here smiling, shifting her weight. Maybe she has to pee.

"Can I help you with something?"

She turns her head sideways, reads the *Metamorphoses* spine.

"Are you reading that?"

I shrug.

"For *fun*?"

"School."

She nods. "What do you think?"

"Um." *Why does she care?* "Kind of depressing."

"Sure."

"And wordy."

She smiles. "Yeah."

"And he doesn't seem to think much of the ladies."

She leans against the desk. "How so?"

Uh. Okay, Mrs. McKinstry. I guess we're doing this.

"Well," I say, "he's no fan of subtlety. His women are wallowing in grief and then—oh, look out, literal metamorphosis!—all of a sudden they're mute. Or petrified, or turned into gold. Or a cow."

She laughs. "You're so right."

Her laugh is not Emily's, not bright and big. This girl's is . . . lighter? Smaller.

"Okay," she says, "but don't you love the *comfort* of it?"

Clearly she has read it for fun. "The what?"

"Well, I mean the whole thing that it's always been this way, it always will be, nothing is static, life is cyclical, no one ever really leaves. . . . It's very . . . I don't know. I love it."

"Guess I'm not to the comfort part yet. People are still just . . ."

"Dying," she says. "Yeah."

She goes back to smiling.

"So," I say again, "is there something I can—"

"Oh! Sorry, yes . . ." She hands me her list. "We've lost

track of this guy." Single depth in Serenity. "He's new to us, maybe we got the row wrong?"

I nod, pull out the binders.

"Rockin' the old school?" she says.

I frown, puzzled.

She nods at Pipey's ancient binders. "No computer?"

I tap the landline phone with my pen. "Just upgraded from rotary. Pretty sure the binders are here to stay."

"Oh my gosh," she says, "my parents are practically Amish. Cell phones give you neck cancer, no TV because it murders your brain, and *computers* . . . People are so mad we don't have a website to order from, but my dad is terrified, he's all, 'Computers have three purposes: porn, fifteen million ways for people to steal your identity, and government spying.'"

Sounds a lot like Wade's asinine logic, except in our case there's also the part about having no money. Which I don't mention.

Hangtown is a black hole for cell service, so I don't actually mind the landlines. We had a computer in Mendocino, but Wade opened some Trojan horse thing, janked it up with a virus too expensive to fix so he turned it off . . . and just didn't ever turn it back on again. His current gospel runs the way of "If binders were good enough for Pipey, they're good enough for us!"

The girl lingers in the doorway. "Otherwise things going well?"

I turn the stiff pages of maps. Where is this guy?

"Hasn't been long, right?" she says. "Few months?"

I nod.

"We were kind of friends with the Hoegreffs before they sold it. I haven't met—is it your dad?"

I nod.

"Oh, so that's fun. Family business!"

I feel myself visibly blanch.

"Well, not *fun*, I just mean . . . like, we have the nursery, my parents . . ." She waves at Overalls Mom, at the van out in the graves. "So I work with them instead of having to get a job at a . . . like, a taco shack or something."

Taco shack?

"I was gone most of the summer, Habitat for Humanity internship, so now I can build anything you want with a drill and some drywall, no joke. And I'm normally only on morning deliveries when I guess you've been in school, so it's . . . We've been ships passing in the night! But my mom told me she's seen you. My stupid brother's at space camp all week, so I'm filling in for him and . . . I'm just really happy to finally meet you. I'm Elanor." She extends a small, pale hand. I scribble *row M, space 81* on her list and draw a little map. Put it in her open hand. She folds it into her apron pocket.

I should say my name. Introduce myself.

"Well. Thanks," she says. "Sorry I scared you."

I shrug.

She leans back in the doorway.

"Smells okay in here. Better. The Hoegreffs were nice but that pipe was out of control."

I nod.

"Okay," she says. "Maybe I'll see you later? Are you here a lot? Like a schedule?"

I nod.

Cold air swirls around her in the open doorway.

She pulls the list from her pocket, memorizes the plot number. "Thanks again." She jogs back through the graves.

I watch her find the space I've mapped, watch her mother fill the flower can with late-season imported daffodils—*expensive!*—and then watch as they turn the van around and head back out through the Manderleys.

The side of the van reads: SERVING HANGTOWN—AND THE SHIRE—SINCE 1958. What on earth is "the Shire"? And how is she here in the morning—doesn't she go to school? Not the high school anyway; there is only one in this town and I would not have missed so close an Emily doppelgänger, not noticed that Princess Leia hair.

I'm so tired.

She talks so much.

But smart.

Like Emily. Too much.

Out my spying windows, I watch the ducks float aimlessly. The plain brown female ambles from the murk and takes a stroll through the babies' headstones, the small section of lawn reserved just for infants and children, a little graveyard day care. The worst. People's kids. That duck is stupid.

Despite Wade's piecrust promise of "Jeez Louise, that'll never happen on your shift, it's all Pre-Need, old people dying in their sleep, don't worry about it!" it's already happened once.

A kid from school. A couple of years older. I didn't know him, but he was an idiot. I know this because he died driving drunk with a drunk bunch of other idiots, but still, how much did that suck for his parents to have to come here and buy his grave from some random kid younger than their dead son? Sixteen used to seem so old to me.

The duck strolls from the babies' graves and nearly gets hit by a truck coming fast, gravel pinging the Manderleys. It parks at the office door.

Oh, man.

I almost wish the Rivendell van would come back.

Two men climb from the truck, shuffle in, sit heavily before me, and one of them says, "I need to bury my boy." Then he huddles over his lap and begins to sob while I fantasize about other after-school jobs I would rather have.

That duck has cursed me.

This is At Need. At the Time of Need. It will be a single grave, single depth. The father chooses a bronze headstone that will be etched with the boy's name, birth and death dates, and kind of a dumb poem the boy wrote last year, which at the time may have held no more significance than the obligatory fulfillment of a lame homework assignment but is now imbued with a sincere reverence. The boy is ten years old. Was.

Okay. *This* is the worst. Somewhere in the middle: old enough for people to really get to know him, young enough to not be a drunk-driving idiot.

While the men are occupied with their crying, I reach quietly into the bottom left-hand desk drawer where I keep my secret At Need stash of York Peppermint Patties and manage to get a fistful of them discreetly unwrapped and into my mouth. Desperate times.

The father and the other guy, the helper, go through the last half of the office box of Kleenex. It is a cube-shaped box with vivid sunset scenes, red and deepest orange on all four sides, black silhouettes of birds taking flight. There are about a hundred more just like it in the supply closet. I make a mental note to ask Wade about getting some less depressing tissue boxes. My God.

Being a witness to people's unyielding anguish feels so intrusive, but lately I have had some measure of success avoiding sponging their agony and giving myself the voyeurism creeps by focusing on things like making guesses at the headstone choice (mostly granite) and being really detailed about the paperwork. I tend to offer tissues with my left hand, my right hand busy filling out forms and arranging graveside services. I keep the men talking, which suspends the crying and keeps things moving, because the sooner I can get them filled out, scheduled, and paid, the sooner they can go home and I can get back to Ovid. Because I have a quiz tomorrow.

And now the thing I almost hate the most: The Walk. To find a nice grave site. Between the stones, beneath what feels like millions of tall pines, I take shallow breaths, wipe my sweaty palms on my jeans, and keep my eyes straight ahead, never on the stones. I concentrate *hard* on getting this part over with, give the men general suggestions with the maps and my own personal opinion; for example, Sierra Sunset is badly named, as it faces east. (Everyone involved at the time knew this, but once he gets his mind made up, you can't tell Wade anything.) Poppy Hill. Peaceful Glen. Serenity Valley.

Eventually it is decided that the ten-year-old will be taking his final rest in row M, space 22, halfway up Sunny Hill. (Perpetually shady. Seriously, Wade.) It has a decent view of the duck pond and is near enough to the gravel path that the grandparents can make the hike when they come visit, which even after just four months on the job I can tell you with absolute certainty they will. Maybe daily at first. They will hang wind chimes in the trees and cheap made-in-China dream catchers bought at Longs Drugs, which bear no resemblance to the actual Native American totems they are impersonating. They will heap the grave with flowers and letters and helium balloons, Monopoly boards open and set up for play, the top hat resting forever on Free Parking, ceramic bears with ceramic tears and sad faces who hold up signs reading "I Wuv You" and "Miss You Tons!" as if the kid has gone away to be a foreign exchange student for a semester instead of having died quickly but horribly from some ridiculous bone cancer they never even knew he had until a month before he died.

At Need.

They will picnic on the grave and talk to it, and after a couple of months they will come every week, then every six weeks, then every holiday, then probably only every Christmas or birthday, and after a while it will just be a grave.

At last we are back in the office.

In my book of maps, I fill in the boy's name on the little

rectangle representing his buried casket. I write in careful block print, in pencil, in case they change their minds. I double-check my math, and then the most gruesome part of all: I announce the total cost. I explain payment-plan options and full payment discounts. Nearly two dozen graves I've sold, mostly Pre-Need but even then it turns my stomach and feels remarkably like collecting school fund-raising walkathon pledges. The embarrassment of asking neighbors for donations in the first place, then the humiliation of knocking on doors to inform Mrs. Nerwinski: *I walked three and a half miles, and according to your generous pledge of seventy-five cents per mile, that comes to a total of* . . . "Two thousand, seven hundred dollars." Standard lawn grave, At Need, single depth, cement liner, midweek graveside service, *Wednesday's Child Is Full of Woe,* and the bronze headstone with five super-expensive extra lines of engraving. Dumb poem.

Thankfully, the helper simply pulls out a checkbook and writes a check for the entire amount. I accept it gratefully, my head ducked in humility. *Thank you so much, Mrs. Nerwinski. I can assure you the entire student body really appreciates this. We'll definitely think of you every time we have an assembly in our new multipurpose room.*

They stand, and I stand. We shake hands. I step outside to watch them drive away past the Manderleys. In the pond the ducks glide, carving dark paths through moss clinging to water lilies. The sky is a million shades of deepening blue.

No one else comes in the rest of the afternoon, alive or dead. Not even close to being six, but the office is getting me down today. Could be the Emily-not-Emily girl. Or the tissue box. Or the dead ten-year-old. I drop Ovid into my backpack, unwrap two or ten Yorks for the walk to the house, and lock the door. If Wade docks my pay, I'll throw him a parade. The stupid icing-on-the-cake money mortifies me. It only encourages the lie that my being here is an actual choice, but he insists I take the money, says he'll get in trouble if I don't. Likely. Every Friday I toss the cash into a shoe box beneath my bed. I hate it. Even though secretly I am beginning to appreciate the fact that it could eliminate the need to ever ask him and Meredith for things like school lunch money or field trip fees, conversations routinely more painful than asking a client if they'd prefer to be on top or beneath their loved one in the event of a double-depth grave.

I hurry, eyes down, over the graves, through the trees—

"Leigh!"

Nearly to the house—

"*Hey!*"

Crap.

"Who's chasing you?" Wade sticks his head out a window of the single-wide he keeps behind the mausoleum and the toolshed, metal siding glowing orange beneath the pines in the late-afternoon sun. This Shangri-la is being prepared for the arrival of an actual employee to replace contracted Jimmy, some unwitting person Wade plans on drugging or otherwise tricking into digging graves under the guise of "park maintenance." He hopes to Arnold Palmer the situation by having the person live here, in the trailer: on hand for maintenance emergencies *and* providing what Wade refers to as "an extra measure of security." Two in one!

Security against *what*, I'd like to know.

Wade is only resorting to this expense because after months of half-assing the running of the place with only my indentured servitude, he's admitted at last that he's going to need more help to half-ass it properly. All this time he's been learning the lessons of: customers do not cotton well to graves dug in the wrong plots, or funerals double-booked or not booked at all even though families have shown up, grieving and bearing huge, expensive flower arrangements.

"How was it?" he calls from the trailer.

I shrug.

"Some guy called before—they come in for a kid?"

I nod.

"Where'd they put him?"

"Sunny Hill."

"Aw, jeez! You sure you're pushing Poppy?"

All the sensitivity of a frying pan to the head. He's really into this Poppy Hill/Sunny Hill rivalry; there's more space in Sunny, but he wants to get Poppy completely filled. I've dutifully avoided Sunny as best I can, but sometimes people want what they want. I don't know.

"Well, there's always tomorrow."

I sigh. "Monday, Wednesday, Friday."

He smiles. "Can't blame me for trying."

Oh, really? I want to say. *Because I think I* can. *I can go ahead and blame you for trying to trick your kid into selling graves more days a week than you promised she had to, and for thinking you could do it by betting I won't remember what day of the week it is.*

I wish I was the kind of person who could look his shenanigans in the face and just be all, *No*. A smart person. A brave person. An *Emily* person.

Emily would never have put up with this garbage. She would say right out loud, "There is no way in hell I'm selling graves for you, dude. Do it yourself."

"Hey," Wade pipes up, "how much Spanish do you know?"

"How much *what*?"

"*Español!*"

"Like . . . words?"

Do two months of refried freshman Spanish in Señora Levet's class count? Because so far, mostly we've been memorizing verb conjugation grids, spending our afternoons singing "Parácuaro, Song of My Father," and exchanging *diálogos* such as:

Me: *¿Te gusta musica?*

Ken Dale, my Spanish partner: *Sí, yo prefiero Sade. Mucho gusto "Smooth Operator."*

Me: *Sí. Yo también.*

Ken Dale: *¿Vamos a la playa ahora? ¿O quizás Taco Bell?*

Me: *Bueno! Sí, como no. ¡Vamos!*

I consider my limited vocabulary, my frequent use of *los* when I mean *las,* and my complete lack of interest in why Wade's interested in my language skills.

"Sure," I sigh. "I guess."

"Fantastic!" he practically sings. "¡*Fantastico!* Study hard, I have a feeling it's gonna come in handy. Might be worth a bonus in your paycheck, if you know what I mean."

"No. What?"

"Just what I said!"

"Okay, doesn't 'bonus' mean extra money?"

He winks. "That's right!"

"So . . . extra money, that's *what you mean*."

"Yes!"

"Then what's with the winking? Who doesn't know what 'bonus' means?"

"It's cemetery jargon!"

What? "Bonuses are not cemetery jargon!"

He hangs happily out the trailer window, laughing. Not *at* me—he just loves being the funniest person he's ever met. I start again toward the house.

"Leigh!"

I turn back.

"You around Saturday? First thing?"

"Saturday?"

"Yeah."

"*This* Saturday."

"Yes, keep up! The nursery charges extra for weekend delivery. Help me load the truck—five minutes. Ten, tops."

I drop my backpack. "Saturday."

"*Yes!*"

I pull my ponytail out, wrap the hair tie around my wrist.

"I guess I could ask Kai . . ." He hems.

"Okay, fine," I say. "Just wake me up."

"Good!"

He jiggles the windowsill, messes with a loose bolt.

"You know Saturday is my birthday, right?"

A loaded pause.

"Well, obviously!" he says, though his tone tells a different story. "Of course! That's why, you know, I can't have you here to ruin . . . the surprise."

"Oh, really?"

"Sure! So we're on? Saturday early?"

I nod.

"You're a good girl!" He waves a socket wrench at me, ducks back inside the trailer.

Eyes up, I march over the mistake headstones. Safe in the house, I slam the door shut.

Waves crash. Gulls cry.

I drop my backpack on a chair, swallow two glasses of water, and follow the sound of pounding surf down the long hall to the laundry room, where Meredith perches on a stool before an easel, ferociously intent on the canvas before her.

Landlocked and yearning for the ocean, helplessly shanghaied by Wade's ninja graveyard purchase, Meredith had one foot out the Manderleys before the first moving box was unpacked. She proclaimed absolution from anything even remotely related to the graves from day one. The minute we moved into Sierrawood, Operation This Woman Is an Island kicked into high gear. She went to work turning the laundry room at the back of the house into a tiny art studio, where she spends her days listening to record albums with titles such as *Ocean Shore Sound Effects for Stage and Screen,* filling the air with a predictable tide, the acrid scent of acetone, and the walls with seascape after seascape, all framed with weather-worn driftwood.

Wade loves to justify his hijinks like he's done us all a big favor—*It's a solid investment, guaranteed income, you love it!*—but has realized at last that with Meredith, he is skating on very, very thin ice, ice with a bunch of long-dead bodies floating beneath it. So he leaves her alone to Miss Havisham it up in the laundry room and makes rules such as *No Talking About the Graveyard in the House When Your Mother Is Home.* Which is fine by me.

I lean in the doorway and watch her paint.

"How was school?"

"Dumb."

"Oh, good."

Wist, wist, wist. She pulls fog up from foamy waves with a fan brush, *wist*ing it into a restless violet sky.

"Kai said to pick her up if it gets dark."

She brushes up some white gesso, moves it around her palette.

"Well," she says, "I'm kind of in the middle of something."

I close my eyes. Count silently to five. "Yeah," I say, "I can see that. And she'll probably walk. She just means if it's dark when they finish. Just in case. Later."

"What's your father doing?"

I shake my head.

Wist, wist, wist.

Poor Kai. Between Wade and Meredith it's a miracle she ever makes it home before midnight. She's on the track and cross-country teams at school. They practice all the time, which is partly what absolves Kai of any obligation to help in the graves, but on the downside has left her more than once waiting on the curb outside school for Mr. I Love My Graveyard! and Ms. I'm Painting Some Seagulls! to remember to pick her up.

"Just please make sure someone goes to get her, okay? Don't make her wait in the dark by herself. Again."

Meredith nods, already back at the shore.

Waves crash.

I lug my backpack upstairs, turn the water on in the bath, and retreat to the cool dark of my room, where moving boxes are still waiting to be unpacked, piled against the walls, stacked in the closet. They still smell like the ocean. I did not pack them and have no idea what's inside—a situation clutter experts say means I should just get rid of it all. Which would leave me with one drawer of clothes, a few pens, and some library books.

Meredith's waves overtake even the sound of the filling tub. I pour in some kind of seashore-themed soap, drop my clothes on the floor, turn off the light, and sink into the dark, hot water. My hip bones knock awkwardly against the tub, Yorks lately being one of the few foods I can stomach. My head beneath the suds, the waves finally give it a rest.

"*Leigh.*"

The bathwater is tepid.

"Sorry, I *really* have to pee," Kai whispers. "Don't listen!"

"Don't *look*!" I pour more soap, swish the water around.

She rolls her eyes, laughs. Still in her running shorts. The sun is nearly set.

"Did you walk?"

She shrugs. "Not dark yet."

"I *told* them—"

"Oh, awesome." She smiles at the mirror. "I *am* a girl!" Six months, three days of remission and the dandelion fluff on her head is just now growing back in silky curls, different from the stick-straight it used to be and finally long enough to hold back with a barrette. I've missed her hair: fair like Meredith's, her eyes as dreamily blue. "I've got chemo curls and chemo boobs," she says, clutching her definitely bigger bosom through her sports bra. "It was good for *something*."

Of all of us, you'd think Kai would be maddest about living here, but she's just—not. Yes, she misses the ocean, too, but she is able to attend school again at last, and she loves this big house; having her own room instead of a towel-covered sofa near a plastic vomit bucket is her actual dream come true. Living in the cemetery, she's never felt so alive.

"Well, sure. That and the whole 'not dying' thing. Close your eyes." I sigh and stand up in the lukewarm water. She smiles, blindly wraps a towel around me.

"You're too skinny," she says.

"Look who's talking." An empty thing to say. She is not skinny. She is Meredith all over—small but not wiry like Wade and me. Lean. Nearly two years my senior, but I'm three inches taller so people always assume she's younger.

She ignores me. Gnaws at my admittedly bony elbow.

"Go put a sandwich in your piehole, dummy. I need a shower."

I have mortgaged my sanity for hers. I'll sell graves every day forever to keep her this happy.

I pull on clean pajamas and summon the energy to eat a bowl of cereal, get in bed, and finally make a decent effort to try to figure out what the hell Ovid is getting at. Because it is true—I do have a quiz tomorrow.

two

"OHHH, LOOK AT THAT goddamn angel!" Wade says. "We need that one!" It's early Saturday morning, and we've left Meredith and Kai sleeping, sun not yet above the dense hillside pines surrounding Rivendell Nursery.

I yawn. The angel probably wants to, too. It waits patiently beside a perplexing gate made of what looks like bent willow branches. The angel is soon to be one of millions of weeping angel statues that Wade, the vocal atheist and self-proclaimed card-carrying Communist, has become obsessed with sticking all over Sierrawood. It's getting a little hackneyed, not to mention crowded, but he insists. "People love that religious shit!"

I follow him along a winding forest path over a rickety bridge to a heavy wooden door. *Rivendell Awaits* is set deep in the stone side of what was once a mill house for the creek flowing beneath our feet. Sagging, toothless jack-o'-lanterns ooze white wax; gauze ghosts swing from low branches. It was Halloween last night.

Still no mention of my birthday.

Tiny brass bells ring in the hazy, pine-filtered light of the mill house, and the thrum of an angel choir . . . Wait, no. It's just Enya. Plants everywhere, dusty boxes of bulbs crowd beneath rickety wooden tables laden with pots of flowering vines, shiny, waxy leaves and blossoms. In the thick glass of every window sparkle crystals suspended from silver threads spinning lazy circles in lavender-scented air; rainbows skim across the ceiling, the mossy stone floor, my hands—everything very definitely alive.

"Wade! How's things?" Overalls Mom steps from a dark recess to shake Wade's hand. I follow as they climb over the plants and out a back door into a wide expanse of grassy field, maybe an entire acre—encircled by a ring of tall, *tall* trees. Mostly pines. I close my eyes and breathe the cold, dusty morning air.

"Leigh."

Wade, arms loaded with six-pack planters of blossoms, jerks his head toward more flats stacked in the grass. "Little less daydreaming, for crap's sake. Let's go!"

Overalls Mom lifts flowers into my arms. "Everything okay?"

I nod.

"You're Wade's oldest, right?"

I shake my head. "Just taller."

"Oh yes, you're the one in the office." She tips her head back and yells, "Hey! Elanor! You two are the same age; you should get together—*Elanor!* Where *is* that girl . . . ?"

She drifts off to search and I make my escape, lugging the flowers back through the cloud of Enya, over the bridge to the truck. I set them into the flatbed and make a move to get in the cab, but not before—

"Leigh!"

She knows my name. Princess Leia rushes out the door, still the tall boots, still the white apron, but this time over an orchid print dress, dark braids still wound behind each ear. She's *fourteen*? Looks twelve.

Over the bridge she comes, wide smile. "Hi!"

Emily.

Out here in the daylight it's even more evident; anyone could see the similarity not just in her face, but also . . . sort of *exuding*?

I can't breathe to speak.

"I saw your dad. You look just like him!"

I nod.

"Come inside, we've got cider from last night."

Wade is nowhere. "I think we're just here for the flowers, we need to get back to Sierra—"

"You've got a minute. My mom's showing your dad some angel fountains. If *my* dad wanders out there and gets going, you might have an hour."

She reaches out. I pull back instinctively—she grasps my hand in both of hers.

"Oh my gosh, you're freezing!"

She leads me stumbling back over the bridge. Inside the mill house she pulls down rubber bats hanging from strings

34

tacked to the ceiling and tosses them onto a pile of fabric on the counter. Heaping it all over a sewing machine in a corner beneath a stained-glass window, she goes to a hot plate behind the register, pours cider from a pot, puts a clay cup in my hands. No handle and a wobbly rim. She sees me notice.

"My brother made that. Sorry. He's not the greatest potter. Boys."

The cider is sweet and clovey.

"Thank you," I say.

"Of course! Did you guys go out last night? Bet you got tons of trick-or-treaters."

There were limp festoons of toilet paper all over the Manderleys this morning, a few soda-can bongs, and a smashed pumpkin beside the pond. All in all Wade was thrilled by the narrow extent of the vandalism.

"We stayed in," I say into my cider cup. "Watched movies."

She nods. "Us too. We watched *The Shining* . . . well, I listened to it. I was at the door handing out candy. I hate scary movies, but it was on so loud I heard the typing and *redrum* and all that. I thought I'd be okay not actually *seeing*, but it may have been worse. I had horrible dreams all night."

The back door sends the brass bells swinging for a tall, black-haired boy—an older, male version of Elanor, probably the potter, who calls over Enya, "Where *are* they?"

Elanor smiles brightly. "Dad says, 'Get out back and finish training the pumpkin vine before it dies or you're in so much trouble I don't even know what.'"

"Elanor, I swear to—"

"Balin, this is Leigh. Her parents bought Sierrawood."

Balin the Potter pushes his hair away from startlingly blue eyes and reaches to shake my hand. "Lucky you." He climbs over baskets of flowers to search the counter. "Give them back. I don't want you touching them; I *need* them right now!"

"Oh, *need*!" Elanor rolls her eyes. She pulls a velvet pouch from a metal cash box, tosses it to him and misses. A clatter of tiny things rolls across the stone floor. Balin is horrified.

"Every single one back in this bag or you're dead!" He holds the pouch open and Elanor crawls good-naturedly to scoop the things from beneath planters and tables and baskets of bulbs.

"Sorry," she says sincerely. "I didn't mean to huck your toys so hard."

"They're *not toys*."

"Oh, really? Dice—for a *game*?"

"It is not a *game*. It's—"

She stands to smooth her apron, picks up her cup, takes a long draw.

Balin glowers, clutches his bag of dice, and storms back out into the trees. The brass bells remain stubbornly cheerful.

"Sorry," Elanor says. "I've sort of got this— I'm compelled to wind him up and I know I shouldn't but it's just so *easy*." She refills my cup. "He's two years older than me but you wouldn't know it, right? Stupid dice. My dad's a Dungeon Master so it means a lot to them."

"He's a master?"

"Dungeons and Dragons."

I shake my head.

"It is *so* awful. Really, you don't . . . ? It's like a game. *Is* a game—ten-sided dice, lots of note-taking . . . seriously, you've never seen this? You are *so* lucky. We homeschool and most of the other homeschool kids around here are Christian and their parents think it's evil so it's hard to find people to join their thing . . . dungeon, coven, whatever. The Master made me play till I got old enough to refuse . . . Oh God, sorry—you're not Christian, are you?"

Homeschool. Morning deliveries. Pottery. Sewing . . . she probably makes those aprons.

"No," I say. "Not anything."

"Oh, thank goodness . . . I mean, not that there's anything wrong with . . . I kind of figured, even though your dad's got his thing with the angels, but the way he talks about them, and then look who's selling them to him in the first place, talk about glass houses . . . Still, I shouldn't—sorry. I need to *think.* My mom tells me that all the time, I need to *think* first."

I nod.

"My parents don't want us going to the Christian kids' houses to play anyway. Bad influence, they think we'll come home lacking any kind of cohesive logic skills or, you know, become born again. Which is pretty judgey if you ask me, but . . . so mostly I'm just here with the Dungeon Dragons. And working. Lots of weddings. Landscaping. Funerals."

At least Elanor's voice is nothing like Emily's. Elanor's has this sort of lilt, and she's got swimmer's lungs. Her words pile into one another without stopping for breath.

Emily would love her. Which makes me feel even guiltier for wanting to, too, like I'm trying to replace Emily, an impossible task and not my aim at all. Besides which, being friends with me didn't work out so well for Emily. Elanor is better off.

My head pounds.

Enya sings.

"Anyway." Elanor brightens. "So where did you live? Before here?"

Where the hell is Wade?

"Um. Mendocino."

Her eyes widen. *"No."*

"Yes."

"I have always, always wanted to go there! My parents never take time off. I've begged for us to all go to the ocean together—and Mendocino is so close—but they think the plants won't survive without them. It's ridiculous. The second I can drive, that's the first place I'm going. You must miss it."

I nod.

"You go to school, yes?"

I nod.

"What grade?"

"Ninth. At the high school."

"Is it fun?"

I shake my head.

"My mom says you have a sister."

I nod.

"Younger?"

"Older. Sophomore."

"I would *love* a sister. My dad says Balin really wanted a sister when he was little but now all we do is fight about dice so I guess be careful what you wish for." She takes my empty cider cup and drops it with hers in a sink full of terra-cotta pots.

The bells ring once more, and Wade finally backs in lugging a last flat of flowers. "Okay, you ready?" he says, as if he's been waiting all this time for me to wrap up some lengthy business.

I follow him to the truck. Elanor tags along.

"Well. Maybe I'll see you at Sierrawood sometimes. You work every weekend?"

I shake my head.

"Just after school?"

I nod. She smiles.

Her mom and dad come out then to lift the bored angel carefully into the flatbed beside the flowers. The dad wears baggy purple patchwork pants and has a long gray ponytail that I have an impulse to snip off with some pruning shears. He lifts wire-framed glasses and wipes sweat from his eyes.

"Wade's daughter?" He extends a calloused hand. I nod and offer him my own cider-warmed one.

"Pleasure to make your acquaintance, milady," he moons, bowing deeply.

In the periphery I see Elanor's head drop into her hands.

I nearly smile.

"We'll call when the cherubs come in!" her mom trills, waving as Wade moves the truck slowly past the willow-bough gates. Cherubs. She's got Wade dialed. He honks.

I rest my head against the door and roll the window down for air, my stomach easing up the farther we get from the trees of Rivendell, from Elanor's earnest, eager urgency. In the rear-view mirror she stands in the road beneath the pines, waving.

"See?" Wade says, claps my knee. "How fun was that, right?"

CR&O

The angel is so heavy she nearly breaks my back, but we get her to Sierrawood and planted safely in the lawn and Wade is right. She is perfect here in the day care, watching over the babies. I lug the flowers from the truck.

"Let's go to Mama Dicarlo's tonight," Wade says. "Birthday spaghetti, yeah?"

Amazing. He remembered. I wonder if Meredith will put her paintbrush down to fulfill her time-honored tradition of box-baking our birthday cakes. Duncan Hines, canned frosting, number-shaped candles. Last year I had two cakes: one coconut made from scratch with Emily and her mom after school, one devil's food from a box at home with the fools.

For the first time in months I think I may be hungry.

"Okay," he says, and cranes his neck past me, squints into the rising sun, searches the graves. He smiles, bouncy and excited. "Ready for your surprise?"

"What?"

"Birthday! Birthday surprise, are you ready?"

"No."

"Want to guess what it is? Do it! You'll never figure it out—guess!"

"I don't know."

"*Guess!*"

"I get to quit?"

"Close! No. Not really. Not at all—trust me. You already love it."

Someone is spinning headstones. For the longest time I thought spinning meant actually *spinning* each stone, but really it involves wearing big goggles and swinging a loud weed-whacker spinning-blade type thing to cut the grass around each stone, crop it close. Headstone haircut.

Wade waves. The person waves back, tugs off the goggles, silences the spinner.

"Okay, listen . . . you are now Sierrawood Hills' official interpreter! You ready?"

"No. Wait, *what*?"

The person is walking through the graves toward us.

Wade gets all sotto voce. "He got here last night. He's got some English words, but I don't know how much he understands, so just *talk . . . really . . . slowly.*"

I wince and wipe my sweaty hands on my jeans.

"Dario!"

He is taller than Wade and a lot younger, but older than me and dark—dark hair, dark skin, dark eyes—smiling in blue jeans and a crisp blue T-shirt, *Sierrawood Hills Memorial Park* in loopy white script across the shoulders. This is Wade's idea of a uniform for us all—members of the most ridiculous softball team in America. "Leigh, say hello to Sierrawood Hills' brand-new director of grounds maintenance!"

I nod.

"Dario," Wade plows on, "this is my youngest, Leigh!" He gathers me in a smothering one-armed embrace. "And today is my baby's birthday! Lucky fifteen today, how do you like that? Brand-new coworker, not a bad birthday present!"

So much for talking slowly.

"*¡Quinceañera!*" Dario says to my blank expression; then abruptly joyful, he clasps both my hands in his before turning to run back up the hill. "Wait for me!" he calls. "Wait!"

Wade is practically bursting with the awesomeness of it all; he can barely contain himself.

"What do you think?" he says, grinning his face off. "He's from *Mexico!*"

"Yeah, I got that," I hiss. "*You don't have to shout it.*"

"He saved every penny he had," he says near my ear, fast, "worked his whole life on a farm . . . or landscaping, I don't remember which, but this kid is industrious and *smart,* knows what the hell he wants, gave all his money to one of those jerk-wads, what is it, a coyote? Who of course took it all and bailed halfway to the border when the feds caught up. San Diego border patrol swarmed them, *for real,* he said, helicopters and everything! So there's ten guys stuffed in the back of the coyote's van and they all scatter, this is the middle of the damn night, and he hides in some rusted-out car in a ditch, right under the hood! Jeez Louise."

"I thought you said he doesn't speak English."

"No, I said he had some words."

"He told you all this?"

42

"Yes!"

"Okay, that's not 'some words,' that's . . . all the words."

He rolls his eyes. "*Any*way, so he crawls through a bunch of drainage ditches and barbed wire for, like, ten hours till he crosses into San Diego and he scrapes a few bucks together somehow or other, I didn't ask, and he buys a bus ticket and twelve hours later he's in Sacramento. Can you believe that?"

"No. When was this?"

"I don't know, like a year ago? It's true! He's been staying on people's sofas, friends of friends of cousins . . ."

"*Cousins? Really?*"

"What?"

"Like all Mexican people are related?"

He tosses his hands, and his voice jacks right back up to full volume. "I'm just telling you what he said, he *told* me this!"

"Fine."

"He did!"

"Okay."

This Dario person answered Wade's ad in the *PennySaver* classifieds the first day it ran: *Yard Work. Xlnt Pay.* (Cash, of course, under the table.) *Bnfts.*

Yard work. Jesus.

I'm just relieved my "interpreting skills" may not be needed after all. I'm perfectly happy letting Howard the coroner keep translating for Spanish-speaking clients over the phone for me, which he's only had to do twice anyway and both times for At Needs who seemed content to just sign at all the Xs, write a check, and call it a day, no chitchat necessary.

Dario comes jogging briskly back over the crest of Poppy Hill, his left arm raised over his head, hand clenched in what looks like triumph.

"Happy birthday!" He offers me his open palm, a tiny clay skeleton balanced there.

A little dead woman, top-heavy in a hat dripping sparkling flowers, bony smile, empty black eyes. I feel the heat and color drain from my face.

"You have the best day!" he says. "The Day of the Angels!" My blank silence confuses him. "*Días de los Muertos*—the Days of the Dead! Your birthday, the first Day of the Dead!" He moves the skeleton closer to my face. "*La Catrina*—she is you, this is you, Our Lady, the patron saint of death!"

I accept the skeleton, hold it in a loose fist.

I have the unsettling sensation of seeing this scene outside myself—it's a movie, my entire life revealing itself at once in all its predestined glory in real time, *in this moment.*

Patron saint.

Of course.

Creepy death/birth? Check. Living in a graveyard? Check. Kai and Emily and oh sure, born on the Day of the Dead? *The Day of the Freaking Dead?* Check. Check! *Check!*

And that makes . . . everything. Every single moment I've been alive is directly related to and for the sole purpose of celebrating, defining, facilitating death.

All around me people get sick, they drop like flies, and I remain untouched.

Proximity to me is poison.

Patron saint. Of *death*.

I *belong* in a graveyard. I'll never get out of here.

"Thank you," I barely whisper. "Excuse me."

And then I walk.

Away from Wade's calling to me to *get the hell back here, where the shinola do you think you're going?* I walk and walk and think. First, how Wade's reports of Dario's English are about as ignorant as his insistence on Dario's having "just gotten here"; a year isn't "just," and obviously the guy speaks pretty good English, easily better than Wade himself, who tends to split infinitives, mix metaphors, and double his negatives like nobody's business.

And second, I think about how Dario has given me so much more than a stupid skeleton; thanks to him I can stop being baffled about the seemingly random losses and sadness and deathiness I leave in my wake.

Not random at all.

Patron saint.

Fantastic.

I toss the skeleton into the wicker wastebasket in my closet, crawl back into my unmade bed, and lie awake in my clothes for a long, long time until Wade bangs on the door and demands to know "What the Bo Jangles is wrong with you? Get out here!"

"Get lost," I hear Kai tell him, and he grumbles off. She unlocks the door with a bobby pin and barges in against my weary protests.

"Birthday lunch, let's go!" She jumps on my mattress.

I pull the covers up over my face.

"And oh, PS," she whispers, lying beside me. "Did you meet him?"

I nod.

"I *like* him! He seems very . . . like he knows what he's doing. Dad better cool it so he'll stay."

I close my eyes.

"All right, so get up. Mama Dicarlo is waiting!"

"Can't." I duck back beneath the blankets. "I don't feel good."

She pulls the covers away, presses her slender wrist to my forehead.

"You feel fine."

"I don't feel *hot,* I feel *awful.*"

"Just power through."

I shake my head. "I don't want it."

"What, lunch? So we'll stay home, that's all right—cake for dinner! Presents!"

The house smells like chocolate. I shake my head.

"Leigh!"

"I don't want it. Just let me sleep."

"You don't want *what*?"

"Anything. Any of it. A birthday."

She squints at me, searching the horizon for the ship of what I actually mean.

"You don't want your *birthday*?"

I curl like a shrimp.

"*Why?*" And right on cue, her lovely almond-shaped bright blue eyes brim with tears.

Even before the leukemia unintentionally depleted Wade and Meredith's entire supply of patience and empathy for anyone but themselves and her, Kai had always been a big crier. They may roll their eyes at my "theatrics," but "sensitive" Kai can cry whenever, wherever, about whatever, however much she wants to. Which is pretty much all the time about everything.

Go to her for sympathy and you'll wind up comforting her proxy grief instead.

"It's all right," I say dutifully, rubbing her arm as she weeps.

"What about presents?"

"Maybe later, okay? Please?"

She finds a package of tissues in the clutter on my floor. Blows her nose.

"But *why?*"

"Just don't feel well. Okay? Okay?"

She nods. "I'll bring your present later, can I?"

"Yeah, sure, thank you." My chest aches.

"You want Mom?"

"*No.*"

She closes the door behind her, goes sniffling off to relay the message to Wade and Meredith, who do not come to my room. A relief. Sort of.

I lie staring at the glitter-infused popcorn ceiling (whose idea was that?), toying briefly with the idea of abandoning my soiled day in exchange for what was supposed to be my *real* birthday—somewhere around late January, early February. I have no problem sharing with, say, Martin Luther King Jr. or Abraham Lincoln. Even stern, ponytailed George Washington would be better than a stupid, creepy, empty-eyed skeleton. I give up, settle on no birthday at all, and seethe.

Dario.

That a-hole has ruined my birthday, dropped it into a double-depth grave of stupidity. Not *a* birthday, but every birthday forever, the actual day of my birth. Like the liners and urns and fresh, upturned grave soil, my birthday is now just one more thing I never want to touch. It is, if his out-of-control excitement was any indication, the Super Bowl of death holidays.

My birthday is dead and buried.

My blame knows no bounds. Or logic. This Dario person is not just the messenger; he is the Grim Reaper.

Or no, wait—that's me.

three

IN RETROSPECT, kudos to Wade for dragging us to live in a graveyard, a genuinely logical next step in my already death-soaked existence. Wade says I'm super dramatic. Wade is the one using headstones for a walkway.

Only months ago we were safe beside the ocean. Home.

Kai and I were born in Mendocino, a cluster of East Coasty–looking cottages hidden among redwood and cypress trees perched on the edge of insanely beautiful cliffs above the wild coast of Northern California. Meredith painted seascapes in oil to sell to tourists. She raised us to believe we were mermaids and made certain, even as toddlers, that we fostered a deep appreciation for the ocean, for this most beautiful place in all the world. She chose Kai's name for its literal Hawaiian translation: *ocean*. We practically lived in salt water, our diapers and hair forever filled with sand. Heaven.

Until out of the blue—leukemia. Every day turned suddenly sad. Kai's thirteenth and my eleventh birthdays and all the days and months that followed I spent beside Kai as she lay on the couch all day, dying. Sleeping, crying, drinking lukewarm 7UP. The house lost its misty ocean coolness; it turned warm and salty and bitter. It smelled of pills and vomit and sweat. She pulled loose fistfuls of hair from her head until it was gone. She slept. Her friends stopped coming around. I became Kai's only friend and lost all of mine in the process.

There was not a Taco Bell within a hundred-mile radius of our town, let alone a decent medical facility, so there were a million road trips back and forth to San Francisco. Wade scavenged enough commissions at the real estate office to keep us well supplied with food, chemotherapy, spinal taps, and little else. I could not bear to bother him and Meredith for things like lunch money or new clothes, so I made myself Land O'Frost lunch meat sandwiches and wore the same pink sweatpants and T-shirt day after day, sometimes weeks between the Laundromat visits we resorted to when first the dryer, then the washer stopped working and we couldn't afford to fix them. At school I hid, embarrassed and unnoticed, alone in the library at recess.

For two years Kai languished but lived. Radiation left her so sick no food would stay in her long enough to matter, until the Halloween I fished a York from my pillowcase stash and we discovered it settled her stomach. We ate pounds of them, hardwiring in us a chocolate-and-mint-flavored Pavlovian sense of relief. Comfort.

Every day I held her clammy hands and read aloud for hours. She loved Laura Ingalls Wilder and begged me to read the Christmas chapters again and again. "Do the one on Silver Lake. Which one do they get tin cups and pennies in?"

Wade and Meredith tended to her medication and hospital visits, gave her every ounce of care and attention they were capable of, and by late afternoon each day were left with nothing, passing the baton to me the moment I stepped in the door after school. I helped her with the schoolwork the district sent home with me each week. Half-watched hours of television went by while fog swept past the windows, sea grass and pounding waves marking every sick, sad minute.

Lonely.

Until one year ago (just as the saga of *Kai's Got Cancer: Year Three!* began), I trudged off to the first day of eighth grade, and the tide turned: Emily had moved to town.

Already small, she'd skipped a grade so seemed even littler. Alone and new in Mendocino, easy prey to incessant bullying by jealous classmates for being a year younger but eons smarter, Emily resorted to lunch recess library hiding, too.

"Are you in trouble?" she asked, surveying my pile of books.

"No," I said. "I'm poor."

She didn't care that I couldn't invite her over, wasn't embarrassed by my secondhand, ill-fitting pink sweatpants wardrobe. We took a collective breath, she grabbed my hand, and we left the library to brave the school yard.

"Nice pants!" mean girls screeched across the tetherball court. I tugged my shirt down over the pink sweats, moved to pull my other hand from Emily's—she held tight.

School became a secretly welcome escape from the illness-laden dreariness of our house. Emily showed me tap-dance routines on the smooth cement of the playground; we read books in the stairwell, passed notes in class, and spent every recess sitting on the edge of the grassy soccer field watching crabs skitter in the tide pools below. I wished Kai could be there and was consumed with guilt for the relief I felt, for being happy in Emily's company.

After a while I stopped resisting Emily's daily invitations to come over to her house after school. Fear of Kai's loneliness let me stay only an hour or two each day before I was back at her side, never a word to her about Emily, wet washcloth on Kai's face, bucket near her mouth. But the gloom didn't dampen me the same way now.

Emily never knew her dad, who had died before she was born, his whole family far away back East and not interested in her or her nomadic "hippie" mom who kept her own last name, and Emily used it, too, ditching what they referred to as the "very WASPy sounding *Martin*" of her dad's family. No siblings, no cousins, just each other. They moved all the time, and luckily for me had found their most recent stint in San Francisco too expensive. Their rented Mendocino cottage was small, but near enough to walk to school and it was cheerful and tidy and smelled like clean laundry.

Her mom worked as a dental assistant and was often home when we got there after school. Emily and I ate macaroni and did our homework and her mom called me sweetheart. "How is your sister doing, sweetheart? Are your parents okay?" I shrugged and gratefully accepted another cookie. Homemade.

I made up study hall excuses for where I was spending my after-school time. Emily and her mom never met Kai, but they sent me home with brownies for her, wrapped warm in paper towels. Wade and Meredith's one brief meeting through rolled-down station wagon windows after a class field trip to the Fort Bragg tide pools was the extent of their contact with Emily or her mom, but they were glad for the free babysitting.

Six months ago, once more without warning, Kai's health swiftly turned. The radiation and the pills gained traction at last; she climbed into a mystifying but definite remission. And almost immediately, maybe just because she could, she started running. Peppering her vocabulary with phrases like *sub forty at the five*, putting miles between herself and the sickness, daring it to try to keep up.

She wasn't even annoyed when Wade pulled an "I'm still young and kicky!" move, laced up his shoes, and joined her. Meredith and I watched them run five- and ten-kilometer races where, always tiny, Kai's efforts were often dwarfed by the long strides of the other girls competing in her age group. Enter Wade (the self-crowned champion of fairness), who shaved a few years from her birth date on the registration forms, pitting her growing strength and endurance against kids who still napped. She won every time. Still, I screamed myself hoarse cheering when her bald head flew past to the finish.

Eighth grade ended, and summer loomed deliciously

hopeful; Kai would not die and Emily had invited me to go with her to Girl Scout sleepaway camp, even though I was not a Girl Scout.

"You can be my distant cousin visiting from France," she said. "Just say *bonjour* a lot and they'll leave us alone."

But Wade and Meredith had other plans. They were exhausted, having fallen at last over the finish line of the endless marathon of yanking Kai back from death day after day, year after year, and they "needed a break." They announced that Kai and I were off to our own personal camp: summer with Meredith's parents.

Secretly devastated to be missing camping with Emily, cheated out of even just a few days from Kai's orbit (then again instantly guilty for such a selfish thought) before I even got the chance to ask if I could go. I hustled Wade and Meredith into a hushed powwow in the kitchen. "Please," I begged, "please can't we stay home? Kai's not ready to be away for so long; this is ridiculous!"

"Kai!" Wade bellowed above my frantic whispering. "You okay going alone to Gramma's? Because apparently Leigh's not up for it."

I gave myself a headache glaring so hard at him. Meredith busied herself unloading the dishwasher.

"You're not coming?" Kai's scared face peered around the kitchen door.

Eyes still slightly sunken, the skin beneath still the purple of a fading bruise. Tears welled there, not on purpose. Genuinely scared to be without me.

"Of course I am," I sighed, hopeful images of canoeing and roasting marshmallows with Emily vanishing in the instant.

The night before we left, I read Kai to sleep, then snuck out for a consolation secret sleepover with Emily.

Her mom ordered pizza; we made popcorn and did not waste a single minute sleeping. Well after two in the morning, we lounged in the pretend camping cabin we'd set up with blankets beneath their dining room table, drawing Magic Marker ponies and doves on the underside, reveling in the delicious scandal of it. *A costly piece of furniture! Defaced!* We'd learned from an Ed Emberley's Drawing book that ponies and doves were the easiest, best-looking animals in our repertoire and therefore they graced the covers of all our school textbooks and spiral notebooks and every note we passed in class. They livened up the underside of the table, for sure.

"Don't go," she pleaded, "I'll be so bored. I won't survive without you."

"What will I do without *you*?" I sighed.

She reached up, added a windswept tail to a trotting pony.

We vowed to write actual letters twice a week, at least.

All summer I received just one letter, a yellow envelope addressed in black Magic Marker cursive. Another envelope came later with two one-way Greyhound tickets, and when Kai and I stepped off the bus we found ourselves far from the ocean and living in a graveyard.

four

I DO NOT SEE DARIO the day after he kills my birthday. Which is to say I do not speak to or participate in actual eye contact with him, though yes, I do visually *see* a lot of him. Watch a lot of him, plot ways to avoid him for the next four years until I can leave for college, join the circus, become a hooker—whichever will get me out of here fastest.

It is Sunday but I'm in the office, doing my spying through the grimy windows because Wade's got the nerve to make me "fill in" while he's off in Sacramento investigating some asinine waterfall feature he's dying to install. I turn two space heaters (Who needs central heating? Not Wade!) up as high as they can go, even though they encourage pipe smell seepage from the carpet and wood paneling. Too cold not to. Dario waves as he passes on the riding mower, salutes as he troops past in the trees, cheerfully lugs shovels, rakes, lengths of irrigation line.

I watch Kai return from a run into town; she jogs past the office and straight through the graves to Dario, who pulls her into a hug. He offers her his water bottle, which she accepts; then he walks beside her up the hill toward the house. They talk; she smiles, laughs. She has recovered overnight from her despair at my abandoned birthday. Traitor.

I pull the York bag to my lap and turn to Ovid for consolation.

We can learn even from our enemies.

Okay, screw Ovid.

Headfirst into algebra's refreshingly nonsentimental variables and coefficients, I look up and Dario is standing at my desk.

"Hello! Working?"

I hate it when people sneak up! Knock louder!

I nod.

"Okay!" he says. "I'm going. To my place. Are you going home?"

I shake my head.

He points to the clock. "No? Six, we can walk together?"

Shake my head. I'd rather walk up alone in the dark.

"Okay. See you tomorrow. Happy birthday—day after!"

He closes the door behind him.

Four years. College or circus or hookering can't come soon enough.

CR&SO

I keep my anti-Dario vigil sacred, skulking around while he tends the grounds. I watch him chat with visitors, *sit* with them. He holds Real Nice Clambake's hand on Wednesdays, talks with her about what a great show *Carousel* is, rights leaning

57

framed photographs piled on graves, untangles wind chimes. The Rivendell crew, of course, adores him. He helps place arrangements and they yammer endlessly about Lord knows what. I hide in the office and watch them; even Elanor is too distracted by his magic to bother me, so at least there's that. Kai gallops over the headstones to him for big hug-fests, the same hugs he greets the mourning families and a delighted Wade with, the way he surely would greet Meredith if she could ever bring herself to acknowledge his existence. Kai natters happily on about how "he is super nice, and funny, and he asks all the time if you're mad at him."

"What's there to be mad about?" I sigh. "I don't even know the guy." Well, besides the penchant for ruining birthdays, and what the hell is the deal with all the hugging? Monitoring and avoiding his whereabouts makes the hours spent in the office much more exhausting. I can only relax when he is busy digging graves, which keeps him in one place for long periods of time, or when he has a day off, which he spends mostly in and around the silver trailer.

Right away he's making that thing a home. From the toolshed I hide and watch him rototill the soil in his front yard, planting grass seed and a million flowers and young trees among the already tall pines. He hangs tin candle lanterns from sturdy branches and strings a tidy row of tiny colored Christmas lights all along the eaves and around the trailer windows. A path of smooth river pebbles leads to his door. The twinkling lights could easily make it a gaudy circus hiding behind the graves, but despite my wanting it to be awful it just isn't. It is cheerful and pretty, the colors sparkle, and it makes me hate him more.

His English, already nearly fluent if a bit noun-filled, improves daily. A radio tuned forever to NPR rests in the open trailer window while he works in the cremain niches nearby or in the shed repairing the lawn mower or prepping liners, and the verbs and adjectives come rapidly. Wade adores him—the son he's always whined about missing out on. He has accidentally hired not only an overqualified dream of a groundskeeper/grave digger, but a very patient person who endures Wade's endless pointless lectures on random crap Wade knows nothing about but loves to relate to a clearly uninterested Dario anyway (the proper way to distill liquor in a bathtub, how to clean fireplace andirons). Theirs is a unique relationship based upon Wade's love of being a know-it-all and Dario's enjoyment in absorbing Wade's crass, slang-laced vocabulary, which, despite the constant taking of the Lord's name in vain, provides a nice contrast to the sedate, properly constructed sentences NPR tends to offer.

"That *kid!*" Wade sighs contentedly after dinner practically every night. "He's got a way with people you wouldn't believe. They just take to him right away, you know? *Man!* Did I find the perfect guy or what?"

"You sound like you guys are dating," Kai says. "Leave him alone, he probably has friends he wants to hang out with." She is so post-cancer sassy.

Wade scowls. "Baloney! He loves working lunches! That kid is going places!"

"Do you have to call him a *kid*?" I say, voicing my and Kai's joint distaste. "He's got to be at least twenty; if he wasn't from Mexico, you totally wouldn't call him that. It's gross."

"Oh for Christ's sake, I would, too!" Wade hollers defensively. "He *is* a kid—you're all kids! My Sierrawood Hills Kids . . . how did we get so lucky?"

Exactly what I'd like to know.

Sierrawood Hills Kids. We're all very special people living in a very, very special group home.

 C&S

"Kind of dark in here," Kai says, stretching her legs before a black office wingback. I toss her a bunch of Yorks. She's right. Winter in a graveyard is just as depressing as one would imagine. It is super dingy, but I refuse to turn on the overhead fluorescent lights. Too clinical. Morguey. Freezing December rains flatten the muddy lawn and send old people to us in droves, two or three a week, nearly faster than Dario can dig. The graves lie cold beneath blankets of brown pine needles; the hum of Wade's leaf blower never shuts up. People come wrapped in twenty-seven layers of sweaters and coats. The poor ducks hang around, hiding in the withered blackberry bushes, and I wish they would get the clue to migrate. They're too used to the stale bread Real Nice Clambake feeds them every week. I'm just waiting for Dario to announce that "December twenty-fifth is the festival of the rare skin diseases!" My birthday is one thing; if he comes near Christmas, I'll kill him.

It is weird, Kai sitting here. She's messed up her calf muscle and has been sent home early from track practice to sit in a

60

bath and rub it. Which is what I remind her she's supposed to be doing instead of lounging around in here yakking with me, but she just unwraps her Yorks, chews. "How is it? You okay?"

"Oh yeah," I say fake-casually, staring aimlessly out at the graves. Clambake tosses an armful of pine needles and dead leaves in the Dumpster behind the office as she goes. I can see the perfect rectangle of cleared lawn over her sister. "It's nice, actually. Wade was right. Hardly anyone comes in, better than the library. Look—rubber pencil!"

She pulls more Yorks from the bag and watches my admittedly excellent rubber penciling. "Yeah?"

She can run a million marathons over Hell's half acres all she wants; to me this remission will always feel unsure. Precarious. I will not disrupt its magical, invisible hold.

"Yes," I say. "It's fine. *I love it.*"

"What about school?"

"What about it?"

"You don't have any friends."

"Do too."

"Oh, really?" She settles in for a formal inquisition.

"Yes!"

"Who?"

"You don't know them. They're freshmen."

"What are their names?"

Oh jeez. "Well," I say, "their names. Are."

"Yeah."

"Lisa! Lisa and Caroline."

"Seriously?"

I would never, ever burden her by saying it, but I wish Kai would at least try to be near me once in a while during the school day. Sophomore classes, alternate lunch schedule, and it's like she's on the moon. But I am grateful she is kept safe, buoyed above the high school humiliation crap by her own firmly established self-esteem, track team friends, and an admiring school administration that hangs banners in the hallways reading: CONGRATULATIONS, KAI, DIVISION IV CROSS-COUNTRY CHAMPIONSHIP QUALIFIER!

Months into the school year and I remain a friendless parasite in this unfamiliar labyrinth, adored by teachers but virtually unnoticed by my classmates except for the few who mock the low-hanging fruit of our living in a graveyard. And then there's Lisa and Caroline, aggressively lip-lined freshman ringleaders who at the start of the year seemed to have enough fun mocking my still poverty-stricken wardrobe, but who now actively hate my guts for breaking stupid standardized test curves in every class we have together, putting their stellar cheerleading careers in jeopardy. They shove me into cold metal lockers between classes, and I am amazed they haven't yet come to Sierrawood to mess with me.

"Mrs. McKinstry," Lisa huffed this afternoon in English Lit, not bothering to raise her hand, "can I move to a new seat?"

"*May* you *please* do what?"

Lisa rolled her eyes. "*May* I *please* move?"

"Why?"

She snapped an enormous wad of gum. "Be*cause* I can't concentrate! Leigh has worn those same jeans like ten days in a row, and the smell is making me ill. For real. They're filthy, there's, like, mud or something on them. Formaldehyde."

Mortuary. You're thinking of a mortuary.

Mrs. McKinstry peered over her glasses at me, then back at Lisa. "Formaldehyde?"

"Yes. Can I—*may I*—just move?"

"No, you may not."

"Then can you move Leigh?"

"Spit that gum out."

Lisa growled and inched her seat as far from mine as she could, pulled her shirt collar up over her mouth and nose. Caroline laughed hysterically, cried her mascara off.

I squirmed and pretended to read, my eyes stinging, stomach burning.

I *have* worn these jeans for ten days. I've been wearing them since before summer and they were my only pair then, too, and now they are also too short. But they aren't dirty. I wash them. All the time. They're just all I've got. I could remedy the situation, but the thought of asking Wade and Meredith or spending that much horrible icing-on-the-cake grave money still gives me hives. I can't do it.

In the Mendocino Cancer Pink Sweatpants Era, Emily's mom begged me to let her take me shopping with Emily. Her well-intended generosity mortified me. "It's just until Kai's better," I pleaded when she was on the verge of calling Meredith to discuss the obvious-neglect-come-on-Leigh-this-is-ridiculous situation with her. "It's not a big deal, I *like* these pants, right now is just not a good time. . . ." I put her off month after month, embarrassed, until Emily finally got her to stop offering. But when the pink sweatpants' elastic waist inevitably gave out and I began hitching them up with a big safety pin, her mom wordlessly handed me a J. C. Penney bag one day after school. I hid in the bathroom to pull on a beautiful brand-new pair of slightly too big jeans. I wore them every day and we never said a word about it. I'm wearing them still.

I will not disrupt Kai's happiness at school, will never let her know my time, care, and attention had ever been divided, that while she lay suffering I was sometimes purposely away from her, wearing new jeans, happy with Emily and her mother.

"Lisa and Caroline are completely made-up names," Kai says.

"Are not!"

"Then why don't you ever go to their houses? Talk to them on the phone?"

I lean back in my black chair. "Kind of busy. Graves to sell."

"See, that's what I'm saying! This sucks, you shouldn't be here all the time."

"No, it's not . . . I mean they're busy, too. Cheerleading."

"Your friends are *cheerleaders*?"

"Yes! I can broaden my friend horizons if I want. We see each other at school; that's our thing. It's our jam." I wrap the story up with an even-breezier-but-still-not-so-breezy-it-sounds-fake laugh, which to my ears does not land but seems to work for Kai.

She smooths silver York wrappers on her knee, folds some tiny origami.

"And you're positive . . ." She leans back in the chair and gives the office another once-over. "This is okay?"

"*Yes,* God!"

She's as eager to be convinced as I am for her to be.

"Well," she says. "You need more light. Get a lamp."

"Yeah." I exhale. "Definitely, you're right. Floor lamp, maybe. I'll tell Wade."

She pinches the corner of a wrapper, holds up a York crane. "Ooh, you could get Grandpa to send you the wagon wheel!"

Grandpa's love of the American West is expressed primarily via his extensive Willie Nelson eight-track tape collection, his cowboy hat and boot wardrobe, and the wagon wheel: an actual wheel from a covered wagon suspended above his and Gramma's dining room table, wired for electricity and fitted with a bunch of red glass globes. Eating beneath it this past summer felt like being in a saloon; it made us want to toss peanut shells on the floor and spit at the stove. I smile, until the wagon wheel yanks me back to the yellow letter, and the sting of missing Emily—but then a van comes through the Manderleys. Kai sits up, turns to see who's here.

Rivendell.

"Oh cripes," I whisper, hunkering down in my chair.

"What?"

"Nothing. Flowers. Go soak your leg before it falls off. I've got homework."

She drops a fistful of tiny shiny cranes on the desk calendar and lugs her backpack off the chair.

"Don't work too hard."

I wave Ovid at her. "Yeah. It's tough."

She reaches across the desk to squeeze my face and kiss my cheek. A sweep of cold air rushes in and she closes the door behind her, still safe. Still happy. Unburdened by me.

Through the windows I watch her slowly walk up the road, her beautiful curls tucked snugly beneath a warm, wool knit hat, blue stripes the color of her eyes. At the veterans section she limps her way through the headstones to the Rivendell van to shake Elanor's dad's hand, his wispy ponytail carefree in the wind. Balin of the dice hops from the van, and she shakes *his* hand. I wait for Elanor to climb out, a flower van clown car—but not today. The three of them chat. Kai laughs. Balin's face stays fused toward hers despite their hilarious height difference, even while lifting pots of flowers to the graves. Man, that guy is lanky. Dark curls fall all over his face. That whole family needs haircuts, stat.

five

TODAY IS EMILY'S BIRTHDAY. December tenth. One guilt-spawned choice of where to spend summer vacation and I've traded all the rest of her birthdays for Kai's.

Dario is down in a grave in Serenity. Real Nice Clambake is out with her sister, Shirley Jones belting from the boom box at the top of her Broadway lungs. I figure out how to use my pencil with bulky warm gloves on, then pour myself wholly into a stack of stapled algebra work sheets.

Ducks quack once in a while.

Wind whistles and moans around the office eaves.

Emily's face is flushed, peeking around the open door.

My heart stops.

"Hi!"

Elanor. Elanor's face.

"Busy?" She steps in, hugs herself warm. Black tights today. Gray skirt, black-and-purple-striped sweater, voluminous wool scarf, swimming-pool blue. The boots.

I rub my temples. She's a ninja. Stealthy.

"How've you been? Is that homework?"

"Yeah." I look past her out the window to the Rivendell van half-hidden in the babies' pines. That thing is so quiet, it's like a flipping golf cart. She picks up the work sheets.

"Yikes. I *hated* algebra. How is it?"

"It's algebra," I say.

"The teacher nice?"

"He's . . ."

She waits. For all the talking she does, she is also an eager audience.

"He's also the football coach," I say.

"Why?"

"Budget issues, I guess."

"Okay."

"He wears bicycle shorts."

"To *class*?"

"And he's sort of a person who definitely should *not* be wearing any kind of shorts in public. Or ever."

She smiles. "Gross."

I am amazed at all the talking I'm doing. Nervous chatting but also . . . I've been wishing I could tell someone, anyone, about Coach Petty since the first day of school. Kai's got no sense of humor when it comes to mocking any athlete ever, and Wade and Meredith—yeah. That's not happening.

"My mom does all the math with us," Elanor says. "I shouldn't say I hated *it*. It wasn't the algebra; it was that I had

68

to do it with Balin and he will *not* sit still for more than five seconds. But we're finally back on separate stuff. Geometry is fun."

"You're *done* with algebra?"

She tilts her head, sheepish. "Eh. Homeschooling. Just goes faster. You're obviously good at it. Lucky." She sets the pages before me. I shuffle them back in order.

Does she have to be so nice?

"Okay," she says at last, closes the door behind her, and slides conspiratorially into a wingback. "What is *up* with Balin and Kai?"

Strange to hear her speak Kai's name . . . Wait, what the—

"Balin and what?"

She leans forward, eyes wide. "I *know*! Kai seems so . . . *smart*. She's so bright and sunny and then Master Gloom and Doom is all shlumping around her but she doesn't seem to mind—like, at *all*. I don't get it! What's going on with that whole thing?"

My mouth works the air but no words come. Luckily Elanor's got plenty.

"I mean, what does she say? Does she *like* him?"

"I . . ."

"Because I'll tell you what, ever since she started coming around—"

"Wait—who's coming where?"

"*Kai*. To Rivendell. I absolutely love her, but it makes zero sense she'd even look at him, and maybe she's just being nice, but . . . what if? It's insane! I love her haircut. Makes me want mine short, except it would never look as good; her eyes are *gorgeous*."

"It's not a haircut." The sharpness in my voice surprises me. She is still. For a second.

She messes with her blue scarf. "Oh. Well . . . how come you don't come with her?"

"I don't . . . where?"

"Rivendell! Oh, Leigh, I wish you would. I mean, I know you're totally busy; Kai says you're working all the time—and I love her to bits, but mostly she hangs out with Balin. It's like she's there *just* to see him, but if you came with—"

"When is she there?"

"After school, I guess? Afternoons."

The pulled muscle, strained, whatever—she has not been at practice helping the coach like she told me; she's been at Rivendell. Flirting. With hair-in-his-face Balin.

"Except this week she said she's back at track practice so instead she came on Saturday. Sunday, too. And of course Balin never says anything to anyone about anything. Acts all know-it-all and chipper. Drives me nuts."

Saturday *and* Sunday. *Just going for a slow run, get this muscle back in business, might be a while . . .*

I want so badly to be happy for her. *Just* happy, not happy-slash-jealous. I should be thrilled she's got one more good thing, a happy secret thing all her own. But then . . . all those endless days holding her hand, lying beside her, rinsing the bucket, and the second she's well, she's gone? Secret friends and crushes and doesn't even tell me, let alone invite me along, not that I would go, but that's beside the point. And sure, Emily was a secret, too, but still it stings. The York I am chewing is now imprinted with what my current author-boyfriend Thomas Hardy would call the bitter taste of her betrayal.

"So does she?"

I pull my eyes from a middle-distance daze. "Does she what?"

"Like him—*like* like?"

"I have no idea."

Again my voice is harder than I intend. Elanor looks at her lap.

What is my problem?

"But," I offer lamely, "I'll let you know if I find out."

She recovers. Brightens.

"Well. If you ever have time to come with her . . . or by yourself, you know, if you want. Weekends are so long, if you came we could—I don't know, mostly I'm working but it would be more fun with—together. You think?"

She stands, straightens her apron down over her skirt, goes to the window. Real Nice Clambake is still out there. Elanor smiles.

"Every Wednesday since I was a baby, she comes to us on her way here. Takes anything in season, roses, carnations, filler flowers, whatever. As long as it's pretty." She turns to me, pulls her scarf snugly to her throat. "All right. You've been assigned your recon mission: Let's get to the bottom of this Kai/Balin business before they get completely stupid and force us to deal with the repercussions of the misguided ardor of their unsavory teenaged loins— God, can you imagine?"

Homeschool vocabulary.

I laugh. Can't help it. "Gross . . ." I sigh.

"I know, right? God." She spins out the door, closes it against the chill wind, waves through the window, and mouths the words *Come over!* I watch her trot toward the van, then turn instead to cross the grass and the land mines of headstones to Real Nice Clambake. Hugs her. They talk, laugh about something. Even slightly stooped with age, Clambake is taller than Elanor.

The office silence is really loud.

Emily would have been nice to Clambake, too.

Aside from straight-up spelling it out to Elanor, *Please forgive me, you seem incredibly smart and nice and I am so very lonely and thank you so much for wanting to be my friend even though I've been nothing but weird and rude to you and while I would also dearly love to get out of the graves once in a while and repot bulbs with you at your beautiful nursery, and that is not me being sarcastic, it truly would be a relief and a fun way to spend an afternoon, I'm afraid I've got this suffocating fear that getting to know you and having fun with you would betray my loyalty to my best and only friend who is gone anyway, and also what if we did become friends and you disappeared, too, and also if I become friends with you it might take away from the attention and care I must ceaselessly give my sister or she will get sick again and die because PS, I am a patron saint of death, so for your own good you should probably avoid contact with me or you'll never make it out alive, so thanks a ton, but as you can tell I've kind of got a full plate of psychosis going on right now, if it ever lets up I will for sure give you a call, how's that?* I'm not sure how else to convince her I am not a good candidate for friendship. I've been dismissive at best, at worst unkind, but she doesn't seem discouraged. At all.

Her impossible likeness to Emily is strange and awful and not her fault, but still here she is, a Lego brick fit of an Emily replacement and I cannot. I will not.

I'm not good friend material.

I'm not good person material.

six

A COLD MONDAY, I'm in the office with Thoreau (*Simplicity, simplicity!*), cementing a kinship with him as I hide from humanity in my very own Walden beside the duck pond. The drowsy hum of the space heaters does not mask the sound of a van through the Manderleys. I drop below the desk, grab *Walden* and the York bag, and make a pillow from my coat to hunker down for the duration.

A knock at the door and I squeeze myself tighter into the leg space beneath the desk. I don't have the energy for this today. *Elanor, please go away,* I will her from my hiding place. *Please, please,* please.

"Hello?" The door opens and someone steps inside— *seriously?*—but it is not her voice, not Elanor.

"Hello? Are you open?"

I rush to stand, forgetting I am crouched in a cubby, and slam the top of my head into the bottom of the desk.

Stars.

"Hello?"

Two youngish women stand in the doorway, purse straps securely on their shoulders, one with a short, sensible shag haircut and the other, the helper, holding tight to Shag Haircut's arm.

They watch me crawl up into my chair. I gesture limply with a pen. "Found it."

Out the open door there is no Rivendell van. Dario nowhere in sight. No Wade.

"Excuse me," I say, "just one second. Have a seat and I'll be right with you." I dash out the door and around behind the Dumpster, where I rub my throbbing head and run my fingers through the mess of tangled homework hair falling in my face, tie it into a ponytail, and curse Meredith's threadbare, boldly lettered *Over 40 and Feelin' Foxy!* T-shirt that I have chosen to wear this day.

"Sorry about the cold," I say, rushing to close the door. I crank the stupid space heaters to ten, regret the very unprofessional buzzing and humming as they warm up, and slide into my seat behind the desk. In my best fake-professional sensitive voice, I ask, "How can I help you today?"

Shag Haircut's husband is dead.

"And do we currently have an active file for your family?"

Because Active File = Pre-Need = Easy. *Please oh please oh please . . .*

At Need.

But at least simple. Practical. Like her haircut. Standard burial, anywhere near a tree would be nice. *Seriously, people and their stupid trees.* Single depth, single headstone. They go for a bronze marker, a pricey but attractive choice. Details of pine boughs and cones beveled into the corners; name, birth, and death, beloved husband, father. Young father. Oh jeez. I write neatly, fill in boxes and lines, date every page.

The paperwork is done and it is time for my stomach to get all nuts because oh God, I have to take them on The Walk, but night is moving swiftly in. I open my mouth to suggest (beg) that they do it tomorrow morning, with Wade, but Shag Haircut beats me to the punch, insisting we go find a grave *right now.*

The women stay close beside me. Shag looks nowhere but at the damp grass; the helper, who turns out to be the sister, makes pedestrian awkward Helper Small Talk: Boy, it sure is cold lately, but thank goodness for the afternoon sun, how do I like working here, what school do I go to, asking without asking *Just how old are you and why are we having to deal with you instead of an actual cemetery professional?*

I keep the women hiking all over Wade's "Let's get it filled!" Poppy Hill. Shag Haircut peers suspiciously over the worn wooden fence that borders our neighbor, the Gold Country Retirement Villa (one of our best customers), shakes her head, marches on.

The sister and I exchange a look and are at once united in a singular mission: Get a grave picked out before nightfall.

Too late.

Shag suddenly stops walking and falls apart right there on

the lawn. The sister drops beside her on the cold, damp grass, and I stand stupidly, watching them cry beneath the trees and the now very nearly black sky.

They weep and weep and I do nothing. What am I supposed to say? What do I do?

Desperate for any distraction, I force my eyes down and read the headstones at my feet.

Here is an elaborate, intricate landscape surrounding some guy's smallish name and death date and a boat speeding along making waves on the glassy surface of a lake. Was his death boat-related, or had he simply enjoyed waterskiing and fishing and other freshwater activities?

Shag cries.

Oh, look, here's a *Beloved Wife, Mother, and Grandmother.* But the dates indicate Beloved was just thirty-one years old when she died. Thirty-one and a grandmother? Two generations of blatant teenaged sex going on in *that* family.

Most of the graves in this row are pretty standard. Older people. Eighty, ninety, *Our Dear Mother, Grandmother, Wife of William, Husband of Ethelyn, Moose Lodge President, Father, Grandfather,* pictures of trees, angels, a dove and a pony, *Daughter, Granddaughter* . . . a dove and a pony a dove and a pony a dove—*wait*— Wait. Wait. Wait.

Wait.

My stomach is ice.

A dove and a pony. The name carved in granite. The dove and the pony. I stare so long, my open mouth is dry. I choke on

77

the cold air rushing down my throat. *Who put this here? I do not understand what is happening. The dove and the pony. All this time, right here with me. Am I awake?*

Shag Haircut sobs and wails.

☙❧

"Don't go," Emily pleaded beneath the table tent last summer. "I won't survive without you."

"What will I do without *you*?" I sighed. "I beg them every day; they're *making* us go."

Wade and Meredith would not give in. No summer with Emily, just a Greyhound bus ride with Kai over the river and through the woods.

Gramma and Grandpa live three hours away in Pixley, a tiny hamlet even farther inland than Hangtown and hotter, which consists of a few homes dotting the sagebrush-covered high-desert countryside and a downtown made up of a minimart, a post office, and a bakery.

"Gramma and Grandpa love you!" Meredith insisted. "They're thrilled to have a whole summer with you!"

If she exchanged the words *a whole summer with* for *free labor from,* she'd be right on target, because what we actually spent the summer doing was cutting wood. Cutting and stacking wood. Sunrise to sunset. In Pixley it snows a ton every winter and most of the houses don't have central heating, so to keep from freezing to death, fires must be built and stoked to burn pretty much twenty-four hours a day, all winter long. The minute Kai and I arrived, the wood gathering began in earnest.

We piled into the cab of Grandpa's blue Cherokee truck,

crammed tight together on the fake leather bench seat. Grandpa drove. Gramma sat next to the passenger door clutching the handle white-knuckled and checking the lock every five seconds. She'd never learned to drive, and the mystery of it all just horrified her. She craned forward, tense, making sure Grandpa stayed on his side of the road and calling out helpful tips every now and then: "Jesus Christ, do you have to go so fast, Wallace?" and urging him to "Put on your blinker!" even though the turn we needed to take was at least a mile ahead. She pulled a tissue from her bra and mopped her damp brow as Grandpa gunned it to forty-five in the sixty-five-miles-per-hour slow lane.

I was forced to straddle the gearshift, a long stick with a ball on top. Gramma warned me every single time we got in the truck, "Don't touch that! If you touch that, we'll crash. Don't even *look* at it; that's not for you. If you touch it, the engine will break and we'll die!" And so I sat, knees apart, feet off the floor. I imagined my skin barely brushing the thing and the truck falling apart around us, sending us all scraped and bloody across the highway.

Amplifying the general mayhem of the trip were the antics of Rene, Gramma's tiny, yipping, stinky French poodle. He ran all over our laps, freaking out and licking us, Fu Manchu snout stained brown from a diet of cooked liver, beef bouillon, and Oreo cookies. I held my knees up, turned my face again and again from his liver lips, and by the time we reached the forest my legs were burning with muscle spasms. The moment the engine stopped ("Wait till Grandpa takes the key out; there's electricity in the motor, and the car will explode if you open the door while it's running. Just *wait*!"), I climbed over Kai and Gramma and fell out into—

Deafening silence. The noise of the road gone, only still air now, and deep black forest soil. Trees. Hazy rays of sunlight through elegant, towering pines, dust spinning like diamonds. A bird sang, took flight. A quiet creek splashed over rocks somewhere close. Bumblebees buzzed. I inhaled deeply.

And then Grandpa revved up the chain saw.

For the next six hours we were a well-oiled machine: Grandpa cut a pie-shaped wedge from one side of a thick pine trunk, then moved around to the other side to cut straight through. For a moment the giant hovered, balanced precariously on itself, until a great shove from Grandpa's shoulder and a shout to Gramma (who every single time chose the *exact* spot where she *knew* the tree would fall to bend over and start picking up kindling)—"Jesus Christ, Irene, get the hell outta the way, here it comes!"—and Gramma dove from the advancing shadow of the falling tree just in time to watch it slam onto the soil.

"Goddamnit, Wallace! You nearly *killed* me! You would just love that, wouldn't you? You'd be the happiest man in town; you'd just clap your hands if I died, wouldn't you? *Wouldn't you?*" Grandpa shook his head and got busy cutting the tree into rounds, which Kai and I raced to gather. We rolled them to the truck, heaved them up and in. All day long Grandpa felled trees, Gramma accused him of attempted murder, Rene ran around pooping, and Kai and I loaded the rounds.

The scream of the chain saw, the sharp splintering of wood, the sweet tang of pine sap, a heavy, brief silence, then the rush of air through green needles, the sharp, deep thud of tree against soil. Over and over and over until dusk, until the truck was full.

Another death ride back to their house, where Gramma called Meredith to report, "Your father tried to kill me today—*again*." Then she settled on their black vinyl sofa to watch TV and work on a tablecloth-size version of *The Last Supper* rendered entirely in white crocheted thread. One hook, thin thread, years and years of devotion. Kai and I took long baths using gallons of Gramma's Prell shampoo and climbed, sore and exhausted, into twin beds where Gramma sat at the foot to listen to our prayers, a confusing but required recitation. According to Gramma, when we lay us down to sleep, we must pray the Lord our souls to keep; that if we should die before we wake, we needed to pray the Lord our souls to take. Then we said "God bless . . ." followed by a litany of names, names of every person we knew or had ever met *and* the pets, because if we didn't include them, God wouldn't bless them, and if they should die tonight, they would go to hell and burn forever thanks to our negligence. I said Kai's and Emily's names twice.

Kai, thrilled to be off the couch and not dead *and* have the strength to run for miles and lift wood, fell instantly asleep each night, while under the blanket with a flashlight I wrote letter after letter to Emily, wide awake in the dark, missing her and her mom, missing the ocean, still hearing the sharp splintering of wood, the rush of air through pine needles, the heavy thud of trees against black soil. Over and over and over, again and again, trees and trees and trees until morning.

The next day was for splitting and stacking at home. Grandpa split the rounds, releasing a sweet ooze of sap and fat white grubs, and we ran to stack the pieces. Splitting, stacking, running for more. The sky was burning pink when we finished for the day, rows of wood, ten feet by six feet by three, stretching beyond the well pump behind the house.

We stacked eleven cords of wood that summer, all of it very unintentionally Montessori of them—these people who, to be fair, as kids themselves had Grapes of Wrathed it from Missouri to California when the effects of the drought and Great Depression had reached the Ozarks and who therefore knew the value of a good day's work, so who am I to judge. But the satisfaction of a job well done was giving way, at least for me, to the monotony and heat, to wishing for more than one day in a row in life that had more to offer than Kai's nausea or endless manual labor.

I daydreamed about swimming with Emily, roasting marshmallows on unwound coat hangers around a campfire, while in real life Kai and I lugged armload after armload of worm-filled wood in the suffocating heat, day after day.

Except Saturdays. On Saturdays we didn't go to the forest, and we didn't have to stack, either. On Saturdays we piled into the Death Mobile to buy milk at the store and pick up the mail at the post office. The third Saturday in June marked three weeks of Wood Stack Camp, and Grandpa decided to get the mail first, then Gramma and Kai went into the store for milk and dog kibble to supplement Rene's liver. I waited with Grandpa and Rene in the truck and he pulled from the pile of bills and catalogs a bright yellow envelope addressed with cursive black Magic Marker penmanship. *Emily, at last,* my heart thumped. Four letters I'd sent her, all unanswered. *Did she forget me? Maybe Girl Scout camp doesn't have mail.* But here it was; here she was! Grandpa tossed the yellow envelope at me. Not Emily's writing after all—Meredith's perfect cursive. I tore it open, devoured the only sentence: *Didn't you know this girl?*

A folded newspaper article dated two weeks prior fluttered to my lap. *Tree Kills Girl Scout.*

Emily is dead.

Below the headline her smiling school photograph, newspaper-grainy black-and-white, unruly curls held back with a clip.

A pine tree, twenty-one inches in diameter and long dead due to drought, fell on the child as she changed into pajamas in her sleeping bag, crushing her.

Awakened by the tree's fall, the remaining campers climbed from their bags and scattered. Camp counselors conducted a head count, noticed the corner of a bright orange sleeping bag beneath the fallen trunk, pulled the child from the immense weight, and performed CPR.

Too late.

She was already dead.

The scream of the chain saw, the rush of air through pine needles, the deafening thud of tree against soil.

In the truck I could not breathe. Gramma and Kai, hefting a gallon of low-fat and a big bag of kibble, climbed up into the cab.

"What's wrong with you?" Gramma asked.

Grandpa looked up from his Fingerhut catalog. "What?"

Gramma sighed. "Not *you*, dummy. Get a move on; don't let this milk spoil."

The road was curvy. I was sicker by the second. Kai whispered, "You okay?" and when I nodded she let me lay my head on her shoulder for maybe a minute. I was just about to cry when she moved her head to my shoulder, murmured she had a headache, dissolved. I wiped her tears with a tissue from Gramma's bra, folded the yellow envelope, stuffed it and the article into my pocket. At the house I tucked Kai in bed, got her two aspirin and a cool, damp washcloth, and locked myself in the bathroom to cry. It didn't happen. Too late. Now I was just nauseous.

I won't survive without you. Hadn't Emily said those words to me, begged me not to go?

Every day, all day, cowering terrified beneath falling trees.

I harangued an annoyed and baffled Gramma, "Is this twenty-one inches? How big is this one? If this fell on you, would it kill you? Is this twenty-one inches?" She gave me her sewing tape measure and I found a trunk that fit. Surprisingly small.

I hid in the pantry with the phone, dialed Emily's home number repeatedly, all hours of the day and night. It rang and rang until a recorded voice claimed disconnection, so I sent a letter, a thick envelope stuffed with ten pages covered front and back in my wobbly grief-penmanship asking her mom to call Gramma and Grandpa's number. Wrote again and again how much I missed her. Missed Emily.

The letter came back in a larger envelope, along with all my letters to Emily. *No Forwarding Address.*

Nothing in the newspaper story beyond the details of her death and the cold final statement: *No services will be held.*

I phone-grilled Wade and Meredith, who expressed a modicum of sympathy but claimed ignorance on all counts; they'd read it in the paper, had recognized her photo from the one time they'd met her, and had thought I'd be interested but couldn't remember what her mom even looked like, let alone if they'd seen her lately or received any phone calls asking for me. ("Who is this we're talking about? Someone from school?") My head throbbed with silent tantrums: *Don't you people leave the house? Don't you understand other people besides you exist in the world?* Wade was nice enough to walk to their cottage for me and knock on the door but reported it empty, once more listed on the rental market. I begged them to let me come home, but they phone-preached from the pulpit of bootstrap practicality to "Get back in the saddle and just be glad it wasn't you."

"Nothing you can do about it now," Meredith said. "You're on vacation! Get some fresh air, wade in the creek, enjoy yourself!"

Her delusions about what this "vacation" involved were practically adorable.

"Leigh," Wade said, stern, when Meredith passed the phone to him, "do *not* bother your sister with this." His voice was tight; my stomach swam. "Just let her be. Keep her out of it. People die every day. You'll be okay. That girl was just a friend from school. You take care of your *sister*. Got it?"

I got it. Neither of them ever mentioned Emily's name again.

I dialed the dentist office where her mom worked. "Honey, I'm sorry," the nice receptionist said. "She never came back in, left her last check, we've got no idea where to find her."

Calls to the *Mendocino Beacon* staff reporter, the Girl Scout site council, and the school district office all ended the same way. *We know nothing. We're sorry. No idea.*

Gone.

The afternoons in the forest crawled dully into one another, trees crashing to the ground all around us as I stood dutifully beside Kai but not paying attention, sickening images of Emily crushed beneath the trees crowding my thoughts with each earsplitting thud until Gramma's shrill hectoring broke through—"Leigh! You could have *killed* her!"

Gramma was on the ground trying to lift Kai, plucking leaves and pine needles from the stubbly fuzz on her head.

I snapped out of my trance, helped pull Kai to her feet.

"Sorry," I said. "What's happening?"

"Oh, nothing much," Gramma huffed, feeling Kai all over for broken bones. "Just great big heavy branches are falling on your sister, knocking her over, while you stand there daydreaming. Pay attention! She could have died right in front of your face, my God!"

"*Gramma*," Kai said, head in her hands, "it wasn't *that* big, it's not Leigh's fault, and no one is dying."

But it was my fault. All of it. I leave Emily for Kai, and Emily dies. I mourn Emily, and Kai is nearly killed.

Wade was right. Keep Kai out of it, keep it to myself, take care of her, or look what happens.

"Show's over!" Gramma hollered, pulling the covers off me every morning at dawn to chastise me for my apparent aversion to physical labor and regale me with cluelessly ironic stories of how as a child in the Ozarks, she and her brothers had helped bury their uncle Mike in practically frozen soil and then slaughtered nine hogs for winter meat all in a single afternoon. If it was attention I was after, she suggested, I'd get a lot more by stacking some wood than I would by lounging around moping in bed till the embarrassing hour of six a.m.

"What do you think happens when you die?" I asked her, pulling the sheet back up under my chin.

She frowned at me and unwound the sponge rollers from her hair.

"Well," she said, "depends. If you've accepted Jesus Christ as your Lord and Savior, you'll go to heaven and live forever beside Him in His glory and be with your family and never feel pain ever again."

Emily alive in heaven maybe? My heart eased up.

"But if you do *not* accept Jesus as your Savior in this life, well then . . ."

"What?"

"Sure as sin you'll burn forever in the black pits of hell, tortured and alone. Forever. *Forever.* So if I was you, I'd get your parents on board and hightail yourselves to church once in a while. Now get out of that bed and come eat some of this bacon. Can't feed it all to Rene; he'll be sick on the rug again."

That she and Grandpa never attended church themselves was a weird non-issue.

Saturdays I did not go to town with them. I sat and did nothing, mindlessly picked up Reader's Digest Condensed Books from the dusty stacks lined beneath the living room picture window, reading them all one after another. *Wuthering Heights. The Three Faces of Eve. East of Eden. Rebecca's* nameless narrator trapped behind the gates of Manderley Estate. I was nameless, too. My eyes bleary, head pounding, I read and read, dissected the narratives for clues, for secret meanings, for fortune-cookie platitudes to save me from the cement in my chest, the freezing cold, panicked, disbelieving ache for my best, my only friend, and for escape from the depressing Pixley house, silent but for the ticking of the giant grandfather clock near the front door, forever counting the seconds, chiming the hours and quarter hours and half hours. This "vacation" was never going to end.

Until it did. On the last day of July, another envelope from Meredith, white this time and no note, just two one-way bus tickets not home to Mendocino, but to Hangtown, a destination we stupidly thought was some park-and-ride situation that Wade would drive the rest of the way home from. We pulled away from Gramma and Grandpa waving on the Pixley sidewalk and I closed my eyes, leaned against Kai's shoulder, and she let me for a while until she got a headache and moved to lay her head in my lap. I stroked the soft wisps of hair just beginning to cover her head and told her again and again, over her muffled sobs, that it was just the altitude making it hurt, that once we got home to sea level everything would be okay. It would be okay. It would.

And maybe it would have.

❧

Shag Haircut is practically keening.

The wind chimes swing and I understand it is night, I am freezing cold and numb and Emily is dead. I chose Kai, left Emily alone, and now here she is. Now she really is dead. She is dead and buried in a hole here where I live; she is *here* and I am here, on her grave, in this random town two hundred miles from the ocean, from Mendocino, alone in the dark but for the still sobbing Shag Haircut. *How is this happening?* Many more minutes pass, each one colder and darker, too dark now to see her stone, to read it, but still I stare; she is calling my name, she is calling me—

"Leigh?"

My heart, my heart stops, oh God, she's calling me from her grave, her cold *grave*—

"Leigh."

Emily.

A narrow flashlight beam slices through the black. A hand reaches for my frozen own.

"Leigh."

I let the hand pull me forward; light spills a pool on her headstone—

"Leigh. What are you doing?"

Dario moves the light from Emily's name on the stone up into my unblinking eyes, does not let go of my hand—

"Do you want to go home?"

I think I may be sick.

"Leigh."

Shag's crying is more insistent.

"Okay, hold on, just—wait. Wait here for me."

His voice is low; he comforts Shag and the sister. He takes them away to the office, and I stay stupidly paralyzed and alone with Emily, on her *grave,* oh God.

Headlights sweep the graves and Shag is past the Manderleys, leaving at last.

Dario is beside me. He lugs me and the flashlight up over the rolling hills of graves. What is he doing out in the dark? His hands are warm in the cold; he stays with me even on the headstone path to our door.

Just be glad it wasn't you.

Wade's ignorance, his and Meredith's denial of Emily's existence, rattles in my head; I pull my hand from Dario's to walk instead toward the Christmas lights.

I hear him hang the flashlight in the shed. He pulls the

silver trailer door open and maybe my vacant, ashen face makes him step wordlessly aside so I can zombie in to stand and say nothing for a long while.

I sit. At his tiny kitchen table. Freezing. Still I do not talk, and neither, blessedly, does Dario. What he does do is crank up a space heater (thanks, Wade) all the way to ten and start pulling things from kitchen cabinets. He heats a saucepan, and a while later puts a steaming cup, *I heart California,* in front of me. My frozen throat is killing me. I take a sip, push the cup away. He moves it back.

"Just drink it."

"Tastes weird."

"No, it doesn't. *Champurrado.* It's just chocolate." He steps back to the counter, keeps his distance, moves dishes around. I breathe steam rising from the cup, lay my head on my arms, wonder vaguely if I will ever be anything but tired. If I will ever remember how to sleep.

Sleep, rest of nature, O sleep, most gentle of the divinities, peace of the soul . . . Oh my God, shut up, Ovid, shut up, shut up—

Too cold, too stupefied to remember to hate him, I am grateful for Dario's silence, and so I try another sip. This is *not* chocolate. Or at the very least is not the Ovaltine Meredith makes. I wrap my freezing hands around the hot cup and watch him rinse off a chopping board, wash a glass blender, wrap a disk of black chocolate in waxy paper and return it to the cupboard. He folds over the top of an open bag of cornmeal and screws the lid onto what may be a jar of anise seed, which

I suspect only because for years I have watched Gramma dump tons of it into the Thanksgiving stuffing. He is fastidiously tidy. I breathe in more steam and sip once more. Molasses. Anise. But still, somewhere in there—chocolate. A longer swallow, and another.

I watch Dario, wait for him to launch into a big patronizing lecture about what the hell was I doing, poor Shag Haircut, and by the by, what is my problem, why do I avoid him, am I mad at him or what? But nothing. He says nothing. The scene is so melodramatic and embarrassing I can hardly believe it, but I am still too cold and numb to knock it off. He wipes the counter with a green sponge, tips the steaming saucepan into another cup for himself, *NPR Pledge Drive Volunteer*, sits opposite me at the little table and drinks. I drink. The space heater clicks off, then three minutes later it comes back on.

Emily is out in the dark. She is in the ground, *Poppy Hill Row L, Space 23*, only yards from where I sit drinking weird hot chocolate in a trailer with a guy I hate. How did she get here? Why not Mendocino? *Why here?* I am so disoriented. Did Shag Haircut's crying bring on a hallucination of Emily's name on the stone in the dark? She's out there by herself, she doesn't have any flowers, there were no flowers for her, where is her mom?

My throat is closing, and the tearless crying that's been going on since summer burns in my chest. Real crying, the kind that makes Wade and Meredith roll their eyes, may be happening somewhere inside me, but it will not come out.

Dario still says nothing, and for the longest time the only

sounds are the heater buzzing and my muffled nonsobs, choked raggedly into my sleeves. He does not comfort me. He does not ask me what my problem is. He just sits and drinks his drink, and I do not sob and do not sob and he brings me Kleenex and a damp washcloth and still he says nothing and I pull my head up and stop trying to hide my face. I sit and not-cry until finally I really am empty, my throat is *really* killing me now, and Dario pours more chocolate. This time it does not taste weird. I drink it all and ask for more. He empties the saucepan into my cup and I nurse it, sad this is the last.

"Family?" he says.

I close my eyes.

"Friend?"

Not hallucinating if he saw it, too.

I nod.

"I'm sorry," he says.

My head throbs. Dario just sits there, as though people come to sit at his table to not-cry and drink *champurrado* every day of the week.

"Okay?" he says at last. I stand. He nods toward the bathroom door and I lock myself into the tiny closet, run the water ice cold and splash my face, which is red and swollen from trying so hard and for so long to either cry or not cry, or whatever I'm doing that I cannot seem to stop doing. I tie my hair back and open the door. Dario is holding a big coat for me.

He is so tall.

The wind rages, branches and leaves cluttering the dark

path. He helps me into the truck and drives me home, which is silly; the house is about two hundred yards away. Still. I climb out and he says, "It's six-forty-five."

"Okay," I say.

"Right?"

"Sure. Is that . . . Do you need to be somewhere?"

"Put it on your timecard. Overtime after six." I think of the shoe box full of Wade's stupid icing-on-the-cake cash and manage half a smile. I pull his coat off and lay it on the seat.

Over the mistake headstones, into the house where Kai stands in the kitchen eating a banana, *I was about to come get you!* Meredith invisibly painting. Wade does not look up from the TV to watch me move my weary body up the stairs to fill the tub with hot water and about a gallon of bath gel. I yell to Kai through the locked door that yes, I am fine, just tired. I stay in until my fingers and toes wrinkle and try desperately to not think of the dove and the pony, Emily's sleeping face down in her grave—and to reconjure my hatred of Dario.

part two

NON-ENDOWMENT

seven

AFTER SCHOOL THE NEXT DAY I lurk near the Manderleys to watch Dario spinning in Serenity.

No gloves. Hands probably still warm.

I run to the house, do not stop until I'm in my bedroom, where I take ragged breaths and lock the door behind me. I need more exercise. All those hours sitting in school, then the office. I'm skinny-fat. My muscles are ribbons, my lungs pathetic.

Meredith's ocean sound track stars a string quartet today. I pull open my closet door. Piles of random school papers, overdue library books, T-shirts. Beneath the pile, my wicker wastepaper basket. Nothing too icky to rummage through and thank God, because of course I find it, finally, at the very bottom, beneath tissues and nail clippings, cotton balls and Q-tips, *Please let it be here please it has to be I never empty this thing which is disgusting but in this case please,* and then there it is, here it is.

I hold it tight in my tremory hand. Meredith's waves roll beneath a mournful cello.

CR ꙮ

Luckily for Wade, a lifetime of his and Meredith's misguided *pretend everything is okay and it will be* Jedi mind trick garbage has soaked into my psyche, so the insane idea of returning to work in the graves after finding Emily there seems just—what I must do. After all, Emily is the dead one, not me. I have nothing to be whining about. I go right back to selling graves and grinding my teeth.

And with no fanfare, starting the morning after finding Emily, whenever I am working Dario is now somewhere near the office at all times.

My feigned annoyance with this new development is dwarfed by my secret, embarrassed relief.

All week I schedule burials, sell a few Pre-Need plots, avoid Emily's grave on The Walk, and when grief and self-pity strangle me, I search the grounds and find him there every single time: spinning, digging graves, planting trees.

Caretaking.

Non-endowment.

Safer than school.

On Friday, the moment the last bell rings, I race to the graves, slowing to a walk only when I see Dario out among them.

He waves.

I raise my hand. Duck into the office.

My ears ring in the quiet. I turn the heaters on high. Wade

could leave them on when he's done, keep it warm for me, but then that's an extra fifteen cents of electricity, so, you know.

The file cabinet practically hums; it knows what I want to know.

I make a neat stack of Yorks. Unwrap each one, a chocolate tower on the desk calendar.

Dario's mowing buzzes comfortably in the background, gives my mind a crutch to hold on to, keeps Emily and the pony and the dove and the trees safely tucked down.

I watch him watch over me.

The file cabinet has three drawers. Alphabetical.

A–J.

Half the York stack in my mouth.

Pipey McPipe Smoker's handwriting is tiny. Very slanted, textbook cursive. Feminine. A sexist thing to think. Dudes can't have nice handwriting? What is wrong with me?

ABCD. E.

My hands sweat.

Put the file on the desk. Rest of the Yorks in my piehole.

Dario is still there.

Ellison, Emily M.

M, really? You go to the trouble of a bird and a pony but *Marie* is too much to bother with?

Date of birth: December 10

Date of death: June 2

The day we arrived in Pixley. My heart sinks.

Date of interment: June 12

Mortuary: Chapel of the Pines

Horribly ironic.

Cause of death: _____

With a pencil, not pen—that would be way too dramatic—I fill in the empty line with my very best cursive. My first, middle, and last name.

Poppy Hill Row L, Space 23. Single space. Single depth.

Date of service: NA

No service. No funeral. Nothing.

Pre-Need. Paid in full January 5, 1962, along with a double depth beside her.

Married couple, *Martin.*

Okay. Unused plot her mom didn't have to pay for. Martin. The WASPs, East Coast by way of . . . Hangtown?

I am in no mood for solving mysteries. This is insane. Why this town, *this* cemetery, and by the way, is life really such a giant screwy web of chance and coincidence, because if it is . . . I don't know. That is just f-ed up.

Responsible party: I recognize her mom's signature, all the school permission slips she signed for me so I wouldn't have to bother Wade and Meredith. *Responsible* party. She couldn't even be bothered to go to Wade and Meredith and tell them herself; had they not seen the article in the paper, would Emily have simply disappeared until I found her in the ground? Why would her mother do this? Where *is* she?

Contact information: Same old Mendocino phone number. Useless. Still, I pick up the office phone. Dial for the millionth time.

The number you have reached has been disconnected or is no longer in service.

I put the file back in another drawer, shove it somewhere between *L* and *Q*.

From the *Ms* I pull the Martin file. Both of her father's parents are dead, interred 1963, 1968. Ancient phone number, different prefix than Hangtown's current, but I try it anyway.

The number you have reached . . .

I get hard-core. Mendocino County coroner. The morgue.

I am not family.

Chapel of the Pines.

Nothing.

Howard the County Coroner is still taped to the desk. His card.

"Howard," I say. "Let me ask you something . . ."

Nothing.

Gone.

How, in this century, can a person vanish so completely?

So easily.

Painful tight breaths. I put my head to my knees.

The mower stops.

I rush to the window.

He's still there. Pulling weeds.

I breathe.

At home in bed that night I read with a flashlight until my eyes grow bleary, then switch it off and drop it into the drawer in my bedside table. It lies there among ballpoint pens,

Emily's newsprint face, and, tucked in the back, nestled in a bed of wadded-up tissue, my Catrina, her flowers a little flattened from her time in the trash basket but still sparkly. I shut my eyes and shove the drawer closed.

CRSO

Blessedly, finally, it is winter break from school. I push my locker closed at the last bell and Kai's beautiful face floats to the surface of the mob of kids. She runs breathless to me, pink-cheeked. It is disorienting to see her here. She grabs me in a smothering embrace.

"Take these home for me, *please,* don't let Mom and Dad see, put them in the office?" A brown paper cone of softly limp, pale lavender roses. "I'm late for practice; I can't bring them—okay?"

I nod.

"Aren't they beautiful?"

I'm not typically a fan of roses, especially lately; they're just so—funereal. But these are gorgeous. Not too sweet, just enough. There is a card. I don't read it, though I'm dying to.

Rivendell. Balin.

Elanor called it.

"I can't tell you who they're from yet, but I will. Soon. I promise, okay?"

"Sure," I say, maybe too brightly. "Sure, I'm— That's exciting. A mystery!"

She is windswept, blissful.

"I love you!" She squeezes my face, kisses my cold cheek, and is gone.

I clutch the roses, shuffle into the library to perform, one-handed, my weekly Internet search for Emily's mom, for the Martins. Only the *Mendocino Beacon* article: *No services will be held.* Nothing else. Never anything. I'm no inter-webs genius, but it's becoming pretty clear that if someone is either a hippie-hobo single mom with no computer or a distant relative by marriage to said hippie who was long dead before computers were even a thing and with a name as common as Smith, odds are I'm not going to find them.

I give up.

I walk slowly out the school doors, stung that the Balin situation has progressed to flowers and still Kai has not confided in me, then ashamed at my selfishness because look how happy she is. That's all that matters.

My stupid heart whines about *Why can't we go back before all this crap?* Back home to the ocean, before Kai was sick, before Emily so I could not know her and then not have to be alone without her. Before this patron sainthood nonsense. Through the Manderleys, past the babies, past the trailer Christmas tree lights, over the headstones. I stash the roses in my backpack and fall into a kitchen chair.

Silence. No waves. Laundry room empty.

"*Meredith!*" My voice is hoarse.

"*What?*" Wade.

"Where is your wife?"

The toilet flushes. He comes downstairs, pulling work gloves back on.

"Mendocino," he says casually, heading out the door.

Takes me a second.

"Wait—what do you mean, *Mendocino*? Where is she?"

He holds the door open with his foot. "*Men-do-cino*. She needs a break. It's been a rough change for her, being . . . here. She'll be back in a couple days— What time is it? Get down to the office!" And he is gone, back out into the graves.

I bite the inside of my cheek. Hard.

I march dully out beneath the trees, over the headstones to the office, *Mendocino* chasing maddening circles in my head.

Kai and I have missed home, haven't touched seawater since leaving for Pixley, but clearly that is immaterial—the ocean is Meredith's thing. She is building an entire personality around missing it. Our childish longings have nothing to do with the actual pain and misery she feels being so far from the waves; can't we *see* that, for God's sake?

Dario is digging Shag's husband's grave.

Two weeks it's taken Shag to decide on a date. Howard's been driven to distraction storing the guy so long, but now soil flies gracefully from the hole, tossed over Dario's shoulder onto the pile from the backhoe. So unlike Jimmy, who just backhoes and takes off, always a big mess left in the grass. Dario is taking his time down in the grave with a shovel. He pulls out stones, probably makes the bottom flat. Smooth. Perfect.

My stomach burns imagining Jimmy lazily digging Emily's grave. She deserved Dario.

I steel myself, stride over lawn and headstones to Shag's grave, and step, unbelievably, to the edge.

My knees are jelly. I watch him carve the walls, the sides, precise corners among the grass and tree roots.

Down in the dark, he shades his eyes from the sun-bright clouds, smiles up at me. Waits for me to say something. The grave hypnotizes.

"*¿Cómo estuvo la escuela?*"

Six feet looks so much deeper from directly above.

"Hey. *¿Cómo estuvo la escuela?*"

Damp cold comes right up from it.

"Leigh."

"What?"

"*La escuela.*"

School. How was school?

"I don't know."

"*Sí, tú lo sabes.*"

Yes, you do know.

"Uh . . . I may have failed an algebra quiz."

He frowns.

I frown back.

"*¿Cómo estuvo la escuela?*" he says again.

Rich black soil. No wonder the lawn is so green.

"*Leigh.*"

"I said! Algebra!"

"*Español solamente.*"

Spanish only. Oh jeez. "Um . . . *¿Creo que . . . no pasó una prueba de* algebra?"

"*Agradable. ¿Te incluso estudiaste?*"

"Okay, wait— *Lo siento.* Slowly."

He calls up loudly and way slower than he needs to, "*¿Estudiaste?*"

Did I study? What the hell—

"*¡Sí! ¡Por supuesto estudio! ¡No es mi culpa que la prueba era estupido!*" I yell down into the grave. A shovelful of soil sails dangerously near my head.

"*La prueba no era tonto, simplemente no quisiste poner el esfuerzo.*"

Okay, first of all, he wasn't there; the test *was* stupid! And, "*Esfuerzo?*"

"Effort. *Tú eres inteligente, un poco perezoso es todo.*"

Perezoso? Wade calling me lazy is one thing, but what does Dario know? "*¿Usted va a juzgar mis hábitos de estudio desde abajo en una tumba?*" The words come without thought, which is pretty awesome because who knew I could say *You're going to judge my study habits from down in a grave?* in Spanish till right then, but also, what is his problem? He doesn't know me *or* my homework ethics! What does he think I'm doing hour after hour in that stupid office? (Well, when I'm not spying on people or reading novels for fun. But other than that.)

He reaches up to lay the shovel on the grass, pulls himself up and out of the grave, and brushes off his knees.

"*¿Cuándo aprendiste hablar español tan bien?*" he asks.

I consider his muddy jeans, the pile of velvety soil, his perfect grave. "I *don't* speak it well. I'm faking it."

"Not bad for fake." I hover at the edge, peer down into the black. Once a casket in a liner is in there, people lie just inches below our feet. Emily beneath the grass. She was so small. Is she in a child-size coffin?

The wind chimes sing. She is eleven rows away.

"There are about a billion butterflies in my town right now. In Mexico." English. "Well, not *in* my town—mine is Pátzcuaro. But near—Michoacán. You know about the butterflies? The migration?"

"Not really. But I bet it's magical and symbolizes something significant."

He makes sure I know he's ignoring me.

"Monarch butterflies. They leave Canada and fly three thousand miles to the forests in Michoacán. Oyamel forests. Balsam firs. Really tall, old pine trees and oaks. They come in autumn right around *Días de los Muertos* and you can't see the branches, even the trunks, just *wings*. It's crazy, they're all moving and fluttering, but slowly, and you stand there and look up into the branches and the sunlight and they fly, they settle in the pine needles and fly again. The air is full of them, the sky. . . . You would love it."

He collects his shovel and moves wide, flat plywood pieces to cover the empty hole until the funeral. He unfolds the traditional big blue tarp—protection against the threatening clouds gathering low beneath the winter white sky so close, barely above our heads. Why are these tarps not green? Knowing Wade, it's all about the blue ones being cheaper. It looks so tacky, the hills dotted with bright blue plastic tents on rainy multiple-burial weekends.

"Do you miss it? Miss your family?" I ask.

He leans on his shovel, wipes the back of his gloved hand across his forehead. "I do. But I love it here."

I hover beside the grave. Step onto the plywood. Bounce a little.

"See?" he says. "Just a grave."

Cloying fallen-tree wood-chip sweetness from a mountain of fresh flowers two rows over.

He tosses the shovel in the back bed of the tractor, pulls his gloves off, and reaches under the seat. Hands me a flat plastic bag: fun-size York Peppermint Patties.

"I was going to leave these on your desk. I snuck a few."

"That's okay."

"They really help," he says. And then he hugs me.

I stand stiff, arms at my sides. Blood thunders in my ears.

His clothes smell like soil. Soil and soap.

I close my eyes. Clench my toes tight inside my shoes.

"*Las cosas serán bien,*" he says. "You'll see."

He drives slowly up the hill toward the shed. I watch until he is gone.

I could see Emily from here if I tried. I don't.

I rip open the Yorks.

Serán bien, my ass. It is too late for things to turn out right.

eight

SPANISH ONLY becomes the unspoken rule for digging graves. He is worse than Señora Levet, who won't even let us go pee if we ask in English. My brain, occupied with vocabulary and syntax, has less room to be scared and actually think about the fact that *I'm digging a dead person's grave,* and Dario knows this. It's February and freezing.

I can't bring myself to help him bury, but I watch the grave-side services from the safety of the office or from behind one of the babies' angels so I can help move the flowers afterward. He always stands at the back of the cluster of mourners during services, near enough in case one of them loses it and makes everyone else domino down the path of out-of-control weeping. In those cases, he moves in swiftly, quietly comforting in two languages, and they lean willingly into him, a stranger in a Sierrawood Hills T-shirt. He waits for them to leave before he touches his shovel. Which often takes for-absolutely-ever, because they stand around talking after the religious part, and then once they move the party down to their cars, they stand around chatting it up some more. It reminds me of waiting after Kai's cross-country races, she and Wade recounting every step of the six, thirteen, twenty miles she has just run: "... *and then at the five K I had this cramp* ..." What about the reception? Aren't there seven-layer dips and Bundt cakes these people need to get to?

When at last they're gone, heavy belts and pulleys and a whirring, groaning motor ease the casket into Dario's perfect, careful grave, fitting it into the liner. Heavy cement lid on top, shovelfuls of soil until only the slim dark mound remains, waiting to be covered in a combination of tightly arranged, boring, from-out-of-town funereal bouquets and the wilder, admittedly beautiful Rivendell ones.

It is mostly the At Needs who stay till the end; and sometimes they insist on watching him bury. At Needs want every single last second they can get before their person turns to past tense. The Pre-Needs mostly take off and he buries them without an audience.

Pre-Need, as a concept, drives Dario nuts. He gets so worked up about it, he has to repeat his rapid-fire Spanish over and over before I get his drift, which is essentially that Pre-Need takes the ritual out of death. Takes away any reason to get out of bed when a person dies. You buy your own grave, schedule the funeral and the flowers, do it all yourself, and what have you left your loved ones with? A blank emptiness where you used to be, and no space to go through the motions of grief without the tangle of emotion. A person needs things to do, he says; a list of chores (*Schedule burial! Buy mini quiches for reception! Pick out headstone!*) gives you air to breathe. Flowers and food and choosing a space—a person needs those tasks.

"I don't know," I sigh one afternoon as we pile flowers on a fairly well attended Pre-Need woman. "For one thing, it's expensive."

"So why not just leave the money?"

"Because! It's *sad*. They're just trying to be nice. It's hard."

He shakes his head, carefully drags a giant pot of overly romantic red roses to the mound.

I'm not so sure choosing a casket to put Emily in provided her mother "breathing room" as much as it probably gave her a permanent broken heart. His logic escapes me.

Shag Haircut's nighttime lawn meltdown is what comes of At Need. Hasty, ill-advised decisions, and not that anyone wants to Pre-Need their own kid's grave just in case, but still. Did Emily's mom put her in some itchy, fancy dress instead of the Mendocino County Spelling Bee Finals T-shirt she wore and washed so many times all year it was super soft and pulling apart at the left shoulder seam? Did she watch Jimmy bury her?

I clutch a paper-wrapped bunch of Rivendell chrysanthemums by their blossoms. Dario eases them from my grip.

"What if they do it wrong?" I say.

"Who?"

"At Need. What if it isn't what you want?"

"Well, I think you have to give people a break and know they'll take care of you."

"But what if they don't? And what if you don't have anyone?"

The flowers are in place. Aside from the chrysanthemums and misguided roses, either her friends and family are all totally cheap or this woman was a lover of gas-station carnations and baby's breath.

"They will," Dario insists. "There's always someone. Everyone has someone."

"What about homeless people?"

"Everyone."

Emily's grave is lonely. No flowers. By unfathomable chance, here she is, here I am, and what good is it? I can't go near her, near her headstone. Seeing it once was an accident. Going back again, bringing flowers . . . that's *visiting*. That's tending. And then she really will be dead.

Mourning Emily, tending her, would leave Kai without my singular attention, vulnerable to every falling tree in the world. I chose Kai. It's done.

Dario folds the blue tarp neatly, respectfully as a flag.

"Why are you here?" I ask without thinking. "This can't be the only job in California. How can you be here every day doing this?"

"How can *you*?" Dario asks.

"I have no choice."

"Of course you do."

"No," I sigh. "I don't."

"Well, whose fault is that?"

"Uh . . . Wade's? Meredith's?"

He shakes his head. "Your job. Your responsibility."

"I'm a minor!"

"You're a patron saint. Act like it."

He pulls his canvas gloves off, shakes the soil from them. Walks me home.

Grave after grave sold in English, dug in Spanish.

The grave-buying public at large seems to mysteriously decide en masse to do their shopping not in the morning with Wade but in the afternoon with me, on *my* days, which thrills Wade and leaves me fatigued and somewhat apathetic—can't fight patron sainthood, apparently. My handwriting takes over the grave binder, every name carefully written first in pencil, then, once they are safely in the ground, in ink. I twist the knife and watch Emily's grave from the office to see if anyone leaves her flowers. Never any. I keep my distant, careful vigil over her unvisited body and remind myself I am securing Kai's happiness.

"I'm sorry," I say to strangers across the desk day after day. "I am so sorry for your loss."

And I am.

While I keep my own loss properly quiet. Nondramatic.

Suppressed grief suffocates, Ovid whispers, *it rages within the breast, and is forced to multiply its strength.*

I am circling the drain. Surrendering to a life of At Need sales in this office forever and ever until I wind up middle-aged, alone, living in the house by myself while Wade and Meredith travel the beaches of the world and Kai spends her life polishing Olympic track and field medals, with her husband, Balin, and their three adorable, well-behaved children.

My three-days-per-week after-school office schedule becomes generally understood by everyone involved as an every-day-per-week after-school-and-weekends-too schedule. Kai still secretly rendezvousing with Balin, Meredith gone to Mendocino, Wade being . . . Wade, and no one seems to care at all, or even register the change.

Well. Except Dario.

My fear of never getting out of the graveyard is eclipsed by his fear that I'll never want to leave. He begins delivering occasional spontaneous, pleading lectures along the lines of "This isn't good for you. Please, please go do something—anything—else. Come with me to Rivendell!" and tossing me *You should be trying to make friends and get a life* looks every chance he gets.

"I won't bother you," I promise. "I'll stay in the office."

He drops back down in the grave he is digging.

"Oh, Leigh," he sighs. "That's not it. At *all*."

He keeps me supplied with Yorks without my ever having to ask.

CR&SO

"Leigh!" Elanor calls, running toward me as I walk through the Manderleys after school this cold, gray Valentine's Day. I manage to keep my anxiety reined in—her visits are predictable, bright, and brief.

"Did she tell you?" she says, breathless. Pale pink dress, gray cardigan sweater. The boots.

114

"Who tell me what?"

"Kai, about Balin? He's enrolling in *school*. I knew it; I kept telling my parents, but all they ever said was, 'There's no way, he's too sensitive!' Oh my God, *sensitive*. He's a big baby and he gets what he wants whenever he wants it— I don't mean that, it's just—if he thinks I'm picking up his slack around Rivendell, he is sadly mistaken."

"Regular high school? He may want to hide his dice."

I'll never see Kai again.

"I know! My parents are all, *Why would he want this?* Which is ridiculous, it's like they're pretending not to know."

Kai is still infuriatingly mum about her Rivendell exploits, but the flowers are now more frequent and pretty blatant, so even navel-gazing Wade and Meredith have gotten the gist of what's up, and it seems just fine by them.

"I like that kid!" Wade bellowed after her this past Saturday as Kai jogged by the mausoleum on her way to Rivendell, under the guise of yet another "long run." She laughed, kept running past the Manderleys and off to Rivendell, and then he turned to me and said, "What the hell kind of name is *Balin*? You name a kid a thing like Balin, you're asking for it!"

"Asking for what?"

He just grunted and walked off into Serenity.

"He's joining the *track team,* for Pete's sake," Elanor says, rolling her eyes. "The guy who can't be bothered to shake the chip crumbs off his sheets, let alone ever actually make the bed—*he's* going to get up at the crack of dawn and go running? Yeah."

"Do *you* want to go?" I'm already exhausted just imagining hiding from her every single day.

"To school?" She makes a face. "No. I see the kids downtown sometimes. I watch them, the way they act, they're just . . . No."

Assholes, I think. *The word you're looking for is* assholes.

I search the green. Dario's in Serenity Valley with the backhoe.

"Oh well. It's his funeral." She brightens, jumps around to keep warm. "Love is in the air!" She gags dramatically and waves, off to pester Dario. "Come visit sometime! Happy Valentine's!"

Last year Emily's mom let us bake on Valentine's Day. Cinnamon rolls from scratch. With yeast. We had to let the dough rise and everything.

"No raisins," Emily said.

"Yes," I said, "and no nuts."

Her mom acted personally insulted. "Raisins and nuts are the whole point."

"Disgusting."

We ate them hot from the oven, straight out of the glass baking dish, pulled them apart with forks—ribbons of cinnamon dough steeped in cream cheese frosting.

"See?" Emily crowed. "Perfect."

Her mom ate three just by herself, smiling sadly in a stupor of sweet warmth. "This is terrible for our teeth. I'll miss baking with you," she said.

Emily frowned. "When are we not baking?"

"When you both have boyfriends and you spend Valentine's with them instead."

"Oh God, as *if*!" Emily moaned. "Every single boy in the entire eighth grade is *still* stupid; you said they'd grow out of it by now."

I dredged a roll through a puddle of frosting. "Sing it, sister."

"Okay, we'll see what happens next year. I would love to bake our way through puberty, but I'm not holding my breath."

"Oh God," we moaned. "Disgusting!"

"That woman needs to date some guys or something; she's the world's biggest martyr!" Emily whispered later in the secrecy of her bedroom. "She wants me to stay forever and be all, *Her and me against the world.* . . . Am I supposed to feel bad about growing up? Because it's kind of not my fault."

"You're all she's got," I sighed, envious. "It *is* you and her. You're a team."

"Not when she's super down in the dumps and making me feel guilty about regular junk. So I get a boyfriend someday, big deal! A normal mom would be happy about that, not *Ahhh! You're leaving me!* Feels selfish."

"Oh, brother," I said. "She doesn't mean it that way."

"She's obsessed."

"She loves you."

"It's annoying."

I couldn't imagine.

Her mom had poured glasses of cold milk, and we toasted to Kai, at home and still not well. To St. Valentine. To baking. To love.

Up in the graves, Elanor sits with Dario in the backhoe. Talking, laughing. I put my hand on the office door.

"Leigh!" she calls once more. "Remember, anytime—seriously, any day, whenever. Okay?"

She's got a death wish and she doesn't even know it.

nine

I CREEP TEN MINUTES LATE into the office, where Wade sits unnaturally straight-backed, stiff and nervous before a young-ish couple slumped near the space heaters.

"Oh, Leigh!" he says, barely masking his totally unnerved, unprofessional relief. It's been weeks since he's had to do a sale. "Leigh's here, here she is, this is Leigh, our . . . office manager. She'll be taking care of you now, so I'll just . . ." He stands, drops the pen where he's left off with the paperwork, squeezes my shoulder, and is out the door, with all the efficiency of an Olive Garden server, *I'm going on my break now, but Leigh's here to take care of you if you'd like a refill on those iced teas, more breadsticks, whatever you need!*

The woman stares vacantly ahead; the man nods.

I shrug out of my coat, drop my backpack behind the chair, and pick up the pen. "So . . ." I scan Wade's terrible hand-writing, stalling in my best grown-up voice. "Let's see where we are. . . ."

At Need, standard burial—but then crossed out, cremain burial, crossed out. Oh jeez.

"I think we're having trouble figuring out which . . . ," the man apologizes. "We can't . . . Could you maybe tell us how they—what it's like?"

Thanks, Wade.

"You know what?" I'm all pretend-calm, fake-not-panicked. "Let's take a look at some markers. That's a good start; then we'll see how we feel. We can take as much time as we need. Okay?"

What is all this "we" crap? God, these poor people, having to deal with my inanity. But they sit up in the wingbacks.

I haul out the catalogs and guide them through the glossy pages of bronze, granite, extravagant but easily chipped marble, the engraving options—*Emily's mom paid extra for the pony and the dove*—and they keep turning the pages again and again to little upright stones, lambs and angels—oh no no no, I skim the paperwork once more, birth and death dates still blank—God, Wade, what have you left me with?

Not even a day old.

All those headstones out in the baby section—yes, they had to get here somehow, but aren't they all from a hundred years ago? Iron lungs, diphtheria on the wagon trail? What about modern medicine?

They are spending more time picking out her headstone than they did holding her. I twist a rubber band around and around my fingers under the desk and share my limited knowledge of the difference between burying an embalmed body and a cremated one. Didn't Howard discuss this with them? Neither option offers any more comfort than the other. They cannot decide.

The three of us are mired in indecision.

I reach blatantly into the bottom left-hand desk drawer.

"Care for a mint?"

We leave it sort of Pre-Needy: they buy a little space, order the headstone, say they'll call when they figure out which option will cause the relatively least amount of horrible, horrible sadness. I do not tell them I will be looking forward to their call. I offer them more Yorks for the road.

I pull my coat on, make certain the Rivendell van is gone, and go searching for Dario.

At the top of Serenity Valley, he does not look up when I sit on a granite boulder two up and three over from the grave he is in. He digs. I hover in the warm hypnotic cadence of shovel, toss. Shovel, toss. Shovel, toss.

Shovel, toss. Shovel, toss. Shovel, toss.

For a long while.

Shovel, toss. Shovel, toss. Shovel, toss.

"Elanor really likes you."

I inhale grave-soil air.

"I could take you," he says. "To Rivendell. You could go with Kai, or— Wait, how old do you have to be to drive?"

I shake my head.

"Yes! Can't you take the class yet? When can you do that?"

"Can't."

"Why not?"

"I can't."

"Don't you *want* to?"

I close my eyes.

"Leigh."

Shovel, toss. Shovel, toss. Shovel.

"Would you want to be buried," I ask, "or cremated?"

"Depends on how old I am when I learn to drive."

"Oh my God, come *on*. Please."

He shakes his head at me. Smiles. "We don't cremate."

"That's racist."

"Hilarious," he says. "My *family*. We bury."

"How come?" I ask.

He shrugs. "What about you?"

I am startled to realize I've never really thought about it. So I do.

"Maybe . . . neither? Oh, could I just be dropped into the ocean?"

"Might wash up later."

"Oh. Right. Yikes."

"In my town people die and we bury them the next day. Sometimes we lay them in the living room first, or at the church. People like to come take a look and say goodbye, like a wake. We use our front room. My dad moves the breakfast table into the kitchen and we dress them in clothes they liked; the women pick things out. Then my cousins and my uncles and my father and I go dig the grave. Every town has its own cemetery; there's no driving to the funeral, no driving to visit, you live near your family. Always. We dig the grave and carry the coffin from the church or the living room, through the streets and straight to the grave, everyone together. When we took my grandmother we had music, a mariachi band walked with us. We bury them, we mix cement, pour it. Some bricks. Then everyone goes back to the house and my dad moves the table and we eat till we're sick.

"And then November comes and it's *Días de los Muertos,* which is a big-enough deal, but in some places like in my town, the first day, your birthday, is for the dead children. *Día de los Angelitos.*"

"Wait, *what?*"

"Day of the Angels."

Time slows, even the birds are silent.

"Are you making this up?"

"I told you!"

"No," I say, so sad it hurts. "No. You never said."

"Best day to be born." He smiles. "It's a responsibility."

Sure. One more I'm spectacularly failing.

Grave soil smells bright. Damp. Cold.

"So my family, for the first November first after a child has died, the godparents go to the parents' house and set a table for them. Fruit and sweets, candy skulls and skeletons and *pan de muerto,* which is just bread baked into a skull—you know, shaped like a skull. Their soul will eat the good part, not the actual *food* of it, but . . . like the point of it?"

"Essence?"

". . . the heart of who left it there . . ."

"The essence."

"*Essence?*"

"Of it."

"The *essence of it.* Okay. And we leave crosses and rosaries so the Virgin will pray for them, and there are a million candles. It's not some happy party, but it's not like here, either. Americans hate a mystery. They've made death so dark and scary. When really it is a door. It is beautiful; it isn't—it's not like here."

Ask that baby's parents. Ask Emily's mother. They know it is not beautiful to bury your daughter.

On the highway, cars pass.

"Then the second of November is all dancing and parades in the plaza and the gardens. Everyone's really happy because it's finally here, this one day of the year the dead get to walk again with the living, walk beside us. You can feel them. It goes on all day and into the night until midnight, but near my home, my parents' house, there is our lake, Pátzcuaro Lake, and in the center is Janitzio Island. At midnight everyone floats candles on the water, little golden stars floating in the blackness. . . . And the *mariposas,* little boats that look like they have butterfly wings because the fishermen use these nets, big wing-shaped nets—they fly in the stars on the water. Little butterfly boats. They float in the dark with the candles and sail to the island. Because on the island is a cemetery, the most beautiful cemetery. You would *love* it."

Oh, good. He's turning into Wade. Perfect.

"Everyone brings more candles to the graves there, and food and rosaries. Grateful that they lived, that we had them for the while we did. And then sometimes we sleep beside them all night because really, they haven't left us. They need us. They are the lights on the water. They need us to help them always stay. They're in the dark, they're with us, only . . . changed."

All things change. Nothing is extinguished.

Ovid is wrong. There is no metamorphosis. Emily is extinguished.

No wonder he got kicked out of Rome. Augustus was sick of that jerk, too.

The shovel flies from the hole and lands neatly beside the soil pile. Dario's hands reach up for the edge and he climbs out. Sits beside me on the muddy lawn.

My throat is tight. "I think I hate them."

"Who?"

"Wade. Meredith."

"No you don't."

"Just him, then."

"No you don't," he says again.

"He's an idiot."

"Oh, now—"

"He *is*. He calls caskets *coffins;* people think he's an idiot!"

"A casket's not a coffin?"

"Coffins have six sides. Dracula uses a coffin. It's all caskets now, four sides. Why do I know this and he doesn't? Stupid."

The wind chimes are still.

"I'm scared," I say.

"Of what?"

"All of it. Everything."

"Sure you're not just lonely?"

I shake my head.

"Well," he says, "what are you going to do about it?"

What *am* I going to do about it?

We sit for a long time unwrapping York after York, an entire Halloween fun-size bag gone.

CR ED

"Jesus Christ, what the hell are you *doing*?" Wade screams—*screams*—to Kai at the top of his lungs from his perch on a leafy branch high in a really tall oak as she runs past, red-faced and intent, hanging back from the front of the crowd of other red-faced intently running girls.

It's the first cross-country meet of the spring semester, home advantage at our school so at least we could walk to this one, and Wade is reveling in what has become his signature unsolicited "coaching" method (racing from one mile marker to another, climbing trees to holler encouraging obscenities as she passes), which the actual coach has given up trying to quell. Kai is far too valuable and the rest of the team just ignores him, so no biggie. He climbs down, takes a swig of Gatorade.

"Move it!" he calls. "We'll go meet her at the half!" I dog-ear my place in *To the Lighthouse*, wishing Wade would take a page from Virginia Woolf and maybe execute a little less dialogue.

"I'll wait at the finish." I shake leaves from the sweatshirt I am sitting on. He waves, runs off to the shortcut to yell more helpful advice. Meredith is home painting, and I have surrendered a Saturday double depth with Dario to cheer Kai on.

I climb to the top of the concrete bleachers, away from the flapping plastic circus flags of the finish line.

"Leigh!"

I squint into the early-spring sun.

Footsteps on the loose dirt track, dark knotted braids, and she bounds up the tall rise of the bleachers.

"Hey!" she pants. "Thank God, I thought I'd have to suffer this all by myself!"

Black skirt. Pale pink blouse. The boots.

She is everywhere. Or maybe there is just one of her, multiplying, a never-not-cheerful *Fantasia* broom bent on driving me out of my nut.

"Okay if I join you?"

I nod.

She sits beside me, turns her head sideways to read my book spine. "For class?" I shake my head. She smiles. "Just smart."

I shake my head.

"So," she says. "School. It's big. Is this where you have PE?"

"Sometimes. If it's not raining."

"It's nice."

I shrug.

"How's work?"

"Busy."

She nods. "Dario says spring may slow down your winter rush. I *love* that guy, don't you?"

Shrug.

The crowd cheers, muted in the distance. She turns toward the sound.

"I seriously don't get it. Do they have to do it so *much*?"

Now I can't help myself—this is a conversation I've guiltily yearned for since Kai got better. "I *know*!" I say. "I love that she loves it, but the *obsession* . . . I just want to shake her and say, *Get a hold of yourself!*"

Elanor laughs, leans forward conspiratorially. "My God, every morning, every weekend, he's *always* sweaty—he pretends he loves it, but I know he doesn't, not like Kai. But if it keeps him near her . . . and I guess the usual high school deification of jocks is a bonus. He seems to have lots of friends at school already."

"Really?"

"They don't know he still has dice in his backpack."

I kick a rock down steps. "How's *your* work?"

"Same. More fun when Kai's there to keep Balin out of my hair. My dad's always saying, 'She brings light to the Shire.'" She rolls her eyes.

"What *is* that?"

"Him thinking he's a hobbit. I don't know, he's . . . well, you met him."

"No—*the Shire*?"

"Oh. *The Lord of the Rings.* Frodo. Rivendell."

I frown back.

"Really? Tolkien?"

"Nope."

"Oh, man." She stretches her booted legs out in the new spring sun. "Well, no worse than dungeon mastery." She exhales. "Rivendell is the Elven Outpost in Middle-Earth."

"Yikes."

"Oh yeah. It's where the flipping *elves* live. You seriously have not read these books?"

I hold up Virginia.

"All right. So, *elves* live in Rivendell and it's all otherworldly peaceful waterfalls and trees and they live forever, kind of. And they're tall, I think. But the Shire is this forest valley where the hobbits live, and they're like people but smaller and more . . . hobbity. The Dungeon Master calls every place he likes the Shire. Our house. The movie theater. Bread aisle at Safeway."

"You live *in* the nursery?"

"Up behind the trees in back. It's a super tiny house so in summer you can't see it."

"Huh."

"Yeah. It's my grandparents', their nursery, my mom grew up in it. They left it to her when they died. Balin and I were born in the house—literally *in* it. In their bed, on a quilt they still have. Gross."

"Wow."

"Yeah. I do love it, I love the house, the trees and all, it's just—the whole Shire thing. They're obsessed."

I think of Meredith, her pounding waves, the seascapes on every inch of drywall. I nod.

"And of course they had to name us Tolkien-y. Balin's a dwarf. I'm a hobbit."

"Oh."

"Yeah. Though thankfully hobbit girls are all named for flowers, so really"—her voice gets dopey-dreamy—"I am a wee golden flower that grows in the fields of Lothlórien."

My every afternoon is swimming in names—first, middle, surnames listed in books, carved in stone, written in grave maps. I've seen some bad ones. I am an authority.

"It's a good name," I assure her. "Classic."

She smiles. "Better than Balin, I guess. Can't get around the dwarf thing too easily."

"At least they thought about it. Wade pulled mine from a hat."

"He did *not*."

"Might as well have." After giving Kai the ultimate homage, Meredith surrendered naming rights, let Wade have the leftovers.

"Well, it's sort of—letting the chips fall where they may? My parents are a mess. Super high-strung. Clingy."

Like Emily's mom.

My parental deficit is too deep to imagine disliking clingy. I study my shoes.

"So," she treads carefully, "how long was Kai sick?"

I kick another rock.

"Forever. Three years? Three."

Maybe if I just open Virginia and start reading . . .

"You'd never know it."

I nod.

"I mean, she's really . . ."

"Yeah."

More distant cheering.

"You know," she says, "she and Balin could talk about running all they wanted if you came over, like sometimes Dario gives her a ride if he's coming anyway, and we could—"

The crowd swells. They're getting closer.

"Not that it's real exciting at Ye Olde Rivendell, but we could find *something* to do."

The longer I sit saying nothing, the more panic rises in my chest—

"But I totally understand if you're busy, it's no big deal. . . ."

My throat burns. "No," I say, "it's not . . ."

The crowd is a frenzied, cow-bell-ringing clump moving toward the finish. We stand.

"Well," she says, "here they come."

We cheer from where we are, clapping, calling their names, my throat still tight. Balin's height gives him a long, loping stride. Kai leads the girls by practically minutes.

We climb down the bleachers. I see Kai in the middle of the field, hands on her knees, head near the grass, trying to breathe.

"Leigh!" Wade hollers. "Come help your sister!" He's forcing little paper cups of water on Kai (who we all know won't drink for another hour or so but he thinks she'll die of dehydration so he tries anyway). She bats him and his cups away from her face, sees me on the bleachers. Waves.

I wave back, try to smile. Elanor squints, searching for Balin in the crowd, and then there he is with their parents, a blur of ponytails and scarves and tie-dye. She sighs and makes a move toward them, when we see Balin bound over to Kai, rub her back, help her up off the grass, hold her hand.

"Huh," Elanor says. "Guess the hobbit's out of the bag."

We shield our eyes from the sun to see them entwine in a smothering embrace. Sweaty. Ick.

"Thought he was a dwarf."

"Hobbit's funnier."

I nod.

"She may be an amazing runner, but she's clearly got questionable taste in boys. Let's go."

She grabs my hand. She's a big hand-grabber.

Her parents move through the crowd toward Wade, toward Kai, Balin's arm around her bird-wing shoulders. Elanor's hand pulls me to them all, and for the millionth time my breath is shallow. I can't do it. I want to go home. I want Dario.

I want Emily to forgive me.

My hand slips from Elanor's as she moves into the jostling crowd. I pry myself free and run back to the graves alone.

ten

MEREDITH HAS TAKEN OVER the entire house. It's gone way beyond the constant sound track of waves and the seascapes—it is sand-colored rattan garage-sale furniture, fish-shaped soaps resting in polished abalone shells in the bathrooms, seashell wind chimes swaying and plinking in every window. We eat off ceramic clamshell dishes, drink from mugs shaped like nautiluses, even the salt and pepper shakers are wee mermaids: Salty's hair naturally blond, Pepper's a flowing cascade of black tendrils falling modestly over her tiny ceramic bosom. Our bedrooms are still our own, but even Wade is smart enough to know that the rest of the house, while we are all free to roam anywhere in it, belongs to Meredith.

And worse, emboldened by her winter escape, she has taken to jaunting off for more weekends back home in Mendocino, shacking up with one artist pal or another at what she has asininely begun referring to as The Sea. Kai and I jealously endure her breezy comings and goings, aching for the ocean ourselves but not permitted to say it out loud.

We harbored a fragile hope, Kai and I, that maybe the real Meredith would come back—the way she was before we left the ocean. Before Kai was sick. At home she had been this self-assured dynamo of exultant energy. Social and confident, she'd been more likely to whisk us off to a tour of the botanical gardens (*My God, have you ever seen such gorgeous rhododendrons?*) or pay-what-you-can belly-dancing class on a school night (*Loosen up, just do your homework in the morning!*) than to offer daily balanced meals, and we'd loved her for it. She was the exciting mom. The "no time for sensitive parental interaction, but how about let's go full moon tide-pooling at midnight" mom. At the ocean she'd always seemed to like going places, doing things with us. Being with us.

But her self-absorption, once part of her charm, has begun to wear. On Kai. Sure, it must be really, *really* horrible to watch your kid suffer with cancer. But "Oh please," Kai moans, "try actually having the crap happen to you, then whine about how tired you are. Jeez!" Still, she nakedly grieves the loss of Meredith's inimitable brand of mothering.

"Why can't we come?" Kai whines, lying next to me on Meredith and Wade's lighthouse-appliquéd bedspread, watching Meredith pack her suitcase. Spring break and the woman can't get away fast enough.

"You'd be bored to death," she says, tucking several carefully folded bras in among a bunch of beach-themed blouses. "Your father needs your help here, and besides, I'll be gone all day painting and then we're going to dinner every night for more silly art talk. You'd hate it." She holds a turquoise sweater under her chin, admiring the effect against her blue eyes in a full-length sand-dollar-framed mirror. "Go to your girlfriends' houses for slumber parties every night, why don't you?"

Slumber parties. It's like she's never met me before.

Kai heaves an enormous, quivering sigh, tears hovering. "I can't. My friends are all going away. On vacations. With their *parents*."

Balin will be off camping all week; Kai's been weeping about it for days.

Poor Kai, having to navigate her first boyfriend bon voyage without Meredith to help her. Though what am I even saying? Meredith and Wade's "relationship" is not really any kind of nautical metaphor to model a dating scenario on. Kai's better off skippering her own *Titanic*.

Meredith rummages through her jewelry box for appropriate seashell earrings. "You kids are so dramatic."

Kai is dumbstruck, unaccustomed to being denied.

I echo Meredith's sigh with my own, sharper one. Her turning Mendocino into a private artist retreat with her old goofy painter pals while we're left behind would normally not bother me so much, but Dario has asked Wade for a few days off to go fishing in Lake Tahoe.

"Absolutely!" Wade gushed. "Take some time, hang out with the guys, toss back a few cold ones, right?"

"What are 'cold ones'?" Dario asked me later as he organized his fishing lures in the toolshed.

This whole spring break is shaping up to be the dumbest thing to happen since . . . huh. Since being made to live in a graveyard.

"But what about Easter?" Kai whimpers.

"Oh, you guys," Meredith moans, worn out from the futility of trying to rally the troops. "Make an effort! You can cook Easter dinner, can't you? Color some eggs, do whatever you want. Baby, sit on this for me." Kai drags herself up and sits on the suitcase, smashing it together so Meredith can zip it up, toss it down the hall, and go to the bathroom to pack her nautilus-shaped toiletry bag.

CR&SO

Early Saturday morning, Meredith and Dario take off for their respective graveyard furloughs and I sit watching Kai through the open office door—with school and track practice on hiatus all week, she's given in to Wade's "offer" of employment. She assures me being in the graves isn't giving her the I-almost-had-a-headstone-myself creeps. But she misses Balin. Misses her whole other Rivendell family. She jabs a trowel listlessly at the soil, pretending to plant flowers in the newest valley being readied for graves, the still unnamed Meadow of Melancholy. Harbor of Heartache. Cadaver Canyon. Whatever. Wade will come up with something awesome.

"Hey! It's looking good!" he calls to Kai, saluting her with a double thumbs-up.

She gives him a halfhearted single in return. Not with her thumb.

Wade steps into the office and rubs my aching shoulders. "Maybe next time, okay? Don't worry. We'll have fun!"

I fold a York wrapper as a bookmark and set Ovid aside.

"Hey," I say. "What do you think happens to people when they die?"

"*What?*"

"When we die. What happens?"

"What do you—like, how it feels?"

"No, *after.* After we die."

He surveys his kingdom of hills and headstones. "Why the jack are you worrying about *that*?"

He gets the look-iest look of all looks.

"Well," he says, "I'll tell you what. When I was ten years old, my brother, Will, was seventeen. He had this girlfriend, Maxine—"

"Wait, hold on—your *brother*?"

"Yeah. My brother, Will. So Maxine was fifteen, I think, and she and Will . . ."

"This would be Will, your *brother.*"

"Shut up, I'm telling you something! *Yes,* my brother, Will, and this teenaged Maxine wanted to get married. So of course her parents were pissed off. My dad told Will he was acting like an idiot, and he was right; I mean, who the hell gets married when they're still in high school, right? Don't you or your sister ever pull a stunt like that. That's a bunch of crap."

"Preaching to the choir."

"All right. So Will whips out a trump card; the next thing

you know, Maxine's knocked up. Now my parents *have* to let them get married, right? Okay, so they get married, and Will quits school and goes to work for the county sanitation department, and a sewage pipe bursts one day in town, it's pouring rain, I mean *buckets,* and the guys are all down in this big hole and the rain's coming down and it's all mud and mess, and then the whole thing caves in."

"What does?"

"The *hole,* the hole they're in! Will's down in it, and the mud slides in and a guy tries to pull him out, but he feels Will's hand slip from his—Jesus, I'm telling you, it was awful. An awful, awful thing."

"Oh my God."

"Oh yeah," he says. "It was this whole big disaster. Maxine heard something was up; she's over at the school in third-period history or some junk. They wouldn't let her leave, but she busted out with a couple girlfriends and she shows up just in time to see them pull Will out with a crane, an actual *hook*—so there's Maxine in a raincoat, pregnant, and Will's hanging from this hook, all muddy, rain dripping off him."

"*Oh my God.*"

"Sure, and then to top it all off, she goes into labor right there and loses the baby! Terrible day. Awful. My mother was never the same."

"Are you making this up?"

"What the—*no!* Why would I make some horrible thing like that up?"

"You never, in our whole lives, ever said you had a brother!"

"Well, I didn't. Not after that."

"*What?*"

"The *point* is—life is screwy. You're going along fine, and out of the blue shit like that happens. Look at all these people." He looks out at the headstones. "Look at your sister; that could have been the *worst*— Look at your little friend, what's her face . . . ?"

My chest burns. The indifference stings.

"Okay, but what *happens* to you? After?"

He shrugs. "Who knows? Nothing. Nothing happens. Science debunked all that Heaven and Hell garbage forever ago. Sleep without dreams or something, I don't know. Nothing. That's what's so jacked up, but that's also why you gotta just do whatever the hell it is you're doing and not worry about stupid people and what they think because who knows what's coming. Have fun, do some stuff, work hard—live your goddamned life."

He moves in for a high five.

I hold my hand up.

"All right!"

He troops happily off to the toolshed.

"*Not after that I didn't*"?

Seriously?

If Kai had died, he'd have gone around denying he'd ever had an older daughter? She just never would have come up again in regular conversation, ever? He is insane, but I don't believe that for a second.

At least I don't think I do.

All morning, people come and go. They visit graves, bring flowers, tidy headstones, chat and sit and mourn. But no one comes to buy a grave. And no one comes to visit Emily.

"I'm going up to pee," Kai calls through the open office door. It's noon and the sun is blazing. I stand and stretch, and I walk to the new Rivendell angel to sit in the shade at her feet.

She is the babies' main angel, the tallest and most beautiful. She is young. Flowing, wild hair frames her face, which turns sadly toward the graves beneath her feet, eyes lonely, empty holes. Lonely for the babies and children resting inches beneath my knees. Here is a mother who misses her children, stays with them always, never sends them away or leaves them, wants so much to be near them she keeps watch over even their sleeping bodies, mourns them.

Dying is such a grown-up thing to do.

"Hey."

Dario is haloed by the sun, backpack on one shoulder, tackle box, wet hair combed.

I pull my ponytail out, worry my faded T-shirt. "I thought you were gone."

"On my way."

"Okay. Have a good time, Grizzly Adams."

"Who?"

"No one. Nothing."

"What are *you* doing?"

I shrug.

"Your mom leave?"

I nod.

He reaches down and pulls a dandelion out by its roots.

"Kind of unfair you didn't get to go."

Thank you!

"Move off that kid's head," he says. "Stay under the feet, above the head." He demonstrates, walks an easy grid between the graves, always moving along the top edge of the stones, right where everyone's feet would be.

Sorry, people's heads. I should have known better.

"Well," he says. "I'm off."

He pulls me up and hugs me. Hard.

My arms stay limp.

Soil. Soap.

Hard to swallow.

Don't leave me here.

"Hold on." He climbs back up over Poppy Hill to a weekend Pre-Need heaped with springtime blooms. And then he walks across the graves toward Emily.

To Emily.

He kneels on the damp lawn in clean jeans. He clears the weeds from her tin cup, fills it with pink and white sweet peas. He stands, brushes mud from his knees, and comes back for his pack.

"Okay?"

My heart thunders, full and spilling, swelling, an unfamiliar sharp warmth.

He starts for the Manderleys, waves over his shoulder. "See you in a few days!"

I wave back, dazed, watching him walk until I can't see him anymore.

The next morning is Easter Sunday, and to his credit, Wade does his best. He buys bags of Cadbury eggs and a precooked ham with pineapple slices on top, and after a healthy debate wherein Kai and I at last successfully convince him of the absolute tackiness of an Easter egg hunt through the graveyard, we instead watch *My Fair Lady* on television and we all like it, especially Wade, who enjoys the song "Why Can't a Woman Be More Like a Man?" a little too much and totally misses the irony of it, but still, it is pretty good, especially since not one song mentions a clambake. He shows us how to make two tiny holes in a raw egg and carefully blow it hollow.

"How do you know how to do this?" Kai asks, light-headed from the effort.

"Boy Scouts or some shit, I guess."

Wade and Kai go for an evening run and I hide in Meredith's laundry room with my hollow egg, put on a record called *Sea for the Senses FX*, and paint vines of pink and white sweet pea winding, curling all around a bright sea-blue shell.

Emily's mom made me an Easter basket last year. Emily brought it with her to school the Monday after spring break—green plastic strawberry basket with pipe-cleaner handles, Easter grass, chocolate eggs. Little chocolate bunny. Emily saved the bunny from her own basket and we went to the field at recess to eat them and compare notes.

"You guys have ham?"

"Turkey."

"Did Kai eat?"

"Just Jell-O."

"Better than nothing."

I nodded.

"My mom is crazy. She goes from never wanting me to grow up, to guess what she put in my plastic eggs?"

"Lithium?"

"Fake nails. Press-on."

"Classy."

The bunnies were hollow dark chocolate. Our favorite.

I wrap the sweet pea eggshell in tissue in a tiny box and go to bed early to lie awake and start waiting for Dario to come home.

CR&O

Tuesday morning Wade comes clomping through the graves in a T-shirt and his Japanese flag running shorts, which feature the rising sun directly in the center of the front—definitely the worst place for it. So gross.

"How's things?" he asks from the open office door.

"Fine."

"I mean, not just work. Are you . . . everything all right?"

I narrow my gaze. "What do you want?"

"I'm just asking!"

"Oh, really."

"Yes! So, you okay?" he asks.

"Sure."

"How's school been?"

"Terrible."

"Fantastic. You busy?"

"Yes."

I prop up my library copy of *Wuthering Heights* to block the view of the flag. Kai is out there weeding lilacs, still doggedly moping about Balin's absence. Jimmy digs a Pre-Need I booked last week. The poor mourners will be here soon, unaware they'll be missing out on a far sincerer burial experience with Dario, but then who knows if it even matters to them one way or another. Eleven up and twenty-three over from the open grave, Emily's sweet peas flutter, still pink.

Wade sits in a wingback. I peer over the top of my book. "What?" I say.

And in this moment that I am so especially desperate to demonstrate my gratitude to Dario, *for* Dario, for his flowers for Emily, to attempt to be a person worthy of anything, my chance arrives. In ashes.

My At Need/Pre-Need/Can't Decide Baby has come back in a tiny metal container, heavier from grief than from the few token bone fragments that rattle dully against the sides like the cubes in a Boggle game when Wade hands her across the desk to me.

"Think you could take care of this?" he asks.

"What?"

"I'd do it myself, but to be honest, it sort of creeps me out."

I just sit, blank-faced.

"Or I could ask Jimmy, it's just—that guy charges an arm and a leg. He's got a one-hour minimum, and this'll take fifteen, twenty minutes. . . . You know, on second thought, maybe I'll just drop it in myself, how hard can it be . . ." And he reaches to take her back.

I snatch her away, hold her to me.

The bones shift to the bottom.

First of all, I want to yell at him to grow up, him being the adult who bought this cemetery on purpose, so what is he talking about being "creeped out." And (b), there is no way in hell I am going to let him be in charge of the final resting place of this barely born girl. She's already been ripped off on life span; she doesn't deserve a grave shoddily dug by a guy who is "creeped out" by it.

"Just show me." His ability to paint me into corners is beginning to rival Meredith's seascapes.

My eyes move to the window, to Emily's blossom-heaped stone.

"Twenty minutes tops, soup to nuts," he says. "Use your gardening trowel, maybe finish with the shovel, and you're done. Ooh, got a little liner for you, too. I'll go get it!" He reaches over, taps the metal box, and squeezes my shoulder on his way out.

"Hey," I say, "don't tell Dario."

"Tell him what?"

"*This.*"

"What for?"

"Just don't. Or Kai. Please."

"Why?"

I don't know why.

"Just don't," I say. "Please."

He shrugs. "All right."

"No, I mean it. You can't tell either one of them, not ever. Promise right now or I'm not doing it."

"You're a team player."

"*Promise.*"

"Jeez, okay, I promise!" He laughs, ducks out the door, sticks his head back in. "You know what this means, right?"

That things have gotten worse than I thought they ever could?

"Bonus! Little something extra in your paycheck, if you know what I mean . . ."

My head drops to the desk and he hikes up the lawn to get the liner, practically flaunting those stupid shorts, right past the arriving Pre-Need family.

I have never suffered more muscle fatigue than the Wade-caused eye-rolling-related strain I've got happening.

I wait until the Pre-Need funeral is over, until Jimmy is gone, until Kai and Wade are in the house for dinner. I lock the Manderleys.

Dario placed her stone weeks ago, and here it is with the other babies, smooth granite, grass already grown up around its edges. Just a few inches tall, the name and one date etched below a sleeping lamb carved on top. Wade is right—the actual digging only takes twenty minutes. I conjure Dario beside me and take extra care to remove every pebble, pull out every root, make the sides smooth. The Rivendell angel watches me dig, sees me place the ashes carefully down in the liner, press the damp soil all around her with my bare hands.

I am the last person to hold her.

I keep the lawn patch in one piece and replace it when she's under, hose the extra black soil away, and when I'm done it looks like nothing's there. Or like it's always been.

The chimes ring.

Maybe I don't want Dario or Kai to know because they are the ones I would want to know the most, and this is not for anyone but her. Just this child. Because she needed me to. Because only I could do it the way it needed to be done.

The baby's family comes in the morning dressed in layers, light sweaters, khaki pants. Cotton skirts. Blue and brown, no black. Five or six people and a guy in a white shirt sporting a whole bunch of beaded necklaces doing some talking, reading from notes. I think of the baby, too late for the NICU.

I think of myself. Two pounds is so little.

"Your whole body was the size of my newborn head!" Emily liked to say.

"Only because *you* weighed ten ridiculous pounds," her mom loved reminding her. "My God, Leigh, you tiny little thing—and look how perfect you are. Modern medicine is unbelievable."

"Modern medicine nothing," Emily said. "Leigh knew what she was doing."

Out on the lawn, the mom stands by herself, arms limp across her deflated belly. She doesn't hold anyone's hand.

I rip open a new bag of Yorks.

Stars are scattered above the trees when I lock the Manderleys.

In Mendocino at the beach, Kai and I once found a nest of newly hatched snowy plovers in the sand, blind, still shaking off bits of shell. Meredith ran to pull us away. "If you touch them, the mother will know. She'll never come back to take care of them. They'll die."

Dario's sweet peas are fading but still there, still marking where Emily lies. But they are neutral; they are Dario handling the baby plovers with gloves on. His kindness is for Emily, but he is taking care of me. Non-endowment.

Through the pines the Christmas lights sparkle. He left them on for me.

If I take care of Emily, will her mother know? Will her mother never come back?

A heap of wildflowers covers the baby. Ducks softly peep and waddle from the pond in a wobbly line, strolling and pooping all over the graves and around the cement angels, around the Rivendell angel gazing fondly down on their plump, feathered bottoms, just more children to watch over.

CR SO

Sunday morning I am out of bed at dawn to see if Dario is back yet, which is stupid because who gets on a Greyhound bus at five a.m., but still.

A sliver of sun pulses orange behind thick clouds, warming the soaked grass. Steam rises from the graves and winds silkily around the black trees. Maybe we do live in the "Thriller" video. The trailer is empty. I sulk back over the headstones.

"What are you doing up?" Wade turns from the kitchen

sink, where he stands eating cling peaches from a can with a fork.

"Nothing."

"Kai still asleep?"

I nod.

"Rivendell kid'll be back soon; that'll cheer her up. Man, those are some good peaches. De*lish*!" He tosses the fork with a flourish into the sink, empty can rattling into the trash. "Get that dishwasher unloaded before your mother gets home, all right?" And he is out into the mist, risking his own run-in with red-leather-jacketed zombie Michael Jackson.

The sun reaches the tops of the pines and burns through the clouds, and Meredith shows up, windswept and refreshed. She strolls in, drops a bag of jelly beans on the counter, and announces, "The headlands are so beautiful this time of year!"

Her breathless accounts of beach strolls and brunches on the bluffs tempt my gag reflexes almost as much as the enthusiastic, welcoming embraces Kai smothers her with. Where is her anger? How about some healthy teenaged resentment? She clings to Meredith's seawater-soaked apron strings; her sloppy, desperate need for Meredith's increasingly arm's-length love makes me sad and pisses me off.

"Hey, baby." Meredith smiles, folding me into a smothering hug. "Hot enough for you?" I pick through the jelly beans for some red and orange ones, comment politely on her newest seascape, and let the screen door slam behind me to go see for the millionth time if Dario is back.

"Hey!" he calls, stepping out of the trailer.

I shove the pot of lip gloss I've smeared on my lips into my back pocket and keep my arms in their static no-big-deal place at my sides while he hugs me, try to downplay my joy: *You're home you're home you're home!*

"So," he says. "How was the week? Anything fun?"

I have a dream that one day medical science will invent a surgery that allows eyeballs to roll all the way to the back of a person's skull. Because then I could give an accurate nonverbal response to questions like this. For now I just lie.

"Fine. Same. You?"

"Oh yeah," he says. "Rented a boat. Fished. Camped."

"Alone?"

"I like the quiet."

"You work in a graveyard," I say.

"Different quiet. My birthday was Easter."

"It was?"

"Yes."

"Easter *Day.*"

"Not every year, but this year."

Rebirth, hope springing eternal, the holiday of *life.* Of course.

"Yours is better," he insists, meaning it. Weirdo.

"Why didn't you say anything?"

He shrugs.

I think of the sweet pea egg, now happily a perfect birthday gift—then wither in shyness. He is an adult, a *man*—he has no use for a flowery painted eggshell.

"So how old are you?"

"Twenty."

My chest clenches.

"Oh," I say, "now you can buy liquor. In South Korea."

"Really?"

"Sure."

"Why do you know that?"

I put my hands up. Why did I *say* it?

"Huh."

"But you're still too young to run for state senate."

"That's too bad."

"Yeah. Well. Happy late birthday."

"Thank you."

He gets up to riffle around in his pack.

"I brought you something."

I twist my ponytail around my fingers and press my shiny lips together. Sit on the top step.

He tosses me a brown-paper-wrapped bundle of tissue bound with red thread, protecting—

One more sparkly dead person, tiny shovel in one hand, bouquet of glittery flowers in the other. I blink. Dario smiles.

"He's a grave digger. See?"

Oh, I see.

"Your birthday one, the lady, she's a Catrina. *Catrin,* it means sort of . . . elegant? Because everyone dies, right? Not just poor people, *everyone,* fancy, *elegant* people, wealthy with big hats and flowers; all of us. José Posada was this artist a hundred years ago; he made a block print of her, carved into wood with ink, *Calavera Catrina.* For political . . . like a joke?"

"Satire?"

"Right. But now people make these from clay, every kind of dead person you can think of. Grave diggers!"

"I get it."

"Your Catrina, she is special. She is Mictecacihuatl, the patron saint. She's the queen. Queen of the Underworld. She watches over the bones. Because she was born, and then sacrificed as a baby."

Nice. Stupid birth/death just like me.

Patron saint of *creepiness.*

The grave digger grins from his tissue bundle in my open hands.

"But that's more Aztec, the sacrifice part."

"Great."

"My friend Ana—friend of my family, in Pátzcuaro—she makes them. She's a real artist. I asked her to send him for you and there he was, waiting at the post office. Isn't he beautiful?"

His smooth bare skull, silver shovel shining, flowers resplendent in his bony fingers, dark pants painted over bone legs.

"Yes," I sigh, holding him to the sunlight, reflected glitter light spinning, shiny stars skimming my skin. "He is."

Dario pulls his Sierrawood Hills baseball hat over his black hair. Sits beside me.

"Elanor come around?"

I shake my head.

"You go see her?"

I stare into the mud.

He shakes his head. "How can you not like her?"

"I do," I admit.

"Really?"

I nod.

"You do?"

"*Yes.*"

"Want to go to Rivendell? I need potting soil anyway. I can drop you off. . . ."

"No. Thank you."

"Or I could teach you to drive and you could get your license and take yourself there, or anywhere you wanted. . . ."

"No."

"Leigh. I don't understand."

"Me either," I sigh.

"Your mom back yet?"

I nod.

"How'd that go?"

I shake my head.

The leaves of the tree saplings lining his walk shiver in a slow draft, rain-soaked and lawn-scented.

"Hungry?"

We walk out the Manderleys and fifteen minutes later we are sipping lemon water downtown in a booth at Denny's and studying tall, glossy plastic menus. When the waitress comes, I announce, "I would like the hot fudge ice cream cake, please."

Dario shoots me a stern *It isn't even eleven a.m.; you are not eating cake and ice cream for breakfast* look, hands his menu over, and says, "Me too."

I am accumulating a debt of gratitude to him I fear I may never be able to repay.

The waitress nods. "Good choice."

eleven

MAYBE "FISHING IN LAKE TAHOE" is code for something sketchy or life-changing, because ever since he's been back, Dario not only has been especially, relentlessly cheerful, but also has a seemingly random and definitely super annoying new obsession.

He is going—*driving*—to the post office every five minutes, which makes me so anxious I can hardly stand it. Because aside from the law he's breaking every single day just by being here at all, he is otherwise a stickler for rules, and when he drives it is understood that he's breaking two pretty major ones simultaneously, but clearly the risk is worth it to him. He does not talk about it. None of us do.

All I know about it is what I've gotten from Wade, which isn't much, because I don't think I *want* to know, and Dario does little more than confirm facts. Plus with Wade, anything I think I know is probably wrong anyway. I know the coyote and the money and hiding and the guns, and this is where my information ends. I could get the actual lowdown in five minutes at the library, but I don't feel like it. Visas. Green cards. Wade remains unconcerned, putting all his eggs in the "Dario knows what he's doing" basket.

"When he drives," I asked Wade once, "like, to town—what would happen if he got pulled over?"

"Nothing good" was all he said. "But it's not like he's driving all over the back forty, just to the store, the nursery . . . the post office so he can send half his damn salary to his mother every week." (Enormous eye roll.) "He's a good driver. He's not going to get pulled over."

"But what would happen if he did?"

"Don't worry about it."

These aren't the droids you're looking for.

Okay, and then there's a second annoying thing, which may be semi-related and is possibly even worse: he's straight up harassing me night and day to join him on the autobahn, insisting I enroll in driver's ed.

"Yeah . . . ," I call down into the grave we're digging, my Spanish faster and more sarcasm-laced every day, "that's a super idea. Let me get right on that so I can kill someone, *quick*."

"Why are you going to kill someone? That's ridiculous!"

"Fifteen is way too young to be driving, permit or not. That's why we have so many kids in here with poems on their headstones."

"But those guys are always drunk!" he insists. "You're not going to be drunk or half-asleep or on drugs; you're going to be an excellent driver, I'll show you!"

"No thanks."

"Elanor says she wants to. She can't wait," he says.

"Good for her."

He frowns up at me.

"Why doesn't Kai drive?"

"Scared." Sixteen but not one to tempt fate, Kai figures cheating death once was the only lottery she will ever win. Driving is pushing her luck.

"So *you* can! Show her it's okay, help her!"

"Don't need to."

"You could go visit your friends."

Is he *trying* to be mean?

"Don't feel sorry for yourself. Elanor's your friend."

I pretend I didn't hear him.

"Listen. That whole situation is just— You're being stupid. But besides that, I find it very hard to believe there isn't *one* girl in your entire school you could be friends with."

"Believe it."

"Whatever. You need to make that a goal. You need friends, ASAP."

Next to *whatever, ASAP* is Dario's new favorite word. English acronyms make him laugh. Wade and I are taking the linguistic bloom off the NPR rose in no time.

"Fine," I sigh. "That's really great advice. I'll get right on it."

"Don't you *want* friends?"

On the hill above us, I see he has graced Emily's grave with tulips, all pink.

"Do you miss your family?" I ask.

He nods.

"A lot?"

Nods again. All I ever get. Never details. It's like he was born on the moon.

"Sure," he says. "I do. But you're supposed to, right? Grow up, have a life, visit. Write."

Ravens caw.

"Leigh. Don't you want to go anywhere?"

I drum my heels against the soil wall.

He stops digging. Looks up at me.

"I want . . . I would like to go home," I say. "To the ocean."

Down in the dark, his face lights up. He grabs my foot. Shakes my leg.

"When can you take the class? Too late for spring, is there a summer one?"

Gramma's voice howls her freaked-out panic. *Don't touch that, we'll die, Wallace, turn here or we'll die, the motor will catch fire, we'll all die!* Patron saint of vehicular manslaughter.

"There are buses. And taxis," I say.

"Leigh."

"Forget it."

"Okay. We'll see."

He pulls his sleeve back from his watch. "Oh, shoot—be back in a minute."

"Where're you going?"

"Post office closes in half an hour," he says.

"Again?"

"Be right back!"

158

How much money does his mother need?

He's up and out of the grave, starting the backhoe, moves it awkwardly around the trees and off to the shed.

"Don't be scared!" he yells over his shoulder. *"No te asustas! Te encantará!"*

No, I will not *love it.*

Stupid post office.

CRLE

Kai's seventeenth birthday is nearly here, and for her sake, I am willing to submit to the ickiness of parting with some icing-on-the-cake grave money.

Every one of her birthdays is cause for relief and celebration, but also I want to help make up for Meredith using the hot weather as an excuse to give the Sea/graveyard split an 80/20 advantage to The Sea, which is seriously troubling Kai. I am troubled as well, though it is less Meredith's absence and more my lack of caring about her absence that gives me pause. Her presence is so rare, it is a novelty, departures and arrivals unceremonious for Wade and me. But poor Kai, even basking in the glow of Balin and the paradise of Rivendell, still refuses to warm to the familiarity of Meredith never being around. The seascapes she produces in Mendocino grow bigger and admittedly more beautiful with each trip, the walls of even the kitchen now crowded with them, and when she *is* here, it's just business as usual with the recorded waves, acetone forever wafting down the hall, the painting, painting, painting. If Wade is disturbed by his mostly bachelor life, he isn't letting on.

The Saturday before her birthday, Kai conveniently dashes

off to a matinee with Balin and I beg Dario to take a long lunch and drive me to town to find her a present.

"See?" he crows. "You could be driving yourself! You could go wherever, whenever you want! Just take the class!"

"Please?" I sigh. "Just downtown. For Kai."

"You can't walk a few blocks?"

"It's hot," I say, my hatred of the inland heat enough to temporarily supersede my fear of his getting pulled over. "I'll just run into the pharmacy and get her some hair clips or lip gloss, I'll be fast, I swear—*please*."

He pulls his gloves off. "I'm going to the post office anyway."

What is *up* with the post office?

He drives slowly, carefully. If he ever does get pulled over, it'll be for drawing attention to himself going way under the speed limit. Or for being a USPS stalker. The wind barely moves through the windows, but at least we're out from beneath the pulsing sun. I lean my head against the door and close my eyes, think hard about the Mendocino bluffs, sea spray, fog, willing myself cool in the comfortable radio drone of Carl Kasell's NPR voice. I feel Dario park in shade.

"Quick stop first."

"Seriously, haven't you been twice today already?"

I open my eyes—

Rivendell.

"I need to get her a present, too," he says. "Just come with. Come in and look."

"No thanks."

"Don't be a baby. Get out here."

"I'll wait."

He climbs out, stands there in the heat rising even within Rivendell's redwoods, guilts me through the open window. "Let's find her something better than pharmacy lip gloss."

"What am I getting her here, daffodil bulbs? Forget it."

"They've got stuff."

"Why don't *you* be friends with Elanor and leave me out of it. God!"

He frowns.

"I mean *gosh*."

I prop my feet petulantly on the dash.

"Leigh."

Always sounds different when he says it. Makes me like it more.

Kai does deserve better than pharmacy lip gloss.

The brass bells ring. The mill house is blessedly cool.

"Dario!"

Of course she's working.

Slate gray skirt, sleeveless lavender blouse, rhinestone earrings beneath each knotted braid. Clean apron. Boots. Blue striped socks, no tights. Too warm.

"Leigh!" She dives to hug Dario, then goes for me.

"We need a present for Kai," Dario says.

She nods. "Balin's been spazzing out trying to think of something good." She kneels at the register, digs around in the shelves beneath it. "He says something from here is lame, which is stupid because wait till I show you, oh my gosh . . . But so I say, 'What about running stuff?' and he gets all huffy. I guess shoes and sweatpants aren't too romantic. I don't know. I told him to wait till the day before and the right thing will just . . . announce itself."

"Good plan," Dario says.

She ignores him and his recently developed sense of sarcasm, tosses a pile of fabric onto her sewing machine, finally fishes a key ring from the register mess, and hurries to a glass case tucked into a corner. "Okay, now look, my mom's friend asked if we'd sell these for her. Delicious."

Jewelry case. Beneath a tall window, sunlight spills rainbows through the crystal suspended above it and into a shallow bowl filled with rice and slender silver chains, some strung with iridescent opals, seed pearls, and—

"Oh, that one," I breathe.

Sea glass. A necklace strung in all shades of blue and green sea glass, the colors we collected at home when Meredith would take us to Fort Bragg to visit Glass Beach, a former dump site, the shore there curving sharply in toward the dunes. We walked carefully on broken shells and filled our sand pails with bits of blue and green and aqua and clear glass worn smooth by years of ocean waves rolling them against the sand, more precious, more beautiful than jewels.

Elanor turns the jumble of keys to open the case, scoops the necklace from the rice, and holds it to the light.

I think of the still-life painting (bowl of fruit, random scruffy dog with one ear cocked, vase of flowers dropping petals on a shiny tabletop) that Meredith routinely paints and wraps for our birthday gifts. Wade signs the card. Not that presents are all-important, and a painting your own mom did is obviously a thing to be treasured or whatever and a decent child would be grateful for it, but—this birthday will not be spent on the sofa near the bucket. The first, after three years, that she won't fear is her last. And this sea glass is just *so* . . . Kai.

It will remind her of the ocean. It is the color of her eyes.

It is ridiculously expensive.

"Want to go halfsies?" I ask Dario, wanting so badly for Kai to have it.

"What?"

"Buy it together, from both of us," I say.

"Dario, you know what halfsies means, don't be dumb," Elanor says. She cradles the glass in her hands, carries it to the register, lays it in a nest of lamb's wool in a slender brown box, attacks the price tag with a Sharpie. "Oh, look, I guess I'm the manager on duty to approve employee discounts."

"Can you do that?" I ask.

"Apparently." She smiles.

Dario and I pool our cash and watch her wrap the box in layers of crispy blue and white and violet tissue. She tosses fairy glitter between each sheet and ties it all in festoons of satin ribbon. She holds it up. "Delightful. She'll love it."

She wipes her sparkling glitter hands on her white apron. Enya warbles. The crystals spin their rainbows.

"Thank you," I say. "She'll be so happy."

Dario kisses her hand soundly. "You are a jewel," he says.

The brass bells ring. A familiar voice.

"Dario!"

Oh for God's sake.

"Helen!"

Dario goes to hug-fest party with Real Nice Clambake near the split-leaf philodendrons, and Elanor takes my arm.

"Don't make eye contact," she whispers, steering me out the back door and waving as we go. "Hey, Mrs. Irvin!" Clambake waves back.

Out in the shady heat of the tree-filled nursery, she leads the way to a hammock anchored between two impossibly tall redwoods.

"She is so hot and cold," Elanor whispers, flopping into the swinging ropes. "Do you talk with her a lot?"

"Clambake? No."

"Is that what you *call* her?"

"Not to her face."

"That song gives me an aneurysm. She's insane! I mean, she's nice, but it's like one day nothing, not a word, and I think, *Great, did I insult her by accident?* and then the next day she'll yammer about nothing for hours. She loves Dario, though, huh? Sit!" She moves to one end, closes her eyes, pushes the hammock, swings back beneath the trees.

"Clambake," she says. Snorts.

"You don't have to stay inside for customers?"

She waves away a fluttering moth. "I'll hear the bells, and my parents will be back soon. She's fine with Dario. Rest for a minute."

I hover. My hands are damp.

"It'll hold us. Trust me."

Won't hold the weight of my guilt. Emily all alone at Sierrawood.

But maybe just for a little while?

I give in, lower myself beside her.

The trees reach endlessly up; near blackness in the thick redwood branches. I close my eyes.

"I don't know how you can wear jeans in this heat," she says. "I would die."

"Yeah" is all I can think to say.

"Though I am the person who wears skirts in the middle of winter, so what am I even talking about?"

I watch our shadows sweep back over the grass as we swing. Forward. Back. Forward. I should say something.

My heart races.

"Did you make that skirt?" I ask.

She nods. "Blouse, too. Kind of screwed up the button-holes, but you can't really tell unless you look closely. . . ." She pulls a pearl button toward me, snug in what seems to be a perfectly stitched hole.

"Pretty color."

"I am absolutely in love with every shade of lilac and lavender. I spend all my paychecks on fabric; it drives my mom nuts. We've got similar coloring, you and me. . . . You ever wear anything violet?"

Either she does not notice or she is being really kind and pretending not to notice that I am wearing the same jeans and one of maybe five T-shirts every time she sees me.

Too smart not to notice.

Kai's got "coloring." *She* is beautiful in anything. I could never wear a color like that. Violet.

"I knitted these," she says, lifting her leg to pull at the thin blue-and-purple-striped socks inside her boots. "I just started. I got this book and some yarn and I thought it was going to be really complicated, but it turns out, knitting? Just rows and rows of knots. It's very meditative. You should try it; you could knit in the office."

"I'm allergic to wool."

"Oh, me too! It's awful, gives me hives. But these are cotton, not scratchy at all."

"Huh."

We swing.

"Do you really work as much as Kai says you do?"

I nod.

"Do you *want* to?"

I think of the baby. "Sometimes there's things people need that . . . things only I can do. I don't always mind."

We swing some more.

"He's a pretty . . . compelling guy. Wade."

"Yeah."

"You're Cordelia."

"Sorry?"

"Yeah," she says, "to his Lear. Except there's only two sisters and Kai's not a total hussy, but other than that. Definitely Cordelia."

Shakespeare. But I don't remember.

She closes her eyes, swings the hammock. "Cordelia is King Lear's youngest daughter. He disowns her for telling the truth; it's like he *wants* her to lie, but she's all, 'Sorry, I can't!' So he says she's dead to him. Super harsh."

"What won't she lie about?"

"How much she loves him."

In the mill house, Clambake laughs.

"Does she?" I ask.

"What?"

"Love her dad."

"Oh yes. A ton. Just—not enough for him."

"Huh."

"It's hard for Lear because Cordelia is his favorite."

"Well," I sigh, "I'm not Wade's favorite. Wade is Wade's favorite."

Another moth, white, flutters around our heads. Elanor holds her hand up, encourages it to land. It flies into my hair, then up into the redwood branches.

"So what happens?" I ask.

"Cordelia ends up dead because of Lear's selfish stupidity, and he goes completely out of his nut wandering the heath alone, railing at the wind."

I imagine Wade alone in his Japanese flag shorts, spinning the green heath of Sierrawood.

"Okay." She sits up. "I'm going to apologize first but ask anyway, even though my mom has said never to, and I'm sure a million people have already asked you a billion times already, but is it . . . How is it?"

"What?"

"Living there. Selling graves. Is it . . . I mean, is it sad?"

On the surface, a self-evident question. But she is the first person ever to ask.

I lean carefully back against the ropes.

"Yes," I say. "Sometimes."

"But not always?"

"And sometimes it's hard for me to leave."

"Like . . . ?"

"I mean, like, if someone's really . . . if they're having a hard time."

"Oh, right," she says. "Yikes."

"If they're having a hard time. They need . . ."

"Sure."

"Just takes a while sometimes."

We push with our feet. The hammock swings.

"You are so brave," she says.

CR SO

Dario dares to drive the actual speed limit all the way to the graves, lest we get back two seconds past his lunch hour. His hands at nine and three.

I lean my head against the door, and the wind through the truck windows moves the ribbons around Kai's Elanor-wrapped birthday necklace over my hands.

In the morning I sign up for summer school driver's ed.

twelve

ON THE LAST DAY OF SCHOOL I watch Caroline sloppily make out against her locker with a greasy-haired metal-shop guy, all the sexy romance of a dog eating spaghetti. She and Lisa sign each other's yearbooks in the throng of laughing, happy kids in the quad messing around, throwing tortillas like Frisbees.

"Hey." Lisa's voice is a siren behind me. She yanks me around by my shoulder. "Stare much?"

"Sorry," I mumble, and move to escape her long reach, but she gets one last shove in; I stumble toward a garbage can, find my footing. Walk fast.

"Run all you want, freak. We know where you live!" Caroline laughs.

As always, Kai is nowhere. Probably already gone, safe at Rivendell with Balin. I empty my locker as fast as I can. I ask the librarian to sign my yearbook, and Mrs. McKinstry, who writes, "Have a lovely summer, don't read too much ha ha but seriously . . . don't."

Through the tall black Manderleys, the impending three years of high school—the rest of my death-infused life—yawn endless before me, dark, scary, and lonely.

Oh, Emily.

"Leigh!"

A loud whisper. Dario crouches beside the pond.

"Hurry! Come here, quick!" I drop my backpack in a sullen lump. He makes room for me in the tall grass, pulls it gently aside.

"Hi!" Elanor whispers, hidden in the reeds beside him.

"What are you guys—?"

"Shhhh!"

"Look how tiny!"

A late batch of ducklings, black and yellow balls of softest fuzz, big bees with feet. They softly peep, skimming the water, and we are still, watching them zoom around looking for bugs, kicking up tiny arcs of cool pond water, followed closely by their attentive mother.

"It's going to be a good summer," Dario declares, stepping back carefully. He helps me to my feet, lifts my pack off the ground, and offers Elanor his other hand. "Right?"

"Yes!" she says.

"You just wait." He smiles at me. "I can tell."

The headstones gleam in the afternoon heat.

"Because of your highly tuned perceptivity and insight about summer fun?" I ask.

"Listen," he says, "if I don't bring the superior Mexican wisdom to you people, you'll never make it."

Wade crests the rise of Serenity Valley on the riding lawn mower, waves, dips back down.

"What are you doing? Are you in the office all summer?" Dario asks pointedly.

I nod.

"Every day?" Elanor says.

"Pretty much."

"You cannot spend your entire summer vacation selling graves!" Dario barks.

"You'd be surprised."

"It isn't good for you."

"Tell Wade that."

"*You* tell him!" he says. "Get out of here, do something fun!"

"Oh, okay."

"Go somewhere with Elanor!"

"Yeah!" she says. "Let's!"

"Hey." Dario suddenly turns to her. "Does Balin drive?"

"My parents won't let him."

"Why?"

"He'll be ready when he's thirty and calms himself down."

"Does he *want* to?"

She shrugs. "Dunno. But *I* do."

He gives me a "See? Told you!" look.

"I have to get to work," I sigh.

"Can I come in for a minute? I've got something for you," Elanor calls over her shoulder, marching off to the flower van, which is parked at the mausoleum.

I shrug my pack on and head for the office. Dario walks beside me, pulling gloves on, a hat over his black curls.

"You okay?" he asks.

I nod.

"Really?"

"What's up with the 'going somewhere' stuff right in front of her?" I whisper.

"All right, okay, sorry. I'm sorry."

"It isn't fair, I don't—"

"Leigh."

"*What?*"

He lifts the backpack off my shoulder and pulls me in for an "everything's going to be all right" hug.

I drop my arms, close my eyes, and let him.

From the office doorway, I watch him walk through the headstones, pull a clutch of roses from an embarrassment of floral riches on a grave in a neighboring row, and settle them into Emily's tin cup. He pulls a few weeds from beneath her stone, brushes it off.

Butterflies.

"Okay, got it!" Elanor makes her way through the babies. I leave the door open and fall into my chair.

She lays a flat package on my desk calendar, same tissue as Kai's sea glass.

A skirt. Two skirts.

"I wanted to make you tops, too, but that's a lot harder without measurements, so—you're skinny and skirt patterns are easy to draw."

One is the same violet as her blouse, the other pale blue. Perfect tiny stitches, a neat pair of pleats runs the length from the waist to the hem.

"They're cotton-poly. I preshrank them so they'll stay that size, which actually is only good if they fit—"

The fabric is so soft but crisp, brand-new, perfect.

I shift in my chair, the tired denim of my Emily jeans familiar, worn thin.

Elanor sits in a wingback.

"I shouldn't have made you *clothes* without asking. It's weird, I'm sorry. I *do* need to think first—"

"They're beautiful," I say. "They're . . . I love them."

Her face lights up. "Really?"

"Really. I do. Thank you."

"Well . . ." She is smiling so hard. "That's— I'm so glad!"

I pull out the Yorks. "Care for a mint?"

"Even though I'm not buying a grave?"

"I'll make an exception."

She accepts a gracious handful. "My *favorite*."

"Are they really?"

"There is nothing better," she says, "than a York."

I have no idea which T-shirt is going to go with these skirts.

CRSO

Dario has decided he needs to demonstrate the delightful health benefits of "going somewhere and doing something fun" by taking advantage of a burial-free Monday for an overnight fishing trip on the Sacramento delta.

I sit on the trailer steps in the early-morning chill,

Christmas lights still on, to half watch him pack while making my way through a stapled pile of work sheets from the new bane of my existence, summer school driver's ed. Five months until my birthday—it'll take that long just to work up the nerve to actually get behind the wheel. But I want so badly to please him, and the news of my reluctant enrollment made him so happy he nearly fell over. Still, I find myself unable to fake any enthusiasm for the inevitable deaths of me and several unsuspecting strangers.

"Okay," I say flatly. "Four people all come to a four-way stop at the same time. Who goes first?"

He tosses a pair of rolled-up socks at his backpack and stuffs them around the edges. I wait five seconds and flip to the answer page. "The person on your right."

"Whose right?"

"Um. That's all it says: '*Your* right.' Everyone's, I guess."

He shakes his head and folds a T-shirt in with the socks. "That doesn't make any sense."

"Whatever, dude," I sigh. "I'm just telling you what it says." I am done trying to get him off my back about this.

The class is completely terrible, mainly because of the films—a bunch of cheaply made cautionary tales that fuel my fear, featuring irresponsible teen drivers listening to music too loud who drive stupidly across train tracks, ignoring clanging bells and flashing warning lights, the last shot invariably a close-up of one of the kids' faces, fake-horrified and screaming, bathed in red brake lights against a backdrop of car-crash sound effects: screeching, metal slamming into itself, shattering glass, and . . . credits! Words roll over blood thickly trickling down a desolate storm drain: *Brought to you by the California State Automobile Association.*

I described these to Dario and to Wade (who is thrilled he may soon have a legally licensed driver to do all his errands for him and keep Dario off the road) and tried to impress upon them both how much anxiety even just the idea of driving is causing me, which prompted Wade's "Don't be so dramatic!" and Dario's "Keep studying."

Kai still resolutely refuses to join me, preferring instead, as any sensible person would, to hang out at Rivendell and run with Balin. Wade and Meredith let her, all the while enthusiastically encouraging my enrollment in Dario's Graveyard Driving School. I try hard not to let all Kai's "Get Out of Driver's Ed and Anything Else You Don't Want to Do" free passes make my jealousy burn even brighter.

From the steps, I see that Dario's tiny kitchen table, normally impeccably free of clutter, is covered with an assortment of things: glass jars of colored water, little pots of paint, blank white cards, envelopes, stamps. A mess. He drops a travel-size toothpaste into a single sock, his version of a toiletry bag.

"I'll teach you," he says. "You get your permit, we'll drive all over Sierrawood so when you drive with the actual teacher, you're extra prepared and confident. Right?"

"We'll see."

"We'll *see?*"

"Maybe I'll fail the written and I won't even be allowed to. *Person on your right.* You never know."

"Oh, I *know*. You'll pass that test and I'll meet you in the driveway." His bag, and the subject, are closed.

I watch him walk through the trees, off to the bus stop and away from the graves, to cool blue lake water and sleeping in a tent.

Up the stairs to my room. I step out of my Emily jeans, toss them on the hamper. On the highest shelf in my closet are the Elanor skirts, still folded in their tissue.

Gray Sierrawood T-shirt, so . . . blue skirt. Not ready for violet. Cotton still soft, pleats sharp, crisply ironed. Simple. Barely noticeable A-line. I can do this.

I tie my plain off-brand canvas sneakers. I put my hair up, grab a few books and an orange from the kitchen, and walk past the trees, past the graves, past Emily, to the office. Wearing a skirt. A skirt Elanor made. For me.

Everything is still early-morning quiet; not even Wade is out yet. I pull at the pleats, mess with the zipper—leave it alone.

My legs, hidden so long in my Emily jeans, are pasty. And bony. They will not be slated to stroll a catwalk anytime ever, but they feel free. Light.

I read. People trickle in to visit graves, but no one comes to me. I turn on my desk fan; warm air circles around my bare knees. I fall deeper into my book and so am jarred by the opening door, a cheerful guy's face peering around it.

"Hi there . . . Leigh?" he asks.

I worry the hem around my seated knees.

"Can I help you?"

"If you're Leigh." He steps in, clipboard in one hand, gorgeous bouquet in the other.

"Oh," I say, "you can just take it out to the grave if you want. Here's a map. . . ."

"Are you Leigh?"

I nod.

"Okay then, sign here for me. . . ." He holds the clipboard before me, sets the flowers in a glass vase right on my desk calendar. I scribble my initials; he climbs back in his van.

Lavender and violet and white blossoms and slender green reeds and ferns, all my favorites bending in the breeze from the fan: cosmos, impatiens, wax flowers. Not Rivendell.

But there is my name in black ink on the card envelope.

No one has ever given me flowers, not ever.

The card is embossed with larks taking flight in a pale blue sky.

THIS IS A HARD DAY FOR YOU. SEE YOU TOMORROW.
SER VALIENTE. BE BRAVE.

About what? I read it again and again. Why is today hard?

I stand in the doorway and look out at the graves.

My face flushes hot.

I didn't forget. I would never forget. I just—

Forgot.

She died this day. This beautiful June day marked by what I have let slip beneath my own selfishness, beneath cotton polyester fabric sewn by someone who is not her, who will never be her.

Em/i/ly. El/a/nor.

I walk, stiff-legged and fast, past Wade at the shed, over the headstone path into the house, up the stairs to yank the skirt off, throw it in the closet, pull my Emily jeans back on.

I sit on the corner of my bed, heart racing, and catch my breath.

Back to the office.

Door wide open, fan still blowing.

The flowers are luminous in the murk of the wood paneling.

Ser valiente.

Days and weeks have turned into an entire year.

This is a hard day for you.

She is never coming back.

⚭

In my Emily jeans, right back to avoiding Elanor, furious with myself because I knew this would happen. What is *wrong* with me? Be loyal to Emily, or leave her lonely and have a living friend. I can't have both—these are truths *I* made evident and still I can't abide?

I choose Emily.

Elanor's parents invite Kai and me to join them at a rented cabin in Lake Tahoe for Fourth of July weekend. Luckily, we end up with back-to-back At Needs—cancer, heart attack—a legitimate work excuse to apologetically decline.

I lean in Kai's bedroom door, hungrily watching her cram sunscreen and extra towels into her backpack.

"This is stupid. You're not in charge of burying anybody. Why can't you come?"

"I know," I say. "I'm sorry." Even Dario has given up trying to figure out what my deal is with Elanor: no more lectures or bait-and-switch Rivendell visits, only audibly heaved sighs every time I decline an invitation or run to hide in the house when the van shows up.

Still, he registers my loneliness. Even Meredith will be with friends for the holiday, drinking boxed white wine from plastic cups at the Mendocino Firecracker Day Parade before picnicking on the bluffs with the other artists, toasting not only our nation's liberty but her own freedom from the oppressive Monarchy of Motherly Obligation.

At sunset on the Fourth, I lock the Manderleys behind the last patriotic mourners and find Dario and Wade have loaded the pickup truck with lawn chairs, a cooler of beer (root beer for me), and King Fong's Chinese takeout. Even on Independence Day, there is no stopping Wade's admiration of the Fong's blatant use of MSG. A prominently displayed placard in the restaurant details the many beneficial uses and "inevitability of MSG in any decent Chinese food," and this strikes a chord with Wade, who feels that avoiding every little thing the FDA says is bad for you when we're all going to die eventually anyway is just "damned ridiculous."

So we eat Dave Fong's shrimp fried rice and have the best

view of the fireworks in the entire county. Far from the crowds and rip-off ten-dollar fairground parking, we luxuriate at the top of Sunny Hill, blankets on our laps, oohing and aahing at the pistils and roundels in our own private box seats, colors and jewels exploding in the stars, dripping into the black and violet shadows of the pines and the mausoleum, the light reflecting in Dario's unblinking eyes.

"I love it here," he says.

"The graveyard?"

"America."

"I bet they don't put on a show this good for Cinco de Mayo," Wade says, struggling with a slippery soy sauce packet.

"We have rockets. But that's not our Independence Day."

Wade looks up from his soy sauce problem. "Yes, it is!"

"No, May fifth is the Battle of Puebla. During your Civil War."

"Against *who*?"

"The French. Our Independence Day is September sixteenth. We beat Spain."

Wade shakes his head, tears the soy sauce open with his teeth, and douses a carton of white rice while Dario offers more interesting facts about life in Mexico. Like how where he is from, there is no such thing as a burrito.

"Bullshit," Wade says, dipping a pot sticker in plum sauce with a plastic fork, never chopsticks.

I am fascinated. "So if I went to your house and said, 'Hey, can I have a burrito?'"

"They would bring you a small donkey."

"Bullshit!" Wade says again, tossing a beer to Dario, who for the millionth time reminds Wade he does not drink. Dario rolls his eyes at me on the sly.

I swoon.

I try hard not to let my thoughts veer to how badly I am treating Elanor, or enviously to Kai swimming in the lake with Balin, their long-haired, bescarved parents on a blanket nearby being all nice and encouraging, offering bean sprout and almond butter sandwiches and vegan marshmallows to roast.

A breeze picks up, smearing the fireworks against their black canvas.

Dario takes his sweatshirt off, lays it across my shivering shoulders.

Later, in the veterans' niche, he finds a bouquet of tiny American flags and I watch him take one to Emily. I imagine it looks nice there, unfurling over the dove.

CR&SO

A particularly sweltery late July afternoon and I trudge home from the DMV, where, despite my best efforts, I have aced my learner's permit test. Wade is knee-deep in a front yard casket liner digging up old geranium roots but offers me a muddy-gloved high five.

"Fantastic!" he sings, tossing some roots out of the liner. "Now work on your sister for me and we'll be all set."

As if. She just laughs and laces up her running shoes.

"Where's Dario?"

"Post office. Back in a minute."

Why do I bother asking anymore?

Wade stretches and leans on his shovel. "You want to start practicing this weekend?"

"Practice what?"

He laughs. "Driving, dummy! We'll go to the school, swing around the parking lot."

I shrug. "Dario'll do it."

He hesitates for the smallest part of a moment—then goes right back to shoveling.

Yikes.

"I mean," I say, "if you *wanted*—"

"No, I'll sign the thingy, say it was me—licensed driver, yeah?" Another trifling law Dario seems willing to break.

"Thanks."

"How many hours?"

"Um. Fifty?"

"Huh. Just make goddamned sure you do *not* go past the gates. At all. Ever."

I resist saying *Yes, I know, I know,* and instead press the bruised issue of "What if we were out and we got pulled over, but I was driving? Would Dario still—"

"Just get your license and we won't have to worry about it." He busies himself with his bulbs, grousing into the soil about certain people needing to get a "passport, for God's sake."

"But with a passport, wouldn't he—"

"Jesus H!" Wade screams, tossing the shovel and jumping out of the liner. "Argh! *Huge* snake!" I rush over to see. "What is it doing in my damn planter?" He runs off toward the shed to find a weapon to defend himself against the monster, which turns out to be a common garter snake, maybe ten inches long. I peer down into the liner to get a closer look.

"Get away from that thing!" he yelps. "It'll bite your face off!"

I follow him to the shed; he rummages through a pile of burlap bags. "What would happen," I say, "if he got a passport and then came back?"

He pulls rakes off the wall, weighing them in his hands.

"Have to get a green card, visa, all that," Wade says. "They'd make him leave after a few months, or he'd need a sponsor or some damn thing. I told him I'd do it, but . . . I don't know. He's still here, so why get him up a tree about it? *This'll* kill it!" He stands tall, wielding a rusty, scary-looking scythe, clearly in no mood to plumb the depths of illegal immigration.

"*Seriously?*" I sigh. "Don't be such a baby."

I grab a burlap bag and jog up the driveway to the liner, Wade calling desperately after me to *Look out!* but obviously glad I have taken the reins. "Don't touch it! It's a dangerous serpent; it's got *fangs!*" I wrap the bag around my hand, pluck the sun-lounging snake from the flowers, and toss it into the tall rough beside the house, where it lands with a gentle thud and skims silkily away, swimming the bright sea of summer grass all the way into the trees toward the veterans.

Wade throws his hands in the air, eyes wide. "Now it's gonna come right back up here! Why the hell would you throw it behind the house? For crying out loud!"

I press the bag into his open hands and start back down to the office.

"Hey!" he calls. "Don't forget to tell your mother!"

"Tell her what?"

"Your permit, that you got your permit! She'll be thrilled!"

Where is Dario?

I keep walking, wanting more than anything to punch Benjamin Franklin in the face for ever insisting America needed a postal service.

thirteen

"I'M GOING TO KILL US BOTH," I whisper, white-knuckled at the wheel.

The Sierrawood truck idles behind the shed; I struggle to shift into reverse. "It's broken." I force it.

Dario winces. "Clutch?"

"*Yes*," I say, casually pushing the clutch in with my terrified left foot. He pretends not to notice.

"Okay, try some gas." The truck jerks backward, dies. "*Some*." In fits and starts, I get down the drive, onto the gravel road, all the way to the office. "Good, good!" he murmurs happily. I get it turned around ("Nice eleven-point turn!") and back up to the shed with much less terror.

"Shifting is scary." I climb from the truck.

"Scary?"

"Won't the engine fall out if I do it wrong? Fall apart?"

He stops walking. "Fall *apart*?"

Oh God. Gramma had no idea how a car works; of course she only said that to scare me into behaving.

"You've got to calm down," he says. "It's not that big a deal. You'll be a wonderful driver."

He squeezes my shoulders, hurries to the trailer to change into clean funeral clothes for a ten o'clock service. I start walking home slowly, and he calls, "Hey, wait—come get these boots for your dad."

Wade has asked to borrow Dario's fishing hip waders so he can search through the grass for more deadly snakes, a ridiculous venture the likely outcome of which I don't even want to think about.

I run to the trailer, pull my hair up off my face in a ponytail, and hover in his doorway. He pulls a box of fishing stuff from under the bed and rummages for the boots. The trailer is, as always, unsettlingly neat except again for the kitchen table, still covered with paper and pens and paint and brushes and stamps. Lined paper. Blue envelopes with nature scenes drawn on them.

Dario emerges from the pile of fishing stuff and hands me the waders.

I nod toward the table. "Art project?"

He shrugs.

"Pen pal?"

"Just some friends in Pátzcuaro. Family."

"Huh." I accept the boots and start for home, then turn hopefully back in the door. "Come get me after you bury?"

"I've got it."

"But—"

"Leigh. Go. Find something else to do." He gathers the letters in a careful pile.

My face burns.

I stumble blindly home, eyes blinking furiously.

My stomach hurts.

Meredith's ocean sounds fill the otherwise silent house, and I wander down the dark hallway to her lair, hovering in *her* doorway.

She is perched before her easel, meticulously darkening deep orchid clouds in a stormy, threatening sky, shadows on a roiling green sea.

Her brush whispers, pulling paint across the canvas in tight, even strokes, *wist, wist, wist.*

Her waves crash.

My dry eyes still smart.

She squints at her sky. "What's up?"

"Nothing," I say.

"Working?"

"Driving."

"With your father?"

"Dario."

She looks up at me. I tug my ponytail out. "Isn't it supposed to be a licensed—"

"Yeah, Wade's just gonna sign the . . . thing."

She shakes her head.

Back to the storm.

Wist, wist, wist.

"Kai off with that kid?"

"Yeah."

"Huh."

Wist, wist, wist.

"You like him?" she asks.

"Balin?"

"Think he's okay?"

"He's all right."

Wist, wist, wist.

"Right before I graduated high school, Raymond Montoya moved in a few blocks from us. His family was really big; he had four or five sisters. Oh, was he a handsome devil. Dark black hair, he was short—barely taller than me—and older. Almost thirty. Gramma was horrified."

Wist, wist, wist.

"He had this red car—I don't remember what kind, but it was little and really shiny. He would pick me up in front of the school and take me to movies, or Broch's drugstore for ice cream. My girlfriends were so jealous. We dated all that summer, but then he started getting impatient with—you know, making out. . . ."

Oh good Lord.

"And then I started taking classes at the city college and he *really* started going on and on with the *I love you, we're going to get married, blah blah blah,* and I thought, *Well, hell, if he's going to marry me . . .*"

"I get it."

"So we do it—"

"Oh *jeez*."

"—and then the next day I call him and his mother says he's not home. So I call again later, and the next day, he's not home and he's not home. This goes on for a week or more, so finally I walk to his dad's car dealership after class one day and he's there. But he *ignores* me. Won't say a word. Laughs at me."

"Oh my God," I say. "That's . . . Did he really?"

She nods.

Holy crap.

Wist, wist, wist.

"So what did you do?"

"Well. I left. I walked home."

"What did Gramma say?"

"Oh good God, I couldn't tell her any of *that,* she'd lose her mind. She was mad enough I was seeing him, let alone . . ."

"Yeah, okay."

"But so I come home and I'm, you know, I'm devastated. Sobbing, I can't breathe, all that. Gramma didn't ever ask anything, didn't say a word. The next day I drag myself to class, and when I get home there's this box on my bed. A dress box. She bought me this beautiful dotted swiss dress from Macy's, all folded into this perfect tissue, really pretty full skirt, pale, pale pink, just . . . oh. I *loved* that thing. *Loved it.*"

Her sky is heavier every second.

"So the next morning, I put the dress on. I'm feeling a little better. I go to archery class and I'm retrieving a wayward arrow—"

"You had an archery class?" I ask.

"It was community college."

"You wore a *dress* to archery class?"

"—and I'm looking for my arrow, and I fall in the bushes and stain it. The entire front, all green. And we did not have Tide pens back then, so, you know."

The orchestra behind the waves swells to an earnest crescendo.

Wist, wist, wist.

She's pulling rain from the clouds down into the ocean.

"I think it's okay," I say. "Balin's a nice guy. I wouldn't worry about Kai."

She drops her brush into a jar of turpentine, rubs her eyes, and studies the waves. "I'm not worried about Kai."

She moves some paint with her thumb, smudges it into the sky. Turns over her shoulder to me.

"Oh," I say. "Okay."

She picks up a fan brush. Back to the sea. Softens the pelting sheets of rain to a fine mist.

Wist, wist, wist.

The waves follow me down the hall and will not let me nap.

ᎭᎬ

Dario and I drive the narrow dirt roads through the graves in the cool of each pink sunrise and the shade of the still-warm lawn-scented evening. We dig graves then, too. People schedule funerals earlier and earlier to avoid the heat; I help put the rain tents up as sunshades. Families crowd under them, toss flowers and shovelfuls of soil down onto their people, and practically run back to their air-conditioned cars. We bury old person after old person. I keep three fans in the office blowing at my face from different angles. The flowers Dario brings to Emily wilt in a few hours.

"Look what I brought you!" he trills into the office the first morning in August, back from his daily deportation-risking drive just to mail a stupid letter or whatever he's doing. I lean my chin in my hand—his *look what I brought you*s typically produce skeletons, and frankly I'm not in the mood. From his pile of mail he pulls a disk wrapped in waxy paper.

"Direct from Pátzcuaro!" Chocolate so dark it is nearly black, the chocolate he uses to make *champurrado*. He tosses me a piece. At his instruction I do not chew it; I let it melt. Barely sweet, it makes Hershey's taste like chalk. "From Ana," he says, breaking a section for himself.

"The grave digger skeleton lady?"

"*Artist*," he says. "Friend of the family."

"She can be *my* friend if she sends more chocolate." I sigh in a stupor of what tastes like eighty percent cacao, and accept another, bigger piece.

He smiles at me then. For a long time.

"Want to help me dig?"

I love it when he asks, though he knows he never needs to. I wait wordlessly while he takes a detour to Emily and covers her stone with borrowed lilacs; then we hike to a Pre-Need on the crest of Poppy Hill.

We are a team of surgical precision.

"Spade. Pick. Shovel—no, spade again."

I hand each tool carefully down and catch the ones he tosses up.

"Seen Elanor lately?"

I pretend not to hear.

"Ella dijo a pedirte que vengas después del trabajo, si te deseas. Ella realmente amaría de verte," he calls from down in the grave.

If I want to come after work, she would love to see me—

"Sí. Gracias."

I concentrate on Emily's lilacs nodding in the breeze on her distant grave, and on Dario in the one at my feet. He digs.

"Hey," I say. "What do you think happens when we die?"

He digs.

Fine. *"¿Qué crees que pasa cuando morimos?"*

"Leigh"—he smiles from down in the dark—"your Spanish is . . ."

"Yeah, I know. Sorry. I'm trying."

"No," he says. "It's beautiful."

My cheeks burn pink. He's just being nice.

"¿Qué te parece?" I ask again. *What do you think?*

He digs. My legs dangle down in the grave.

His resplendent Spanish floats up from the grave, some of which my sieve of a brain keeps hold of, but still plenty slips past.

"The Purépechas were the first to live in Pátzcuaro, and they called it Tzacapu-ansucutinpatzcuaro, which in the first language means *Door to Heaven,* but word for word is more . . ."

"*Despacio,*" I remind him. "*Por favor.*" Slowly. Please.

I wish I could keep up. Speaking, limping through a conversation is one thing, but I long to hear—understand—at once in both languages.

"It's something like, *Place where the blackness begins.* It isn't only for the migration. The monarchs come to our trees because they are the souls of the dead. They're home to be with us, and never as many as the millions that arrive on your birthday. Because they *know* beginning then, and for all the Days of the Dead, the Door is open. If you listen very carefully, their wings whisper to say they're with us. They're not afraid."

I cannot remember the last time I saw a butterfly.

The lilacs on Emily's grave unfurl in the light and heat.

And then my breath catches.

People. Two people, acid-washed jeans, matching choppy haircuts, even from here I can see *so* much eyeliner, my heart stops thumping and slows. I stand, dumb beside the open grave, and their eyeliner-rimmed eyes are searchlights, coming to rest on me, an unmoving target—

I do not think. I drop to the ground and into the hole.

Down into the grave.

Mid shovel plunge, Dario backs against the head wall. My hands go to his mouth, and then to mine. My eyes are wide and so are his. He is completely still, and my light-headed, incredulous state makes me really wish I could be a third person and get to see this happening, because how hilarious is it that we're hiding from some stupid girls down in a grave— *Oh my God in a grave in a grave—*

I reach up the soil wall, flail for the edge to pull myself out, out of *the grave*.

"Seriously?" He lifts me by my waist, up and out, right into the damp black soil pile. I gulp clean, non-grave air.

They're coming.

"What is *wrong* with you?" he calls up in exasperated English.

Caroline first, Lisa dutifully in tow.

"Help," I whisper. *"Ayudame."*

"What?"

Too late. Caroline towers above me as I cower in the dirt.

"Hey, Leigh. What's up?"

Lip liner, too, nearly as black as their eyes.

"Yeah." Lisa smiles. "How's things?"

I barely hear them over the thumping blood in my ears. My hands are so sweaty. Why? What can they do? What am I afraid they'll do? I'm not in trouble; they're just stupid girls. What is *wrong* with me?

"Fine," I mumble. "Good."

Dario stays quiet down in the grave.

Get up here, please help me, what are you doing?

"Great," Caroline says, snapping a wad of gum.

My hands are shaking.

"My boyfriend's grandpa is buried here," Lisa says, "which sucks for him. Kind of a dump."

"Can I help you?" Dario is out of the grave, his full height between them and me. Caroline steps back a little.

"Uh, no thanks, amigo. We're good."

He smiles.

"Friends from school, Leigh?"

"*No,*" they spit in unison.

Through the trees I hear a car pass through the Manderleys. A van.

Rivendell.

"Then you should probably go back to visiting your loved one," Dario says.

"I said we're good."

I wonder randomly in the midst of my panic, *Where is Wade when stuff like this goes down?* He misses everything exciting.

My terrified, pounding heart clings desperately to the new, wholly separate situation of the Rivendell van's arrival. Lisa and Caroline step closer to me; Dario moves them back; they are talking, but all I hear are Elanor's boots on the grass. I've successfully avoided her for weeks, but still she waves, walks smiling beneath the pines to me, straight into this foolishness, and she is holding a package, sparkly-tissue-wrapped, ribbon-tied. Her smile changes as she nears the sharp voices of the girls.

"Hey!" she says. "Hey, Dario . . . hi, Leigh."

Silence. They turn to her.

Then Lisa: "Who is *this*?"

"Okay, definitely time to go—" Dario moves his arms toward them, sort of herding them back and away.

"Do not *touch* me!" Lisa screeches.

"Leigh?" I give Elanor the best *Let it go* look I can muster. "Are you okay?"

Caroline steps from Dario's orbit into Elanor's. "Nice hair, Corky."

Lisa laughs.

Elanor is puzzled. "Friends from school?"

"No!" they shriek once more.

Dario moves again to herd them.

"No, wait," Elanor says. "I know you."

Caroline narrows her Magic Markered eyes. "No," she says. "You don't."

"Yes." Elanor nods. "Yeah, I do. Both of you!"

Lisa is confused. "Uh, in your dreams."

"No." Elanor shakes her head. "I do, I see you all the time. You're *those* girls. You'll be knocked up and on welfare before you're eighteen, and living in a mobile home that you'll burn down by leaving a lit cigarette in the baby's crib, causing you to move all your kids into the cramped quarters of a two-door Datsun. You'll spend the rest of your lives working for tips in a strip club but strictly as waitresses, since no one will want to see skanky stretch-marked middle-aged moms gyrating their hoo-has on a pole with the raging yeast and urinary tract infections you'll have, since you'll never learn to stop wearing your pants so tight no matter how fat you get on all that government cheese."

She's going to get us killed.

But they don't seem angry as much as they are confused.

"I'm clairvoyant." Elanor shrugs. "It's kind of my thing."

Dario is charmed.

"And on that note . . ." He smiles, turns Caroline and Lisa

sternly by their shoulders, and marches them, against their shrill protests, all the way to the Manderleys.

"Nice to meet you!" Elanor calls cheerfully. "And you're welcome!"

Dario stands at the road and makes sure they keep walking.

"Oh gosh," Elanor says. "You must *really* love school."

She peers down into the open grave. "Looking good in there."

Still sitting in the dirt pile, I breathe in. Out. In. She sits beside me. In a clean dress. Right in the grave soil.

"Working a lot? How've you been?" she asks.

"Sorry, I know it's been a long . . . Yeah. Tons of work," I say.

Dario is chatting with Elanor's dad.

"Hey," she says. "It'll be okay."

I moan, miserable.

"They'll forget about it in a day," she says. "Everyone worries so much what other people are thinking about them— 'Are they plotting against me? Do they think I'm lame?' and whatever—but the thing is, they aren't. They're just not; no one is. People can't be bothered, and you know why? They're too busy thinking about themselves. You wait; they'll forget all about you."

I drop my head to my knees.

"Oh, Leigh. It's a *little* bit funny. . . . They're ridiculous!"

My head is pounding. "I know, but you can't just—*do* that."

"Do *what*?"

"*Say* stuff like that to them. It's not . . ."

"What? What are you supposed to do? Shut up and take it?"

"No, but—"

"They're just jealous! You're so smart and funny, and they're peaking in high school. That is the truth. Those girls are nothing."

"That's not how it works."

"Okay, are there special rules for them we all must follow?" she asks.

"No, but . . . I mean, there are ways to get by."

"So they're to be protected while they treat people like crap."

"It's hard to explain."

"No, I get it. No one's allowed to upset them, hurt their fragile feelings?"

"Elanor. They're going to kill me now. *Kill* me. They'll come here or they'll wait till school starts, but they'll kill me."

She frowns. "You're being metaphorical, right?"

How does she not get this? "It was bad before, but now it's . . . You've made it so much worse."

She is stung. "I'm sorry. I didn't think."

"It's just—school is hard."

"Of course. I mean, I'm sure it is."

"It's not like being home every day where everyone loves you."

"I know."

I press my aching temples. "But you don't."

I feel her turn to me.

"No, you're right—because being homeschooled makes a person sheltered and naive."

"No," I stumble.

"It's okay."

"I only meant that school is more . . . It's real life. And it sucks most of the time."

She sits up. "School? *School* is real life."

"Well . . . yeah," I say.

"So then my existence is—what, fake life?"

"*No . . .*"

"Because in *real life* everyone spends all day, every day, in . . . like a tuberculosis quarantine with thirty other people all the same age sitting in rows of desks doing mindless work sheets, bells ringing to tell you where to go and what for, and when and for how long. *That's* real life?"

"No, but—"

"And because I've not been made to feel insignificant for not winning the approval of a mindless peer group and have therefore made it through adolescence with an actual personality and my self-esteem intact, and can subsequently afford a modicum of sympathy for said mindless peers, I am not aware of the actual suckiness of this *real life*?"

"Elanor—"

"What?"

I don't know what. "I'm sorry. I'm sorry."

We sit and watch Dario help her dad unload the van at the mausoleum.

"I've tried so hard to be your friend," she says, deflated.

"I know."

"I don't understand what I'm doing wrong."

"*Nothing*, you're not doing anything wrong," I say.

"Feels like I am."

"No."

"Are those girls your friends?"

"No."

"Do you have any friends?"

I want one, I want so badly to say. *I wish it could be you.*

But I hear myself say "No."

"Oh." Her voice is high.

"Okay," she says, and stands, brushes off the back of her skirt. "Maybe someday I'll be able to demonstrate how quickly I can access the hive mind and *then* I'll be friend material. I made these for you." She lays the tissue package in the dirt.

I let her walk away. I do not call her back. Her narrow shoulders are down, her usual strong posture curved inward. Wilted.

My stomach burns.

She goes to the mausoleum and helps Dario and her dad finish hanging wreaths. Then Dario waves at the van moving slowly back out onto the highway.

My hands are muddy, but I pull the ribbons anyway, unfolding the tissue of Elanor's gift.

Socks. Knitted. Narrow rows of blue and gray and white stripes.

Cotton. Not scratchy at all.

Dario comes back through the trees, carefully around the graves. Sits beside me at the open grave.

"Elanor," he says. "I love that kid."

I nod.

"You all right?"

I shake my head.

He puts one arm around me and pulls me close to him.

I give in, laying my head wearily on his shoulder.

The pines sigh.

"Well," he says, "I'll tell you one thing: those girls were *total* bitches."

fourteen

OUR NEXT PREDAWN driving-straight-to-my-death session is all arm patting and "Great turn signal!" Dario chooses abundant kindness over rehashing the awfulness of The Bitches. Elanor's voice *I've tried so hard to be your friend* and the socks and skirts and Caroline and Lisa and *God, am I really as mean as they are?* and Emily all run a constant crowded loop in my head as I park beside the shed. Dario hands me a celebratory York, and something silver—not a mint wrapper—catches the light.

"What is that?" I reach for his arm. A bracelet. Wide, flat band of silver. He pulls it off, hands it to me.

Polished, etched with pine boughs. "Since when do you wear jewelry?"

"Isn't it beautiful?"

"It's a *bracelet*."

He smiles. "Ana made it—friend of the family."

Again with this "friend of the family" song and dance. Why does he always qualify her?

"Catrina Lady."

"Yes! She's a real artist. All kinds—Catrinas and jewelry from silver, bracelets and necklaces, everything. She works the metal herself and does all the details, the etching. She liked this one. She didn't want to sell it, so she sent it to me."

A nameless unease slides into my stomach.

He pushes the bracelet back over his hand and walks cheerfully off to bury someone in Harmony Haven.

In the office I draw skirts on people's Pre-Need file folders. Socks. Boots like Elanor's.

Emily may have worn that spelling bee T-shirt like a uniform but always with a cute cardigan sweater. And jeans that fit. Sometimes a skirt, or a sparkly barrette in her dark curls.

I bet Ana the Jewelry Lady wears skirts. And those gauzy, off-the-shoulder embroidered blouses women always wear on TV when they go on cruises to Mexico.

I fall into the cool of the house for a lunch of grapes and water, the only things my stomach can handle after yesterday's mayhem in this suffocating heat, and find Kai languishing on the sofa, cool damp cloths on her forehead. Bob Ross is painting on TV.

"It's your own little world," Bob murmurs gently from his televised art studio. "Just tap a little paint into the bristles; we don't need a lot."

I clutch my bowl of grapes and drop myself onto the rattan love seat. Meredith's favorite thing in the entire world besides painting is watching other people paint. I have forgotten Bob Ross until just this second, amazing given the hours and hours we spent lying on the sofa watching him when we lived at The Sea. I am five years old again and home in Mendocino.

"Oh, Bob, you devil!" Meredith would sigh. Not one for seascapes, Bob focused mostly on cabins in clearings in the woods, but still Meredith worshiped him. A microphone clipped to his canvas picks up the supple whisper of his paint-brush, and his voluminous brown Afro bobs, his soft voice reminding us that "we don't make mistakes; we have happy little accidents."

Saturday afternoons home from the beach in Mendocino, Kai and I freshly hosed off on the front lawn. *No sand in the house!* We lay together—Meredith, Kai, and me—dozing with the distant crashing waves and Bob's tranquil, breathy solil-oquies: "Let's pick up a little cadmium blue," Bob whispers. "Just a dab—and we're going to gently sweep in the sky . . . just softly. Back and forth, back and forth. Just that way. Beauti-ful . . . that is a beautiful, happy sky."

I study the wallpaper of Meredith's seascapes, Bob's voice curls around them, and oh, I think I get it.

Meredith's weekend life in Mendocino is not a secret *other* life—it's just her old life. She has no friends here. She has a house in a graveyard and two happy little accidents and no ocean. No wonder she wants to be alone there with her art friends and The Sea, free to paint without us ruining the time-machine illusion with our crying and cancer and crankiness.

Kai chokes back an onslaught of tears. I move instinctively to her side.

"What?" I whisper. "You're okay, what is it, what hurts?"

"It's my fault," she sobs.

"What is?"

"Bob Ross! It's my fault we left. She's going home. She won't come back. It's my fault. That's why she won't take us with her. I made us leave in the first place. I'm sorry!" She holds on to me, cries enough for us both.

"Listen," I say. "First of all, really? Cancer is your fault? You want to pin blame for that crap, look at Gramma's genetics—*all* those people had cancer back in Ye Olden Days, but unlike you, they were wusses and totally died. Well, wusses *and* they had no modern medicine, but still. And number two, Meredith is a grown damn adult and seriously, she lets a *graveyard* slip under the radar? Wade is not that stealthy. If she'd paid better attention, we'd still be home right now. Let's be pissed at *them*!"

She sniffles. Nearly smiles.

"And okay, if we had gone home, yes, obviously awesome, but . . ."

"I would never have met Balin."

"There you go. To every season . . ."

I can't tell who I'm channeling more, Dario or Ovid. And why can't I make *myself* believe any of this? Would I exchange Kai for Emily? The ocean for Dario?

"Hey." Kai sniffs and wipes her eyes with her sleeve. "Did you see Elanor yesterday? She and her dad left for here, and when they got back to Rivendell, she was crying."

Oh God.

I shake my head.

"Weren't you working?"

"Was she *crying* crying? What did she say?"

"She didn't say anything, and yeah, *crying*. She just went straight to the house; we didn't see her anymore all afternoon."

"Jeez. That's . . . I hope she's okay," I say.

Kai stretches the full length of the sofa. "Me too. You need to stop hiding here with Dario and get to know her. You would love her."

"I do not *hide* with Dario—"

"All right."

"You just want me there so you and Balin can make out uninterrupted."

"Maybe you don't want to go so you and Dario can be alone here and not be interrupted."

I get up from the couch. "You are both stupid."

"*What?*"

"You and Meredith, you think everyone . . . just because you're boy crazy and she ruined her dress, you think I can't have a friend who isn't a girl, it has to be about making out and—"

"She ruined what? Leigh, I was kidding."

"You are not! And neither is she. I'm sick of it."

"I am not *boy* crazy. Just Balin crazy."

"I don't care!" I say.

"Okay."

"I have to go to work."

"Okay."

"I do!"

"*Okay.*" She pulls the bowl of grapes to her chest and closes her eyes.

What is wrong with me? We were having such a nice time; why can't I keep my trap shut?

Elanor was *crying*?

I ruin everything.

Bob signs his masterpiece and tucks his brush into his Afro. "Happy painting," he says, "and God bless."

I let the screen door slam behind me.

fifteen

THAT SILVER BRACELET fused to Dario's arm is a shiny, beautifully crafted harbinger of doom. He's constantly touching it, the foreign dread in my stomach as sharp and bright as the light the stupid thing catches as we drive and dig graves, and as he waves out the truck window on each of his hundred trips per day to the post office.

He is happier every day, exponentially so. My fear of the answer won't let me ask him directly what the hell is up, but I keep a detailed watch just the same, because is he on a Meredith-style path to the hell away from here?

I hide my disappointment when he steps in the office door at lunch and pushes his hat off his sweaty hair to say, "Hey, okay if we skip driving tonight?"

"Okay." I shrug. "Sure."

He smiles. Squeezes my shoulder.

Just twelve weeks until my birthday. Twelve weeks to figure out how not to kill myself and everyone else on the road.

I need to calm down. He is not Meredith. He isn't leaving.

I'm sad to miss driving, not for itself but for being with him, the only person not currently mad at or hurt by me.

The first twilight stars pierce the blackish-blue beginning of night as I lock the Manderleys and pass behind the mausoleum to the Christmas lights to say good night to Dario and ask if we are driving in the morning.

Boxes. Moving boxes on the trailer lawn, boxes, full of things. Furniture. Everything.

The radio is on, propped in an open trailer window. The BBC, his new favorite.

I hover near the shed. He is shirtless. Only jeans. Dark curls falling in his eyes.

He hops down his two steps to hang his backpacking tent in a tree, then into the trailer and out with his sleeping bag, and hangs it, too, in the low pine branches.

My heart aches for Emily's bright orange bag, for her changing into her pajamas inside it.

"It's not really that fun," she comforted me as she packed last summer. "Girl Scouts is getting kind of boring. I feel like I'm too old." I lay on her bed, idly organizing her barrettes into color and sparkle groups, wishing so badly I could go camping with her for the week instead of being dragged to Pixley.

"But don't you get to hike and swim and all that? Make crafts?"

"Well, yeah, the actual camping's fun, I guess. It's the during the year part that's pointless. The meetings. I'm sick of selling cookies."

"Do *not* cut off my Thin Mints."

"Whatever, I'll buy you some!"

"Maybe— What if I could do it with you this year? Go to the meetings and everything? Kai's better; she might go to school, even. Maybe Wade and Meredith will let me."

"Oh my gosh, if you get to do stuff, we'll ditch Girl Scouts and do swim team or something! Would Wade and Meredith go for that?"

I sighed. "God, I don't know. Maybe after Pixley they'll calm down and be normal. I hope."

"Well," she said, tucking her pajamas down into her bag, "nothing wrong with a little hope."

The last sliver of sunlight is gone, only lamplight spilling from the trailer windows, and the Christmas lights twinkling, and I watch Dario bring out bedsheets, shake them open, cover the boxes and furniture.

I make my dark way to the house, to bed, filled with disbelief but hoping as hard as I can.

Please don't leave me.

ରେ ଥ

The sun rises over the sheet-covered boxes. I wait by the truck until he comes bright-eyed out the trailer door and tosses me the keys, bracelet gleaming.

"Let's go!"

Not a word about the boxes, the empty trailer. He climbs in. I drive.

Down into the valleys, up over the hills, through the

graves and trees and flowers. I stay on the right side of the road, use my mirrors with precision, shift up and down with finesse.

"You were born to this," he says. "You'll get your license and they'll never see you again—you'll be off on a million adventures!"

It's like he's never met me. *A million adventures.*

I park beside the shed.

"Leigh! Isn't it exciting?"

I take a breath. "Are you leaving?"

"Not for maybe half an hour." He yawns and steps from the truck to stretch his arms.

"No, your . . . everything. Is on the lawn."

He is genuinely puzzled for a moment, then—

"Oh!" he says. "Sorry, I was— Come see." He takes my hand and pulls me along with him.

The entire length of my arm tingles warm.

Into the trailer, empty but for canvas tarps on the floor, blue tape around the windows.

He pulls a gallon-size paint can to the counter and pries the lid off with a screwdriver.

"Magic!" he whispers.

White.

"No! Wait, that's primer. Wait!" He taps the lid back down and pulls another can up.

"Okay, *this* is it."

I peer inside. He stirs the color with a clean stick: bottomless turquoise blue.

A brave color. The color of a sunlit sky. The sunlit sea.

"What do you think?"

I stare into the can. "For the *inside*?"

"Do you like it?"

I consider the walls around us. Paneling, not unlike the office. Dark, fake pressed wood. But here is this paint, this color to make the tiny rooms as bright and beautiful as he has made the outside. To make it a home. To *stay*.

I am so relieved, I nearly pass out.

"I love it," I sigh happily. "I do. It's so beautiful, I can't even— I *love* it."

And then I reach up, heart racing, not thinking, and move my arms around him. Hug him.

He laughs, startled, and hugs me back. "Leigh," he says. "Everything's going to be all right. I promise."

I almost believe him.

☙❧

First day of school and Kai leaves before dawn to run with Balin, so I eat my toast alone and walk slowly past the trailer, and just as I hoped, Dario comes out to walk with me.

"Just ignore those girls," he says. "You have lunch money?"

I had to remind Wade and Meredith that Kai and I were off to school this morning.

Through the Manderleys, I cross the highway, and he calls from the duck pond, "Hey, want to help me paint tonight?"

"Yes!" I call, my chest a little lighter at the thought. "*Yes!*"

He salutes me like a sailor.

By the time first period English begins, I'm so scared I

can barely keep my eyes open. I sit in the front row, as close to the teacher's desk as I can get, and they walk in, see me. Lisa smirks. Caroline glares. They sit in the last row.

Ignore me.

Thank. God.

"Leigh, dear," Mrs. Edwards sighs, faced with my long-winded, waited-all-summer-to-talk-to-someone-about-it dissertation on how maybe Anna Karenina is right about deserving her lame husband *and* death because look how selfish she's being, and PS, those trains are clearly *signs* broadcasting her fast-approaching, inevitable, impending doom, the cruel futility of life even existing at all in the face of death because really, if there's no escape, what's the point of any of it. "Perhaps a less Talmudic analysis of the author's intent might allow you to enjoy the book a little more." And the predictable chorus of laughter is punctuated by an exasperated sigh from Lisa and a less-than-subtle snicker from Caroline. They do not care that I hear. Still, I pretend not to.

Class ends, the crush of bodies into the hall, I prepare for their ambush—

Nothing. They walk right past me. I do not exist.

All day, every class, nothing.

At the last bell I run to the graves, still alive, never happier to be so invisible, so very inconsequential, to not matter at all.

Maybe Dario really did scare the crap out of them.

Or maybe Elanor was right.

The intense heat has mellowed once more to an Indian summer; still, I keep my office fan blowing. The pleasant hum flutters the tissues in their sad box; I try to read and not think about Elanor. Her kindness, her smartness, my dumbness.

Her Emily-ness.

All the ness-es.

Two Pre-Needs, and three hours later Dario steps in and pulls his hat off. I drive through the graves and then to the Christmas lights.

We prime the trailer walls.

The fake paneling is so awful. There's some crazy varnish on it, but Dario doesn't want to strip it; he just wants to pile on as many coats of primer as we can, and so we do. Fans blow the warm early-autumn air from the windows and each coat dries quickly. The paneling sucks it up, and we slather on more. Takes forever. The BBC fills us in on various international diplomacy crises. I concentrate on reproducing Dario's even, vertical brushstrokes, while he periodically tosses me pieces of Pátzcuaro chocolate. The walls are white, white, whiter. We do not talk. We paint. Rollers, brushes. Up, down. Up, down. My shoulders drop; no racing thoughts, no panicked worry. My mind is blessedly quiet, and stays quiet even later as I lie down and actually sleep. Painting primer is my new favorite thing.

All week Lisa and Caroline give me no notice, Dario and I paint coat after coat of primer, and I sleep nearly five amazing hours every night. On Friday afternoon, Dario meets me walking through the Manderleys and idles the truck on his way out.

"Primer's dry," he says. "Color tonight?"

"Absolutely," I answer dreamily, eager for the drowsy, hypnotic painting spell, which maybe is partly due to paint fumes, but who cares. I wish we could ditch the graves and just spend all day painting. "It's a date."

"I'll come get you," he calls, rolling forward. "Be ready!"

"Where're you going?"

"Post office!" He waves, turns onto the highway.

Even this doesn't ruin my mood.

Emily's grave is piled high with what look like posies. White and pink.

I turn on my office fans, unwrap a few Yorks, fall into some Emily Dickinson, and wait for Dario to come get me.

The Rivendell van passes slowly by the window, Elanor's mom driving. I strain to see through the trees if Elanor is with her, but she parks down in Serenity. I can't hold a pen or turn a page; I just sit, heart pounding, and wait until finally the van comes over the valley and back through the Manderleys.

If I had any kind of spine and wasn't so ashamed, I would go to Rivendell and apologize to Elanor for treating her so horribly, instead of hiding in this stupid office.

I try to read, manage only the same few pages again and again as the hours drag past.

"Ready to go?" Dario says at last, tossing the truck keys to me.

I drive. We paint.

The color is a little watery with this first pass, not as saturated a blue as swims in the can.

"Just wait," he says. "You'll see."

It dries quickly on the primer. Still, our shoulders are too sore for another coat tonight. It's Friday, so I linger. He pours us iced sun tea, steeped all day with lemon wedges in a glass gallon jar on his lawn, and we sit before the fans on the newspaper-covered floor to admire our work.

It is late when he walks me over the mistake stones to the house. I creep quietly through the door.

"Leigh!" he whispers.

"What?"

"Be up early to drive?"

"Yes," I yawn.

"Okay. Good night. Thank you."

"Good night."

He walks back through the trees to the Christmas lights.

The house is quiet, just one light on in the kitchen, and I go silently to the bathroom to fill the tub, hot, tons of soap, and sink in. I close my eyes and let my tired arms and shoulders float.

Love will enter cloaked in friendship's name, Ovid whispers in the bathwater steam.

I wish I had some Enya.

The bathroom door opens.

"What are you doing?" Kai whispers, pulling a sweatshirt over her pajamas. "It's after midnight."

"Nothing," I say, low, and gather bubbles over me. "Go back to bed." My ultimate dream in life is quickly becoming having a bathroom of my own.

"Did you just get in?"

"Dario's painting the trailer. The inside."

"Really?" She goes to the mirror, picks up a hairbrush. "What color?"

"Blue."

"Boy blue?"

"I don't know what 'boy blue' means, but it's like aqua blue."

"Oh, *really*."

"It's beautiful."

She nods. "Ana will love that."

The bathwater is suddenly cold.

"Ana who?" I know damn well who.

"*Ana.* You know, the bracelet lady."

"Why does *she* need to love it?" I ask.

And how would she even know about it?

"Have you not *seen* the bracelet? It's the shiniest thing in America."

"So?"

"So . . . it's totally love jewelry," Kai says.

This bath is ruined.

"What are you— *Love* jewelry?"

"You don't give jewelry to a dude unless it's for love."

"No," I say, my voice a little more insistent than I intend. "It's . . . she's a friend of the family; jewelry is her *job*; it's her thing; she just sent it to him for—"

"*Love.* Love between two *lovers.* I love it." She brushes her hair, pins it into a Grace Kelly updo.

My throat is dry. "Did he *tell* you this?"

"No. But why else would he be spending half his life at the post office? *Love*. Sad for him she's in Mexico, but oh God, a long-distance affair . . ."

She slides a sparkly comb into the updo.

My fingers are pink. Wrinkled.

She perches on the edge of the tub. "Calm down, I'm not looking. Don't you think it's romantic?"

I shrug.

"How's school? Still hanging with the cheerleaders?" she asks.

Shrug.

"Leigh," she says. "You okay?"

"I don't know."

I blink. Hard.

"You know what? Let's go somewhere. You and me."

I shake my head.

"Anywhere you want. Movie? Make Dad take us to the river? Somewhere out of Sierrawood. Come with me to Rivendell. Please?"

I rest my forehead on my knees. "Can't."

"Yes, you can! You're here too much. I wish . . . Elanor would be such a good friend."

"I know," I say, just before my throat swells predictably closed.

"Leigh," she whispers, sitting on her knees beside the tub. "You're too skinny." She soaks a sea sponge in the soapy water and rubs my aching shoulders. Washes my back. "You need to eat something—*besides* toast. And Yorks."

It is easy to forget she is my big sister. My *older* sister.

She helps me stand, wraps me in a towel, and pulls the stopper. The tepid sudsy water swirls around my feet and down the drain.

ᢒᡝᢒ

Warm rain overnight and Dario uses every funeral tarp we have to cover his worldly possessions out on his lawn. Our Saturday-morning drive session features me steering the truck, splashing through each muddy puddle, Dario's braceleted arm hanging out the open window. The clouds thin and reveal a glowing autumn sun. The headstones shine in the wet grass; trees with lingering leaves show off bright patches of red and gold.

"Paint tonight?" he says.

We brush and roller the blue slowly around the windows and doorframes, the air not as warm but still moving enough to dry every wall. He is careful not to get paint on the bracelet but will not take it off.

By sundown a second coat is drying on the trailer walls, and we take a tea and chocolate break before starting the final pass.

"It's a good color, right?" he asks.

"Yes." I lay my head back to rest on my bent arm. "It's beautiful."

"Not too much for such a little space? I don't want to make it feel smaller."

He seems genuinely concerned.

"Why?" I murmur, half-asleep in the fan-manufactured breeze and paint fumes. "Does it feel smaller to you?"

"Not so far."

"Well, you're the one living with it. But it seems good to me."

"Just nice to have another opinion. A lady's opinion."

My closed eyes roll back. "Yeah, I'm quite a *lady*. It feels like the ocean. Like swimming."

"The *ocean*. That's high praise."

"I love it."

"You do?"

"Yes. I wish my room was this color."

He stands back from the wall, considers it. Refills my tea glass.

"When . . . I had a friend who, when she turned thirteen, her mom let us paint her bedroom. Any color she wanted," I say.

He sets the tea down.

"What did she choose?"

"Oatmeal."

"Cereal?"

"Like light brown."

"Okay."

"Because they were renting their house from this really old lady who sort of fancied herself an 'artist,' and the way she expressed this was by painting every interior wall a different primary color."

"Primary?"

"Red, yellow, blue. But dark, you know, really intense. Like a circus."

"Yeesh."

"My friend's room was a super bright yellowish-green. So we walked to the paint store and she got some sample cards. I remember all of them. Ecru. Eggshell. Cotton. Cream. Toast. Wheat. But she *loved* Oatmeal."

"Well, sure."

"Her mom was all upset; she thought it was crazy that her kid wanted oatmeal-colored walls."

"Why?"

"Well, I guess because she was thirteen. Thirteen-year-old girls are maybe supposed to want brightness. Attention, to be noticed. But Emily wasn't like that. She didn't need it."

He nods.

"Her mom kept saying, 'It's not the *color* so much; it's what it *says*—what it's *saying*. Seriously, *beige*?'"

He nods.

"I think after months of living with the insanity of that neon green, she just wanted something quiet."

He nods.

"It was really pretty. Semigloss, smooth like glass. I gave her glow-in-the-dark star stickers and her mom practically cried, she was so happy when we turned the lights off and there they were, all over the ceiling."

The fans blow, oscillating across the wall, across our faces.

"Okay," he says. "Last coat tomorrow and I'll be sleeping under the ocean waves."

He holds out his hand, helps me to my feet, walks me home.

"See you in the morning!" he whispers.

The rain and cooling weather have dropped so many leaves, even with the pines I can see the Christmas lights clearly from the porch, the entire outline of the trailer. So close.

"Good night," I whisper back.

೧೮

I wake in the Sunday predawn dark, ravens going berserk in the pines outside my sheet-covered window. Nearly six anyway.

The truck is not in its spot at the shed.

I tap on the open trailer door and step inside.

The blue is beautiful, ready for its final coat. Dario's makeshift bed of blankets and sleeping bags is on the newspaper-carpeted floor where the kitchen table once was, books and paper and pens near his pillow on a cardboard box labeled with tall Sharpie letters:

Ana.

Knots tighten in my chest.

I step back out the door, down the steps. Hop around in the early-morning cold. Sit on the trailer steps, wait awhile, go to the pile of grave liners. Sit on the edge of a lidded one.

The pines sway. I don't look up.

I hear the truck through the Manderleys.

"Sorry!" he calls, pulling up beside the shed. "Look what I got!"

In the truck bed, wedged awkwardly beneath sheets and ratchet straps—

"A *mattress.*"

"Practically brand-new, found it in the *PennySaver*—box spring, too!"

He unhooks the straps and pulls the sheets aside.

Ah, the *PennySaver*. You just can't beat that thing for finding used home furnishings and graveyard jobs.

I don't mind telling him how sketchy it is to buy a used mattress, which he takes total issue with.

"It's got plastic around it, barely been used, so why waste all that money for new, and PS, I'm already sleeping on a used one."

Touché.

"Kind of big" is all I have to say about it. His fold-out in the trailer can't be more than a twin; this one is easily a queen. Where is he going to put it?

"Well, hopefully I'll have a real bedroom one day and it won't seem so big."

"One day when? You just painted!"

His head falls back like a Pez dispenser. "Not *tomorrow*— but I don't want to spend my entire life living in a trailer."

My cheeks burn. Of course he doesn't.

I help him pull the hulking thing from the truck and wrap it in sheets and tarps to rest against the side of the trailer; then he tosses the keys to me.

"Let's go."

I drive. Eight weeks till I have my License to Kill. Autumn leaves swirl up, the road and graves covered with them.

"My grandparents had this really tall wrought-iron bed," he says, "and when they had parties, or like at Christmas, all the cousins got to sleep in it while the adults were up talking and playing music all night."

Such a Laura Ingalls Wilder memory. I like it when he tells me things about when he was little, which he barely ever does, and only when it is something really good.

He applauds my use of the emergency brake and promises we'll work on parallel parking; then I am off to read and sell and unwrap Yorks. He hikes over the hills and down into the valley with the leaf blower, clouds of scarlet and saffron and daffodil-yellow, October just days away. This bird's nest of suspense and intrigue is making me so nervous. Pull one thread and it will all unravel in a giant mess of . . . messiness. It sweeps circles in my head, my own voice and Dario's, Kai's, Elanor's. Emily's.

The bracelet. The blue paint. The great big giant bed.

The Ana box.

Something is *up*.

All afternoon I watch him clear the graves of color. Visitors come and he silences the leaf blower until they've gone. Wade spins headstones. I schedule a Pre-Need service, order a headstone, answer the phone, reorganize files. Read.

The sun is low and red. The leaf blower is silent. I pack up my books, pocket a few Yorks. The truck headlights shine in the windows.

I drive us to the shed, to the Christmas lights. We begin the final coat of blue.

I beg him to change the radio to something less talky and more music-y.

"You don't know what's good for you," he says, but moves the dial anyway from the BBC to a semi-old-people station. Simon without the Garfunkel. A James Taylor ten-in-a-row.

James is "Up on the Roof" and the sun still hovers over the trees, filling the house with the rosy evening glow of *Maybe everything is going to be okay.* I concentrate hard on quieting the nagging voices, let the painting bliss wash over me, up, down, across, up, down. The beautiful blue is deeper, truer every moment.

We've finished the bedroom, the bathroom, the kitchen, and move to the front room.

James gets off the roof and now the radio is full of "You are my only one."

The *Ana* box is on the floor beside the paint cans. My roller stops midway up the wall, paint dripping across the newspaper-covered floor. I sit down.

It's what the color says. What it's saying.

Stupid James Taylor and his hidden clues about other people's lives.

"You're leaving."

He turns over his shoulder to me. "No."

This color. The great big humongous *queen* bed.

"No?"

"*No.*"

Wait. "She's coming here?"

He sets his roller in the tray. James keeps singing.

Now she has a name *and* a bed.

I don't feel well.

"To *stay*?"

225

He sits beside me on an empty paint can. His eyes are at once anxious and determined.

"Listen. I am not leaving. I'm not. Okay?"

I nod.

"Please don't say anything to your dad," he says. "Is that all right?"

I nod.

"Please. Not yet."

"Okay." *What am I not saying?* "Is she your girlfriend?"

"Where'd you get *that*?"

My heart sprints.

"Kai." I nod at his wrist. "She said this is a love bracelet."

"A what?"

"Is it?"

The fans whisper at the damp blue walls.

"I guess so," he says.

James is still "You are my only one"-ing it and I climb over the newspaper and roller trays to turn him off, and maybe it's the paint fumes but I am suddenly burning up and sick to my stomach. I do not sit; I stand.

"She's in Mexico?"

"Yes."

"When is she coming?" *Please say she's not; please say it's just love letters, or better yet just letters.*

"Soon," he says. "I think."

"You don't know?"

"Well. It's— You can't say anything. Please. Promise me you won't."

226

"Okay."

"Because I haven't talked to your dad yet, and I need—"

"*Okay.*"

Dario knows by now that with Wade, it's better to just do whatever and apologize later than to ask and give him a chance to say no.

"He won't care anyway," I sigh. "He won't be mad; he'll love it. Just tell him."

"Not yet. Promise."

"Okay."

"Because I need your help."

"Okay."

"I wasn't going to tell you any of this yet, but now Kai's got you all worked up. . . ."

"Okay, *what?*"

"Ana is coming."

My chest constricts. "Okay."

"To live. *Here.*"

My this-is-no-big-deal casualness is wearing thin.

"She'll like the paint," I say. "Wade'll be thrilled."

"I have to go get her."

"Sure."

"I have to *go get* her."

"Okay."

He pantomimes *travel* with his roller. "I have to go there and get her."

"*Okay!*"

He sets the roller in the tray.

"Leigh. I have to *go* there, to *Mexico,* and *get her.* I have to get her *out* of there. I have to bring her back here with me. The same way I came the first time. Same as before."

I wish I hadn't turned James off.

"Please don't tell anyone. Please. Okay?"

Wet paint on a wall can very easily look stripy. It takes a lot of concentration to get it even. Up, across. Up. Across. Even strokes. Back and forth. Over and over.

"Leigh. I need your help."

Even I understand going in and coming back across—with another person in tow. Even I know that is dicey at best, completely dangerous at worst. Impossible.

"People do it all the time," he says. "They work here for a while, they go home, visit back and forth. They do. All the time."

I swallow. Make a genuine effort not to be sick. "When?"

"Soon."

"How long will it take?"

"Not long. Two, three weeks. Maybe. Not long."

His uncertainty makes me mad. A person needs to be confident when planning to do something on purpose that may or may not involve them being killed, otherwise—it *really* pisses me off.

"What're you telling Wade?"

"Sacramento. That I'm meeting family there, staying for some kind of emergency."

"Great."

I pick up my roller. Paint. Kind of angrily.

"You can buy me time if you don't tell anyone anything; I'll be back as quickly as I can. But if something happens, if I can get to a phone, will you—"

There is a piercing ringing in my ears. I put my roller in the tray, pick up a brush, and cut in the corners around the windows.

He takes the brush from my hand.

"We're getting married. At my parents' house in Pátzcuaro, and then after . . . then my cousin Aurillo will pick us up in San Diego and we'll come home."

All this spilled in one breath. Freezing waves of *I am so stupid* knock me down, drag me under.

"Okay, so then she *is* your girlfriend."

"Leigh."

"Is she asking you to do this? Can't someone else bring her over?"

"No, it's not— She's not asking. She's only doing it for me. If it goes badly, it's going to be my fault."

"Goes badly?"

"Just . . . not how we plan."

"Why not just stay there with her?" I choke through my swollen throat. "She's your *wife*. Or whatever. Doesn't she get a vote?"

He looks exhausted. "She *wants* to come; she wants to *be* here. It's just the getting across . . . but it's not impossible. I want her with me. Here."

I bite the inside of my cheek and taste blood.

"I'm coming back. I will."

The blue's fumes are making my head swim in this new universe where people have secret girlfriends in faraway places and risk deportation to bring them to live in graveyards. Everything is nothing, sea grass floating aimlessly in the water, no rock, no seabed to anchor to.

Everyone good always leaves. Or dies.

There are a million ways I can try to help. I can promise to be the one to fix it, take care of things here, assure him *Yes, yes, of course I will help you,* a million kind, comforting things I can say. But now it is too late; all I see are his boots down in the grave beside my feet, his hand holding mine to take me from Emily to the safety of the Christmas lights, the flowers he brings to Emily, the flowers he gave to me, no more Christmas lights, alone in the graveyard while I sleep, or don't.

"Please don't go."

"I'll be back."

"You won't."

"I *will.*"

His shoulders, his arms again and again holding the weight of my aching head, my sadness, my selfish, lonely heart.

Two days later he is gone.

part three

AT NEED

sixteen

"DARIO'S GOT SOME kind of family hoopla going on," Wade barks from the bathroom door while Kai and I stand brushing our teeth at the sink. A very official Sierrawood employee meeting. "We're all going to pitch in and keep things running till he's back."

He is gone for good. Happy at home in the warm sun and trees of Pátzcuaro with the butterflies in their oyamel forests. He's living out his autobiography called *Dario's Wonderful Life Not in a Graveyard*, home where he never has to dig graves for strangers, only for people he knows, for family.

It's only been days, but I know this. I *know* it.

October is cold and the office is freezing. I huddle over the heaters with my old frenemy Ovid, reading nearly on autopilot. I still hate him, but I can't help reading him still, searching for the comfort Elanor was so certain of but I can never see. Familiar if nothing else. Ovid will never leave me, no matter how many overdue fees I rack up.

Elanor.

I watch Kai out in the graves with the leaf blower, willingly giving up a couple of Rivendell afternoons each week because it is for Dario, so she is being very lemons-into-lemonade about it.

Wade is "pitching in" by screwing up all my headstone files while I'm at school, chewing all my pen caps, and eating all my Yorks. He grumbles and crabs around and complains to cover up how much he misses Dario. "Can't make a ding-dang phone call from Sacramento? What kind of 'family emergency' breaks your phone? Is he on the moon?"

No one knows anything about anything. Except me. Including me. The two days before he left I spent hiding in the house. I faked being sick while he begged me via Kai to come talk to him; my only contribution to the cause is silence. It is easy for me to say nothing, to know nothing, because truthfully, I don't. Maybe he never will be back. Maybe he is in jail; maybe he is dead. I know nothing, have no idea where he will be or when, what he is doing, when the wedding is.

The wedding.

I draw butterflies in the margins around the funeral times on the desk calendar. Monarchs.

My driver's ed handbook lies open on the calendar. Useless. I don't know the answers to any of these stupid questions. I'll never pass the test without him. I don't want to anyway; if he's so hot on me driving, he should have stayed to make sure I did it.

Through the window Kai waves and lugs the blower to the shed, done for the night. I imagine a stranger out there with the spinner. The new guy Wade will have to hire when Dario decides to stay in Pátzcuaro to be with his *wife*.

Elanor is wrong. I am not Cordelia. I am more Lear than Wade could ever be.

I gather my books and stand to go. An hour early, but I couldn't care less. My Emily jeans slip down my nonexistent hips and I yank them up. I need a new belt. I need a new stomach that can handle food. I need a new everything.

The sky is darkening. I make my way alone beneath the trees, through the graves. Over the feet, between each space, stepping carefully around people's heads.

I look straight ahead. Away from Emily's abandoned grave, no one now to bring her flowers. I try hard not to see the dark Christmas lights, ignore the periphery, walk steadily forward and concentrate only on getting home, which is how I trip and nearly fall over the yapping mop that comes running from nowhere to nip crazily at my feet.

"Off, off!" I scream, shrugging out of my backpack to wield it and defend myself. But the beast is tiny. A dirty white poodle with brown liver stains around its mouth.

"Rene!" Gramma calls shrilly from the porch. "Knock that off! You remember Leigh!"

CR SO

Empty Kentucky Fried Chicken buckets fill the kitchen sink. Meredith, Wade, and Grandpa each like different kinds, and so there are all these little containers instead of just the one big one: Extra Crispy, Spicy, what have you. The only thing I am attempting to hold down is plain mashed potatoes, or whatever KFC is trying to pass off as mashed potatoes. Lately I am realizing that restaurants, real or fast food, are all just kind of gross.

Dario, even in his quest to experience all things American, would never touch this stuff.

Emily's mother would have fried the chicken at home, in a cast-iron skillet.

Elanor has probably never eaten fast food, not once in her whole life. These buckets of death would make her hurl.

Loneliness sits cold in my lap.

"I meant to tell you," Grandpa says. "You would not believe how much fell overnight! Four, four and a half feet *overnight!*"

"Oh, Wallace, don't exaggerate, you fool. *Four feet.* My God!"

This spirited debate is centered around the recent early Pixley snowfall, Gramma's resulting fear of Donner Party–style cabin-fever death, and their subsequent open-ended stay here in the cemetery. With us.

Kai and I haven't even been given a chance to whisper-fight about whose bedroom they'll be taking over.

The phone rings. Wade reaches across Grandpa's plate for the wall extension.

"Yellow!" Wade hollers before swallowing.

Gramma rolls her eyes.

"*Hello?*" He frowns. "She's in the middle of dinner. You can call back." Hangs up.

"Did you just hang up on Balin?" Kai whines.

"They asked for Leigh."

"Who did?" she says.

"The person who just called! Jeez, you guys, keep up!"

I rub my temples. *"Who* asked for me?"

Wade shrugs.

"Was it Elanor?" Kai asks hopefully. I shoot her a look.

"It was a man, and whoever he is, he better not call during dinner again."

Kai turns to me, eyes wide. Even Meredith looks up. Gramma's plastic spork hovers over her coleslaw.

"A man?" Kai says.

"A *guy*. I don't know."

Kai and Meredith eyeball me.

"So," Gramma lays in, pushing her plate aside and turning her chair to face Meredith.

Here we go. Meredith's Awesome Life and Gramma's Opinion of It: Unsolicited.

She pulls the Last Supper from her crochet bag into her lap and stares Meredith down. "Let me get this straight: you're just going to let yourself be dragged to live in a *graveyard*—for the rest of your *life*?" Right in front of Wade, who laughs.

Meredith blinks.

Gramma is incredulous. "What the hell is *wrong* with you?"

Meredith swallows an entire glass of water at once and excuses herself to go paint.

Good Lord.

Kai's eyes are round. Nice mothering. I think I'd rather

be ignored. Then again—the devil you know, the devil you don't—who knows.

What *guy* would be calling me? The only guy I know is busy getting killed in Mexico; he would have spoken to Wade.

I rest my head on my arms.

"Leigh, get your hair out of the biscuits," Wade says. "If you're so tired, go to bed, jeez!"

So I do.

CR&SO

"Move over, my pillow's hanging off the edge!" Kai whispers later in the dark. My room, deemed *Too G.D. messy for guests; what's with all the boxes?* by Wade, now houses me, and Kai, and all of Kai's stuff. Including her giant body pillow.

"It's like three people in here," I moan. "Do you need that thing?"

"I can snuggle next to you instead," she offers, and hugs my entire body.

"Hot, hot, too hot!" I throw the covers off.

"All right!" She laughs. "Just stay there. I'll fix it."

I lie still and she shakes the sheet and the blanket in parachute waves above me, smooths them flat, and drags her stupid pillow back under. "Okay?"

I nod.

"If Rene pees in my room, I'll kill him."

"Sorry. I can see if they'll switch."

"No," she says. "It's all right. I'm sure he won't. Maybe just poo."

We breathe in the dark. My eyes will not close.

"You didn't eat much dinner," she says.

"Not hungry."

"Okay."

An owl hoots.

"Leigh," she whispers.

"What?"

"Why didn't you say goodbye to Dario?"

"I don't know," I say.

"Are you tired?"

"Yes. But I can't sleep."

"Me neither." She rolls over. "Were you mad at him?"

"Who?"

"Dario!"

"No."

"Was he mad at you?"

"*No.*"

"Okay."

"I don't think so."

She turns back to me. "Who called at dinner?"

"I don't know!"

"Why was Dario mad?" she asks.

"I don't— He wasn't. I was sick, I didn't feel like talking, no one was mad, and I don't know who called."

"Okay."

"*Okay.*"

I can hear her wheels turning in the dark.

"Did you know his birthday was in April?"

I nod.

"He's twenty," she says.

My heart thumps beneath my threadbare T-shirt.

"Yeah," I say. "I know."

"Years old."

"*Yes.* I know."

"Well . . . do you miss him?"

"Don't you?"

She lies on her back and reaches absently for a long swath of my hair, twirls it in her fingers.

"Yes," she says. "I do. A lot."

Her hand in my hair sends tingles through my scalp and makes me suddenly drowsy.

"Leigh," she whispers.

"Hmm?"

"Where is he?"

My heart starts back up. I am wide awake, but I keep my eyes screwed shut.

"Who?"

"Where *is* he?"

I lie there for a while, eyes still closed.

"Sacramento," I whisper. "Right?"

She divides my hair into three sections. Braids it, tucks it beneath my pillow. Turns on her side to face me.

"Tell me the Plum Creek Christmas?"

The wind whistles low around the corner of the house. The pine branches reach and swing against my window. In

Mendocino we slept every night beneath open windows, the waves singing us to sleep.

"Well," I whisper, "Pa had gone into town for molasses and salt pork. He had no idea a blizzard was coming. . . ."

She is asleep in less than a minute.

seventeen

BITTER, WINTERLIKE COLD seeps in overnight, and with it, more clients. All old. Jimmy digs sloppy graves left and right for me to finish, and I do; I hose the far-flung dirt and move the flowers, carefully covering the black soil. Alone. I work nonstop before and after school, all weekend; the shoe box beneath my bed has a twin, both crammed with icing-on-the-cake cash. Tens, twenties, fifties. Need more room. A boot box, maybe.

I draw more butterflies on the office desk calendar. In flight, wings spread, they creep into the scheduling notes.

Gramma and Grandpa have settled into a comfortable routine. Grandpa's blue Death Trap Express truck sits covered in dust beside the grave liners. Gramma is content to work on the Last Supper in front of the TV night and day, while Grandpa is thrilled to be given free rein to fix, repair, clean up, and just generally mess around with anything he feels like anywhere in Sierrawood. He is equally delighted to have so many strangers to chat with; as Gramma likes to put it, "That man loves to run his mouth to anyone sorry enough to stand there and listen."

And thank God, because Real Nice Clambake does not like this Dario-being-gone business.

"Do you know yet?" she asks, her powdered, wrinkled face peering around the office door, not stepping in. "When he'll be back?"

"Not yet."

"Have you heard from him?"

I shake my head.

"It's his family? Someone ill?"

"Yes"—I nod energetically—"but he hasn't . . . I'm sure he'll be back. It won't be long. Not long now."

"Not the same without him, is it?"

I shake my head.

"Well." She nods at the space heaters. "Stay warm."

Now Grandpa's out there with her, they talk and laugh and it makes me feel a little better.

Kai is weeding the babies. Weeds growing in such bitter cold—stupid. But they do, crabgrass and just regular longer grasses that need to be pulled out because they look so tacky, especially around the babies. Around mine.

I cannot bear to look toward Emily on Poppy Hill. I am worthless.

I am starting to forget her voice.

The phone rings; it shrieks in the stale office warmth. I nearly die of a heart attack.

I press my open palm to my chest, slow my breath. "Sierra-wood Hills, how may I help you?"

"Hello." Man's voice.

"Yes," I sigh. "Hello, can I help you?"

"Hello?"

People, really? Get a decent phone.

"Yes, hello!"

"*¿Quién estoy hablando?*"

If you don't know who you're talking to when you call a cemetery, I probably can't help you, but I keep up my end of the song and dance. "Uh . . . *Este es Colinas Sierrawood.*"

I am not in the mood for this.

"*¿Este es el cementerio?*"

"*Sí,*" I assure whoever it is. "Yes, *este es el cementerio. ¿Cómo puedo ayudarte?*"

Silence. But a gravelly one. White noise. A separate conversation happening in the background, too fast, muted, I can't understand a word.

"*Perdón. ¿Hola?*" I say. "*¿Está ahí?*" But they do not respond. Distant laughter. More quiet rapid-fire words.

The line goes dead.

Fantastic. Go get your grave somewhere else, then.

I sleep maybe six or seven minutes all night, restless beside Kai. My broken sleep is punctured by dreams of myself, middle-aged and digging graves alone, single-handedly running Sierra-wood and caring for the ten or fifteen feral cats I've rescued from behind King Fong's, which I brought home strapped to the rickshaw I pull behind the bicycle I ride everywhere since I never learned to drive a car. Then dreams of Elanor waiting outside the office door, calling my name over and over; Dario sprints past cacti in vague darkness, pulling a girl in a floating white veil behind him, and she is tripping and pulling him back and then his body twists and stiffens in a hail of bullets. Emily holding hands with Elanor beneath the trees in Rivendell. I wake over and over, sweating and anxious. Tired.

I give up well before sunrise and go to the bathroom to wash my face. My reflection is startling. With the deep frown lines between my eyebrows, the deep shadows beneath my eyes, and my rapidly declining weight replaced with the weight of the fifty million secrets I'm carrying, I look older than seventy-year-old chain-smoking bitter farmwife from the Ozarks Gramma. So, not real good.

I drag myself downstairs to lie on the sofa, and there she is. Bitter Ozark Farmwife herself. Hair in rollers, TV on, Last Supper on her lap and Rene at her feet. He stands up, barks. Once.

"Oh, shut it!" Gramma hisses at him.

He lies back down.

"What are you doing awake?" she whispers.

I curl up at the other end of the sofa. "Couldn't sleep."

She shakes her head. "Kids should have no trouble sleeping; when I was your age, I worked a full day sunup to sundown and fell into bed every night, glad for it!"

I yawn.

She crochets.

"Might be that you're trying to sleep in a *graveyard*. Could keep a person up."

She's got a point.

"And what's your mother doing out so early? She took off before I even put my teeth in."

I sigh. "Mendocino."

"Mendocino what?"

"She goes."

"To Mendocino?" Gramma asks.

I nod.

"Why?"

I shrug. "All the time."

"Really?"

I nod.

"Alone?"

"Yep."

"When's she coming back?"

I shrug.

She crochets. "Well," she says.

Amen, sister.

Still.

"She misses it," I say. "She visits her friends."

"She ought not to have let your father drag her here, then. This house is ridiculous; it's a tacky gift shop! I tried to find a cup for my coffee; I'm drinking out of a G.D. seashell!"

I nearly smile.

"All these paintings. This ocean thing, you kids' names. It's too much."

"Not me"—I yawn again—"just Kai."

"Not you what?"

"My name's not about the ocean. Kai is."

She pushes Rene off her lap.

"Do you know what we called you for two months? The Baby. 'What's your new granddaughter's name?' and I'd be so embarrassed; every time I'd have to go through this whole song and dance, 'Oh, they haven't thought of anything yet, blah blah.' *The Baby.* Honestly." She studies the thread in her hands, unties a knot.

"Because why bother naming me if I was just going to die."

She shrugs. "I don't know if it was *that* exactly, but . . ."

The crochet needle clicks against her wedding ring.

I take a breath.

"Would God really send a little kid to Hell?"

She puts down her crochet hook. Sits and *looks* at me.

"Your father." She clucks her tongue. "This graveyard business is making me irregular and I can't abide. But I tell you what. You were born and he stayed beside you night and day for three months. Had to take you in a helicopter to San Francisco, no decent hospitals in Mendocino; then they shipped you where they make the wine . . ."

"Napa."

"*Napa.* Kept you in an incubator to finish baking. *Three months.* He barely showered. Left your mom by herself in

Mendocino with Kai, wouldn't let the nurses hold you. They said he just sat there with his hand on you, reading to you all day."

"No, he did not."

"Yes, he did so! He read you every magazine in the waiting room, and then he found a book someone left—that man read the damned *French Lieutenant's Woman* to you. Out loud. *Twice.* That's where he got your name."

"I'm sorry—this is *Wade* we're talking about?"

"*Yes.*"

"I'm the French lieutenant's woman? That is not the ocean."

"No, not that trashy . . . *Leigh-on-Sea.* The guy who wrote it was born in a town beside the ocean in England; it's at the mouth of a river—"

"The Thames?"

"Who knows? But sometimes people call it just Leigh, or Leigh by the Sea. So he decided it meant you next to Kai. Couldn't go with something nice and simple. Megan. Jane. No. You are Leigh by the Sea."

I don't know if I buy this—Wade's hand on my infant body no bigger than a burrito, reading something that isn't *Runner's World* magazine, care and attention for someone who isn't himself or Kai? Impossible.

The morning news is back on. Rene barks at the newscaster.

"You look horrible, by the way. I can see every bone in your body. What is wrong with you?"

I shrug.

"Do we need to take you to the doctor?"

"I don't know."

She shakes her head. Picks up the Last Supper. "How you do *feel*?"

Her hands are gnarled. Age spots, liver spots. But they move easily. The apostles' faces look so real.

"Bad," I say truthfully. "I feel awful."

"Well," she says, "what are you going to do about it?"

Rene rolls over on his back, paws up. Gramma reaches down and rubs his belly. He squirms. Dog-smiles.

People keep asking me that.

It is a good question.

What am I going to do about it?

eighteen

I KEEP FORGETTING to buy Yorks. Selling graves without them is infinitely more difficult; taking The Walk with people, nearly impossible. I pull out a stack of Post-its, make a list:

1. Yorks
2. Cheerful Tissue Boxes
3. New Grave Seller

I stick it to the desk calendar on my ballpoint-pen butterflies, where Wade is sure to see it.

It is the last Wednesday of October. One week until my birthday.

Days', weeks' worth of homework lounge undone and uncared-about in my backpack. My butterflies are taking over the calendar, so intricate they could leave the paper; the grave files are backed up and disorganized. I couldn't care less.

The phone rings. I let it go to the machine. Wade's voice drones in his version of "sensitive and professional," but which is actually super monotone and very graveyardish. "Please leave a message at the beep. Thank you, and have a pleasant day." So lame. If they're calling here on purpose, odds are their day hasn't been pleasant so far and will likely get worse once we call them back and they have to come sit here and look at the horrible tissues.

The beep.

Nothing. But *loud* nothing. Not static, sort of amplified ambient room sound. I reach for the button to end the call, but then barely audible—voices. I lean toward the speaker.

Spanish.

Whoever he is, he better not call during dinner again.

"Wait!" I plead to no one, grab the receiver. "Hello?"

The voices stop. Loud quiet.

"Dario?" I whisper.

Dial tone.

My hands are all jittery; I can barely replace the receiver.

The silence presses into my ears, makes me have to yawn, and then—

Singing.

Not from the phone. Outside.

Shirley Jones.

Our hearts are warm, our bellies are full,
And we are feeling prime.

This was a real nice clambake,
And we all had a real good time.

Wednesday.

"A Real Nice Clambake," the actual song, is cranked up and halfway through its first verse. I stand in the doorway and watch Clambake sit on her sister's grave.

I do not think, just walk to Clambake and stand there on the grass beside her.

"Hi, sweetie!" she calls above the din, but does not turn it down.

"Hi." I wait with her.

Throw'd in ribbons of salted pork,
An old New England trick.

Holy cats, this song is complete lunacy. It goes on and on. Clambake smiles, straightens flowers, polishes her sister's stone.

BELOVED WIFE, MOTHER, SISTER
JANUARY 30, 1935–MARCH 2, 1990
SINGIN' IN AN ANGELS' CHOIR

The engraving's kind of cornball, but as a rule I forgive corn in old people.

Remember when we raked them red hot lobsters
Out of the driftwood fire?
They sizzled and crackled and sputtered a song
Fittin' for an angels' choir.

There's a bunch more nonsense about clams and gullets, and then at last the *real good time!* comes blessedly to an end. Clambake presses the stop button on her tape player and stands, brushes grass off her polyester elastic-waist pants.

"Hi, honey!" she says again. "Dario back yet?"

I shake my head.

"Oh," she says. "Well." She bends to pick up the sweater she's sitting on, and her tape player.

Got her on a not-chatty day. Fantastic.

"But I wanted . . . I wondered, could I ask you something?"

She smiles. "Of course, dear heart, what do you need?"

I have lost most of my momentum getting through the twenty-seven thousand verses of that insane song.

"Um."

She waits.

"Do you . . . I mean, you come visit a lot?" I'm so lame. She knows I know she's here every week. But she nods.

I glance down at the headstone.

She shifts her sweater and the radio into her other arm. "Never missed a week in well over twenty years. Anything else?"

Stupid, stupid song. I was so raring to go ten minutes ago.

She walks slowly to her car. Puts the radio in the trunk and shuts it. I tag along, take a breath, and go at it from another angle.

"If your kid died, would you visit her? Or him?"

She shrugs. "I don't have any kids."

I stop myself before blurting, "Oh, really? Why?" I don't know that I've ever met an adult without kids. Do people do that? Seems a practical choice. Or maybe she couldn't have them. Either way, thank God I didn't ask why out loud. That is incredibly rude. I really need to think more. Always think first.

Elanor doesn't think first. Just says what she means.

"Okay," I say instead. "But if you did. Wouldn't you come?"

"Well," she says, "of course. Of course I would. I mean, good grief, I'd hope so. Wouldn't you?"

I nod.

She frowns. "Something wrong, sweetheart?"

I shake my head. She moves to get in the car.

"What do you think happens when you die?"

The poor woman. She holds the door handle, stands there for a minute.

"Well, my family is Jewish. So."

"I'm sorry, I don't . . ."

"Oh, well. It's sort of . . . You know, the Egyptians were real overboard on death. Mummies, pyramids. Death, death, death. My people hightailed it out of there, and maybe we wanted to be as *not* like them as we could. The Torah just doesn't talk about it. Death. Or after."

"But—" I scramble desperately. "Okay, so then—what do *you* think happens? Like, what's your sister doing? Where is she? You really think she gets lonely?"

She ties a filmy floral-print scarf around her hair.

"You know what?" she says at last. "I just haven't the fog-giest. I really couldn't say."

Oh, for crap's sake. She's *old*! Where's the goddamned wis-dom and comfort?

"You feeling okay, honey?" I nod but cannot speak for the closing of my throat.

"All righty, then." She pats my shoulder and gets in her bucket seat, then puts the key in the ignition.

I squeeze my eyes shut and raise my voice. "What about the song?"

She rolls her window down.

"What about it?" she asks.

"How come?"

Now she reaches for my hand and squeezes tight.

"Because she loves it. She *loves* that show. You ever see *Carousel*?" I shake my head. "Well." She puts the car into gear and rolls slowly toward the gates. "You ought to. Rodgers and Hammerstein. We saw the original cast; our parents took us and oh, was it *wonderful*. We got all dressed up, new coats, brand-new shoes, everything. New York was so exciting then. . . ." Her eyes are dewy, she is still clutching my hand, and I'm walking fast beside the car as it inches toward the highway. Then she hits the brake hard. "You listen to me, young lady." She aims an elaborately manicured finger firmly at my face. "There is *nothing* better than a good musical. It's the best thing there is. You understand?"

I nod.

She smiles, satisfied.

"If you talk to Dario, make sure and tell him Helen misses him!" She waves out the window.

No one else anywhere in the graves. No Wade, not even Jimmy.

Kai running. I think I wish the Rivendell van would come.

I wish I could talk to Elanor.

I wish Dario would come home.

I wish Emily would come home.

Almost completely dark now. I walk in the gloaming. I do not run. I lift my heavy backpack, lock the office, lock the Manderleys, and move forward through the graves, along the road, past Emily.

Where is her mother? She was like a mom to me, too. My mom. Doesn't she miss me?

"Leigh."

I stand on the headstone path. Look up.

"What are you doing?" Meredith stands on the porch, silhouetted before the bright living room windows in the fast-fading dusk.

Inside the house, Rene yips.

"Mother, tell that dog to shut up!" Meredith hollers toward the window. "Little bastard," she mutters, leaning over the porch railing to whack her shoes together. Ocean sand shimmers out; dusty little explosions pour into the grave liners below.

"*Leigh.*"

When did she come back?

She moves down the porch steps, frowns at me and my frown lines. Takes my backpack off my shoulders, moves me along the headstone path toward the house, to the door. "It's too dark to be down there so late. Who the hell's coming at night to get themselves a grave? Rene, shut *up*! Your father is ridiculous. When is Dario coming back?"

I don't know that I've ever heard her say his name out loud.

Over Rene's yapping there is piano music, a familiar plinking tune from the television. It's the theme to *Murder, She Wrote,* our favorite show in the world because all the exterior scenes of Angela Lansbury riding her wicker-basketed bicycle along the cliffs above the ocean were filmed not in made-up Cabot Cove, Maine, but in our neighborhood in Mendocino. We search obsessively for reruns just to get a glimpse of our street. Of our beaches.

I love that song.

Unpredictably, my shoulders drop. My stomach drops. The disorienting sensation of standing at the ocean's edge, retreating waves pulling sand beneath my bare feet, sinking, moving sand in water, unsteady, and tears spill from my tired eyes and do not stop. Actual tears.

It does not feel good. It is not some magical dreamy euphoria. It is kind of dumb.

I sit down hard on the porch steps. Poor Meredith stands for a moment, and then she is beside me. She tosses her shoes at the door, one arm around me, and she pulls my head to her lap and her cool, soft hand pets my hair.

For a long while.

Angela Lansbury is mad about something. I hear her speaking sternly.

Meredith is so small. Not tall. Small around. She is wearing my favorite dark blue sweatshirt, the one she has always worn from when we lived at the ocean, white words printed: *Mendocino Public Library*. It is threadbare, soft as flannel. Meredith is cold and oceany. She smells oceany. Salt and sand. I hold on to her and she doesn't move away.

I must be cutting off her circulation but still she lets me cling. Her cool fingers find my eyebrows through my mess of tangled hair and massage the crease there. I try hard to breathe. The sun is gone.

"Do I need to buy you a dress?"

I shake my head into her knee.

"Really?"

"Oh my God." I sigh. *"No."*

She tucks my hair back behind my ears, like she always did at the beach when the wind whipped our hair around and we'd forgotten a hair tie.

"Why are you here?" I ask.

She rubs my back. "Gramma's bogarting the TV."

"No, *here*. Not Mendocino."

"Oh. I don't know. Just felt like it."

My nose is running. The silhouetted birds of the depressing office tissue boxes taunt me. I wish I had some right now.

"Well, for Christ's sake," Meredith says suddenly, quietly. "Look at that." She nods at the grave liner below the porch.

Japanese irises are blooming, unfurled and white. In the coldest air we've had all month. At night.

I love Japanese irises. Deceptively spindly, bony little stems and a tiny white blossom, they are virtually indestructible.

They thrive on being ignored; lack of maintenance only seems to encourage their growth, so they are planted in a lot of ugly places: highway medians, parking lots. But still they are beautiful. Even here, reaching up into the dark and the cold from a cement casket.

"Huh," she says. "What the hell." And still she doesn't move.

I cry on her some more and never say what the waves roll over and over in my exhausted mind: *I will never get out of here.*

She rubs my head and strokes my hair and lets me stay.

Eventually I get up. Untangle myself from her.

"Leigh," she calls.

I turn back.

"You should eat something."

I nod.

"Yeah," I say. "I know."

I go upstairs, take a bath, and crawl into bed beside Kai.

I reach into my drawer for my flashlight and line everyone up: Emily's face. My Catrina. My grave digger. I close the drawer and sleep. Hard. Long into the morning, through my first two classes. When I finally wake up, my head aches from crying so much. From crying at all.

On the kitchen counter, there is an excuse note for the school secretary about a fake dental appointment written in Meredith's unmistakable penmanship.

CR80

Late afternoon I am back in bed. The cold sun blinds me, spills from the hallway onto my face when Kai opens the door.

"Hey. Are you sick?"

259

I shake my head.

"Because Dad says to say, 'Where the hell are you?' Did you even go to school?"

My head is killing me.

Her cheeks are pink; she is radiating cold and an unfamiliar urgency. She drops a pile of envelopes on my dresser. "He's in the office totally out of control. He had to do an At Need, and he made me get the mail. What are you doing?"

My hollow chest, my red swollen eyes, my stupid sore body; all this crying is getting me nowhere, and sleeping has only made it worse.

Ovid and the butterflies, all that metamorphosis crap. Pointless.

Kai lies down next to me. Moves my hair off my forehead, pulls off one of her bulky woolen mittens, reaches into the pile of mail.

"This came today. Just now."

A package. Small butcher-paper-wrapped parcel addressed to me.

Stamps, all different sizes, watercolor butterflies, orange and black.

Mexico postmark. I sit up.

"You got the mail? Not Wade?"

"I did."

"Don't say anything."

"I won't," she says. "I swear."

I rip the butcher paper open.

Familiar red thread, nest of tissue.

Ana.

Dario.

A skeleton. A little girl riding a pony. There are flowers in her hair, flowers in the skeleton pony's tail, glitter and bony smiles.

She is Emily.

"She's so beautiful," Kai whispers. "Why is she dead?"

"Because I'm . . . because of me."

"What?"

"I don't know. I don't know why. I don't know."

What am I going to do about it?

Empty as I am, apparently tears are never ending. Who knew? I cry. And cry and cry.

Amazingly, Kai does not.

"Leigh. You have to tell me."

"What?"

"Everything."

She is in her track shorts, even in this cold. She must have skipped practice to bring the package to me. Didn't go to Rivendell. Came here instead. For me.

She gets up. Brings me a cool, wet washcloth.

☞☜

We stash the package in my closet and wait until the sun is nearly set behind the pines around Dario's trailer.

"This is breaking and entering!" Kai chatters, pulling her sweatshirt tighter around her.

"We're not breaking anything." I find the key in a cremain canister beneath a river rock and unlock the door. We step inside.

"Wow," she breathes.

Evening light seems to pulse within the blue walls, makes the color practically vibrate.

He has finished painting: blue tape gone, newspaper off the floor. The tiny bedroom area is filled almost entirely with the *PennySaver* queen bed, neatly made. New blue-gray bedspread, two plump white pillows.

Two.

Kitchen immaculate, as always. Clean white cloth on the table.

"Okay, let's see."

Kai pulls a paper package from her coat, folds back a nest of tissue, and here are the crystals she's brought from Rivendell. Ran all the way there and back, she is so fast.

We hang one in the kitchen window, one in the bedroom, one in the window above the table.

"What is this?" she calls, and holds up a plain paper bag. *Leigh* in tall black letters.

Three one-pound bags of Yorks.

Two disks of Pátzcuaro chocolate.

One folded piece of stationery.

Kai reads over my shoulder.

I forgot to tell you. There are these other butterflies that come for Los Muertos. They migrate the same path, not nearly as many and they're not as showy as the monarchs, so they don't get the same attention. They've got dark wings with little blue dots along the edges. They're called mourning cloaks. I'm not kidding, that is their real name. Mourning cloak butterflies. They are beautiful.

Pass your test.

"What does *that* mean?" she whispers.

"Which part?"

"All of it."

I unwrap a disk, put a piece of chocolate in her mouth.

"What the . . ." She closes her eyes. "Oh my *God* . . ."

"I know. Don't chew."

She takes the letter from me, sits at the table. "Is he coming back?"

I fill a jar with water. Arrange the stargazer lilies I've borrowed from Clambake's sister. Roses from the veterans, daisies from Shag Haircut's husband. They are cheerful on the white tablecloth. On the kitchen windowsill, below the spinning crystal, I set the blue sweet pea egg carefully on a saucer.

Out the open door the river rocks line the smooth pebble path from the door, flowers blooming in the cold among the stone. The blue walls sing.

I break a piece of chocolate for myself.

"Yes," I tell her. Tell myself. "He is. They will. He promised."

CR₈O

263

Back at the house, Wade is making biscuits from a cardboard tube. Rene jumps around barking, begging for bits of raw dough. Gramma and Grandpa sit on the sofa watching *Entertainment Tonight*. Waves and acetone signal Meredith's presence in the laundry room.

"Leigh!" Gramma calls over the din. "We were just talking about you!"

Fantastic. I pour glasses of milk for myself and for Kai. *That chocolate.*

"Why is your father telling us this garbage about your birthday?"

"What garbage?"

"You don't *celebrate* your birthday anymore?"

Wade smiles to himself, happily arranging raw biscuits on a cookie sheet, two inches apart for optimal browning. Wade, Meredith always says, just loves to stir the pot. I bump into him a little harder than I need to as I put the milk back in the fridge.

"I don't know, Gramma," I say.

She rolls her eyes. We all come rightly by it with the eye rolling.

"What the hell are you talking about? What's there to know? It's your *birthday*! What's the matter with you?"

"Oh, Mother, leave her alone." Meredith strolls in, grabs a roll of paper towels and an orange. Gramma purses her lips and goes back to her manic, tightly wound crocheting.

I imagine Elanor leaning over to put a hand on Gramma's

arm, easing the tension on the hook. *Not so tight, Irene; it'll be prettier if you let it go a little.*

"Disrespectful. God puts you on this Earth, gives you a life—*two* lives!—and you're just throwing it in His face. In your mother's face!"

I slide into a chair. She crochets furiously, Rene pouting at her feet. Grandpa dozes beside her. "And aren't you supposed to be in Mendocino?" she practically shouts at Meredith. "What are you doing here?"

"I live here, Mother." Meredith sighs.

Kai turns to me, eyes round. *She lives here?*

"And Leigh isn't throwing anything in anyone's face," Meredith says. "Let her be." She heads back down the hall to her seascapes.

Gramma shakes her head and clucks her tongue. Meredith standing up for me tingles the back of my neck, leaves me slightly woozy.

"I don't mean it that way," I say.

Gramma turns to look at me over the back of the sofa. "Well, what in God's name way *do* you mean it? Your sister knows what gratitude is; that girl is glad every second she's alive, aren't you, Kai?"

"Leigh's grateful, Gramma."

"I don't mean to not be. . . ."

"Don't listen to her," Kai whispers, and grabs my hand, kisses my knuckles noisily.

My eyes well up and spill. For the millionth time. I let

them. Gramma reaches into her bra and I gratefully accept a warm, wadded tissue.

"Wallace!" Wade calls from the kitchen. "Come have some biscuits!" Grandpa puts his hands on his knees and shoves himself up.

Meredith's waves crash. The sun sinks below the kitchen window.

"These are some very flaky biscuits, Wade," Grandpa announces.

Wade smiles. "Aren't they?" he gloats, pleased with himself. "Not bad from a can."

"Hey," I say to Biscuit Jones. "You busy later?"

"What for?" He slathers butter on a huge hunk of biscuit and tosses it down his throat.

"I need your help."

He chokes. I whack him on his back.

"You need what?"

"Dude." I hand him a glass of water. "I'm not saying it again."

He beams.

nineteen

"JESUS, WHAT HAVE YOU two been doing all this time? I thought he was *teaching* you!" Wade is white-knuckled the next day, pale as I kill Dario's truck for the third time in two minutes. I have only days to get this right.

"He *did*. Better than the class instructor." I shove the brake back on and start over. "It's been a while." I get it going and try to ease the clutch out but it dies again, jerks us forward.

"You're going to kill us!"

"Shut *up*, I'm trying!"

"You're not gonna pass if you can't get out of the parking lot."

"It's your duty as my father to do this, so just knock it off. Hold on a second." I give it a little gas, gently, *gently* pull my foot back, and—

"Duty, my ass! I *offered*, but oh no, 'Dario'll do it,' and I'll tell you what, when I was your age— Okay, now there you go. . . ." He grips the dashboard with both hands. We move out onto the dirt road and slowly up over Poppy, past Emily, past Serenity, past the veterans, past the babies. I've got it. I remember.

"Shift down for this hill."

"I can't yet, just hold on—"

"No, do it—get off the gas and do it!"

"I can't!"

"Oh yes, you can, too! Is this how you're going to be on the freeway? All timid and *I can't change lanes, I'm not ready*? For Christ's sake, this is life or death! You have to think fast! Just do it! Do it!"

"I'm not gonna be shifting down in the middle of the freeway!"

"You *might*! Traffic jam, accident, you don't know what's going to happen. Let me see you do it!"

I take a breath, shift from third to first and kill it. *"See?"* I burst into fresh tears. Wade sucks. I want Dario back. Dario never made me cry. About driving.

"Yes! Good! There you go!" he yelps happily. "That's it!"

"It's *dead*!"

"That's okay! You gotta have balls; go ahead and kill it! That's why we're here and not on the road yet. Go. Do it again! Do it!"

I slump in the seat.

"No, now look. Sit up straight. Adjust your damn rearview and drive this thing. *Drive* it. Nothing bad will happen if you stay in control. Tell it what to do. It can tell you're scared. Who is in charge? *Who* is in charge?"

"Me," I whimper.

"Who is in charge? Who is driving?"

"Me."

"*Who?*"

"*Me!* Me! Okay okay okay, just let me . . ."

He is wide-eyed and clearly scared, but he is *really* trying. And he is right. I know he is, but I cannot seem to find my proverbial balls, the lack of which, until now, has benefited Wade more than anyone. I turn the key firmly, Dario's voice in my head, *Clutch in, key, shift, gas* . . . I am in charge. I am in charge. I am in charge.

The engine turns over. I take us around the hill again, all the way to the shed, past Rene tied up and yipping in what was once our front yard but is now Rene's petrified poop pen. I make a confident, successful four-point turn that Wade nearly comments on but has the sense at the last second not to. Because I am on a roll. And four is better than five. Or seven or eight.

I drive past the office, through the Manderleys, and onto the highway. In charge on the highway. In my periphery I see Wade instinctively move his hand to his pants pocket, where his wallet is not. Awesome. No license. He says nothing. He is confident we will not get pulled over. His belief in my ability to not get us killed bathes me in warmth. The hours, days, and weeks driving with Dario come back. I am driving.

He will come home.

I honk and brazenly take my hand off the wheel to wave at some pedestrians.

"All right now, don't get cocky," Wade says. I give him a sidelong glance and see his seat belt dangling, unfastened.

"Hey!" I say. "Get that thing on! What's the matter with you?" He makes a face, keeps his eyes forward.

"Seat belts are stupid. Goddamned death traps. Put your blinker on and turn here." I signal and turn left onto a surface street heading downtown.

"How are they a death trap? *That* is completely stupid. Put it on!"

He shakes his head. "Say you drive off a cliff into a lake and you break your arms in the fall. You can't get out of the car to swim up because *why*?" He reaches up, jerks the dangling strap a little. "Because you can't get the seat belt undone. So you drown in the car. That's just great. Or the car catches on fire and you break both your arms. Can you get out to rescue yourself from the flames? Nope! Screwed again! Trapped, all safe and sound in the fire with a strap across your chest. Burned alive. Horrible way to die. No thanks."

My eyebrows are so high, they are hidden in my hair. "Each of those scenarios involves both your arms being broken."

"Exactly."

"And what lake are you driving around?"

"You'd be surprised."

"What if the DMV guy gets mad when I don't wear a seat belt?"

He is totally affronted. "Of course *you* wear your seat belt! You *always* wear your seat belt. Don't ever let me catch you without your seat belt! Jesus Christ!"

"But you said—"

"That's me. That's for *me*, dummy! *You're* not going to break your arms; you're a goddamned good driver. A *good* driver—yes, you are. I'm a horrible driver; I'll definitely end up on fire in a lake with two broken arms, so I need to be ready for that. But don't *you* dare drive without your seat belt on. Ever. You understand me?"

I do.

"All right, then." And with barely any terror in my heart at all, I take us all the way back to the cemetery, alive and well.

೦৪৪৩

Rhetorical question of the day: What kind of parents ditch you on what was once your birthday, just twelve—okay, now *eleven*—minutes before your driver's test, which only hours before they *promised* to take you to?

Kai comes huffing white clouds of breath and slams the front door against the cold.

"He's not in the office!" She tosses her arms in disbelief. "This is so stupid! What time is it?"

The microwave's green digital numbers glow the sick nervous color of my stomach. "Ten minutes. I have to be there in ten minutes. *Where are they?*"

"All right!" She matches my volume but undercuts my desperation. "We'll get there. We'll just . . . we will."

"I knew he would do this. I *knew* it! Why do I ever listen to him?"

"Because we're dumbasses who never learn," Kai sighs.

Even in my unglued state, this makes me smile for a second—at *last* some age-appropriate resentment.

I try to gather myself, regain composure, *think*. "Okay. Okay, we'll walk. Right? You run ahead, tell them I'll be right there, and maybe they have, like, a test-taker car I can use."

She shakes her head. "You'd know better than I would, but don't you have to have a car? I mean, don't you need to drive the one you'll be using?"

The three-ring circus of anxiety, lack of sleep, and irritation at Wade and Meredith reaches an apex of lunacy. I hold my head in my hands.

Pass your test.

But something is going to fix this. I can tell.

Silent seconds go by. And then:

"What're you kids up to?" Grandpa yodels, and pushes yipping, jumping Rene to the floor as he and Gramma come schlepping through the door, home from their weekly grocery store visit.

I pick up Rene, turn everyone right around, and herd them all back out the door.

ॐ

My legs burn from the effort of keeping my knees from touching Grandpa's truck's gearshift. We are smooshed so close together in the cab of the truck, we can't move our arms, and so Rene has free rein to run and jump all over our laps, licking our faces with his stinky liver lips. Maybe we should stack some wood while we're at it.

"Rene, get *off*!" Kai yelps, turning her head from his slobbery, spazzy love.

"Wallace," Gramma says. "Here it comes. Put your signal on." Grandpa drives on, humming happily. "Did you hear me? Wallace. Are you listening? *Wallace!*" she screams, clutching the dashboard. "Slow down! It's here, here it is, you're going to kill us, here it is, turn! *TURN!*" The DMV, still three blocks away, sends a shivering thrill up my spine.

If I weren't so sardined, I would pat Gramma's leg.

"Here we are!" I sing. My heart is suddenly warm, my stomach calm.

"Here we are!" Grandpa echoes. He parks the truck in a testing spot, smiles at me, thrusts the keys ceremoniously into my hands, and tips his straw cowboy hat.

"Be careful!" he yells at my face. "Have fun!"

"Totally!" I yell back, and I run for the DMV doors, waving to them, and to Rene, still barking his head off.

 files

I make a luxurious left turn into the DMV lot and park like a boss. Lovely. The test guy scribbles notes; the only sounds in the cab are pen against paper and my heavy, relieved breathing. I have held my breath, apparently, for the entire trip.

Aced my written. Remembered my hand signals. Parallel parked with confidence. Changed lanes without hesitation. With balls.

At last Test Guy looks up, unclips his seat belt, and opens the door. "That your family?"

Across the lot, a group of people stands near the low

cinder-block DMV building. They are huddled together in the cold. They are holding what looks like a sheet cake ablaze with candles. I squint at them. At Gramma and Grandpa. At Wade and Meredith. At Kai holding Rene's squirming body. I sit back and sigh.

"Yes."

"Well, come on in for your picture." He takes another look at the fools. "Sure nice of them."

I climb out of the truck to a wobbly, chattery-teeth version of "Happy Birthday." It *is* a sheet cake, covered with coconut flakes, snow-white and fluffy. Store-bought. Tiny candles blaze and sputter in the cold November air. Meredith smiles and sings. Wade smiles and sings, lifts the cake in the air. Kai is annoyed; she was not in on this. But she sings. Gramma scowls and sings. Grandpa sings super loud. Rene howls. I stand on the sidewalk, hands in my coat pockets, politely attentive until they finish.

"Leigh," Gramma says before I even make a move for the candles, "I want you to have this." From her giant purse she pulls a gift-wrapped package with a stick-on bow. "You need it more than I do." I tear it open.

Grandpa holds one end, I step back with the other, and the entire Last Supper unfurls, enormous, eerily accurate. Finished at last.

I kiss her leathery cheek.

Kai mouths the word *yikes.*

I step forward, take a breath, direct all my collected confidence right at Wade.

"I quit."

His face falls. "What?"

"Okay. Now ask me back."

"*What?*"

"Ask. *Ask* me."

"Ask you what?"

"Just . . . all right. I'm hiring myself back."

"*What?*"

"I'll stay as long as I need to, not a day more. Got it?"

His mouth snaps shut.

"And I'm painting in there. White. Or blue. Or wallpapering. And I want new chairs, not leather and *not* black. And for God's sake, we need new tissue boxes."

He turns to Kai, who nods sternly. My wingman. Winglady.

"And keep out of my Yorks."

"But—"

"Hands *off.* I need them to do my job, which is sometimes very sad. Sometimes *I* am very sad. And that is normal, it is not dramatic, life can be sad, and also I am *selling graves,* I get to be sad sometimes. Understand?"

He doesn't understand. But he nods. Meredith nods.

The most they can do.

It is enough.

I blow out all sixteen candles in a single breath.

twenty

"LIGHT THEM AGAIN," Kai says.

My hands are frozen, gloveless and stiff. She strikes a match and passes it carefully to me.

I relight the dozen white candles that are having a really hard time burning in this chill, slow night wind. In the dark. The way Dario told me.

On Emily's headstone.

Kai and I have brought lilacs, candles, individually wrapped hunks of Bubble Yum bubble gum. She really loved Bubble Yum. We've brought her some Yorks. And my grave digger, happily grinning with his silver shovel. My Catrina, her hat dripping sparkling blossoms, nestled cozily beside tiny sparkling Emily herself, content on her pony.

In the tin flower cup, Kai arranges a bouquet of slender wires supporting tiny trembling butterflies: lacy orange-and-black-patterned wings fashioned from delicate feathers attached to little black papier-mâché bodies, the type of thing one would stick in a potted plant to be pretty.

Among the monarchs, one plain. Black wings.

Mourning cloak.

"Rivendell," Kai whispers. "They have *everything*."

I pull my coat close to my body. Poppy Hill spills down into the moonless black silence of Serenity Valley.

It is my birthday. *El Día de los Muertos.* It is Emily's day, the Day of the Little Angels.

"Don't be scared," Kai says. "She's okay. She'll be so happy you're here."

I don't say I'm having trouble believing her, even though I want to. Badly.

The wind moves right through our coats but we stay. With Emily. Still no moon and the clouds are thicker every moment.

The candles flicker. I light them again.

"Okay?" Kai says.

She takes my hand. Still here.

My heart pounds, hopeful for a sign, trying so hard to feel her here, even just a little. More wind. More chimes. Darkness and candlelight.

We concentrate on Emily's stone, peaceful and bright, busy and still.

The Rivendell butterflies make shadows in the candlelight.

I breathe the cold air and let Dario in.

Tonight, and for all the Days of the Dead, the Door is open. If you listen very carefully, you can hear them whisper. Their wings tell you everything is okay. They're not afraid. They're with us. They're not afraid.

Your birthday is a gift. It is your responsibility. You chose an early arrival; it is your responsibility.

She is your responsibility.

I chose my arrival.

I *am* a patron saint.

I have responsibilities long neglected.

There is a reason the coroner's office sends the At Needs to me and not to Wade. They need me. They need *me*.

I was born to this.

This is why we came from The Sea. Why Emily was my friend when no one else would be. Why she is here and nowhere else. I was meant to watch over her.

The candles take hold. The flames reach up.

She is here. I can feel her beside me.

I don't even have to try.

CR SO

Hours later I learn that the most jarring sound in life is a telephone ringing in the middle of the night.

I am half-asleep and the ringing breaks the heavy quiet of the house, splits it into a million shards of panic. I lie in the dark trying to catch my breath as it rings. And rings. Kai breathes deeply, soundly, beside me.

Ring.

Do they not hear that?

Ring.

People maybe need to lay off the sleeping pills.

Ring.

I roll over and look at the clock. Who would call at this hour?

I am out of bed and down the stairs in two seconds, dive for the phone—

Dial tone.

"Who was it?" Meredith's totally wide-awake voice calls from upstairs. What the . . . They're just lying there in bed hoping I'll answer it? Jerks!

"No one!" I yell, trudge back up the stairs. "Missed it."

Ring.

I nearly break my face on the receiver.

"Hello?" Nothing. *"Hello?"*

Silence.

That silence.

"Leigh?" Whispered.

"Yes," I whisper fiercely back. "I'm here. It's me, I'm here."

"Leigh."

"Yes, I'm here!"

"Happy birthday."

"Where are you?"

Static.

"Dario. *Dario!*" I whisper.

"Leigh?"

"Yes."

"Did you pass your test?"

I have to sit down.

CR SO

I dress in the dark. No longer rigid, my muscles unwind and accept the temperature. Dario is right. "It's just weather," he always says. "It isn't out to get you."

"Be careful," Kai whispers from under the covers. "You have keys?"

I hold them tight inside my pocket. Keys to the Death Mobile, my birthday gift from Grandpa.

"Call when you get there—call on the way. Okay?"

"*You* better answer."

"I will. Hurry and come back. But don't worry, I'm a really good liar."

That is not true. She sucks at lying; it's one of her best qualities.

I make my silent way out of the house into the *yes, technically morning but still night* dark, the trees, the graves.

Map, keys, money, water. Map, keys, money, water, Yorks.

I roll in neutral, no headlights until I'm past the mausoleum.

The engine idles at the Manderleys. I pull them—frozen and heavy—slowly open, and turn, out of habit, to Emily.

There is light at her stone.

Not candles. Flashlight. At her grave.

I stand in the headlights, not moving, not breathing.

The flashlight goes out.

I inhale. Step forward.

"Hello!" I call.

Ravens fly up from the pines.

Nothing.

It is so dark.

"Hello?"

The light comes back on.

Moves toward me.

"Leigh?"

Not a woman.

Not Emily's mom.

Tall. Black hair in the headlights.

"Leigh," Balin says.

We breathe clouds at each other in the headlights.

"Elanor's sick."

My heart slows to a stop.

She's dying, proximity to me . . . "What kind of sick?"

"Not *sick* sick. A cold, it's nothing. She's home in bed."

I exhale.

"That's why I'm here," he says. "Because she's sick."

"Okay."

"Dario asked her. He said if he wasn't back yet, would she make sure there were flowers yesterday, but she was *really* sick then. She was so mad she missed it, but at least today was better than nothing, she said. . . ." He pulls a folded paper from his pocket. "Row L, Space 23. Poppy Hill."

Familiar as her name.

"So. Sorry it's a day late. She made me come in the dark so you wouldn't see me and then know it was really her and think she was being weird. I don't know. She's embarrassed. What are you *doing*?"

The headlights are blinding.

"I have to . . . I have an errand. I don't know," I stammer. "I'm sorry."

"Okay."

"Thank you for the flowers."

He nods. "We overordered for a wedding, so there's tons. You'll like them."

I nod.

"I need to leave," I say. "Are you— Can I give you a ride?"

Silence as I drive him home, all the way until I turn the headlights off at the willow gate.

"So. Graveyard errand?"

"Field trip."

"Oh, really?"

"Helping a friend."

He nods. "You okay?"

I press my forehead to the wheel. "I think so."

"Listen," he says. "Elanor's . . . I mean, she's a good person."

"I know," I say. "I know she is."

"Don't tell her I said that."

"I won't."

I can't seem to lift my head from the wheel.

Crying. Again.

I feel his hand on my back, a steady weight between my sharp shoulder blades. Makes it hard to cry quietly. This poor guy, he'll never do another favor for Elanor after this.

"Are you . . . What can I do?" he asks, but I'm too weepy to respond. And then low, "Oh, thank God."

I lift my head.

In the gray shadows Elanor is a tiny snowman swimming in what looks like five pairs of flannel pajamas.

She swings the willow gate wide and goes to the passenger window.

"What did you *do*?" she growls through the glass at poor Balin.

He turns to me. "Okay?"

I nod.

"All right." He climbs out of the truck. "Not my fault!" he tosses back at her, latches the gate behind him.

She stands shivering. Her hair is loose, bed-messy, and falls all the way down her back. Her nose is pink. She's got a giant wad of tissues.

"Sorry." She chatters. "He is so— Wait, did you *drive* here?"

She is overtaken by sneezing.

"Elanor."

"What?"

"Bless you."

"Thanks."

She folds her arms tight around herself. An owl flies low, wings wide.

"I'm so sorry," I say at last. "I'm stupid, I don't know what I'm doing, I'm sorry . . ."

"No," she says.

"I don't . . . I don't know. I'm sorry."

"Okay," she says. "It's okay!"

"No," I moan, "it's not . . ."

"Leigh!"

More stillness. She's just standing there shivering, and at once I want something so badly I am nearly afraid to ask.

Nearly.

"Are you working today?"

She shakes her head.

"Oh," I say. "Okay. So are you doing anything for the next"—I unfold the map in my lap, redo some mental math—"twelve, fourteen hours?"

She eyes the map. Swipes her nose with the tissue.

"I'll go get dressed."

twenty-one

MERGING ONTO THE HIGHWAY at five-thirty in the morning when there are practically no other cars on the road is so much easier than it is during the middle of the day. I drive exactly the speed limit, staying carefully glued to the rearview for signs of Highway Patrol. CHiPs. The Feds. The Fuzz. I ignore the driver's ed films and Gramma's hysterics, *Don't go so fast, look out, here comes a stop sign, look out for that guy in the next lane, he's probably high on meth, don't touch the radio, concentrate, concentrate!* I reach for the tenth time into my backpack to feel my license. Bottle of water. Meredith's seashell toiletry bag stuffed *I just robbed a bank*–style with icing-on-the-cake grave money. I am okay.

Elanor reads the maps. Black skirt. Blue sweater. Blue-and-white-and-black-striped tights. The boots. Hair wound back into the braids. She is not messing around.

We are okay.

The highway is a straight, undulating black ribbon through hilly fields of cattle, churches, new housing developments. There are no stars, only low black clouds, heavy, exceedingly cold. The wind through the open window whips my hair around my face. In my urgency to get out of the house, I have forgotten to put it up or even bring a tie to do it later. Elanor is right on with the braids.

Twenty minutes in, I remember to breathe. Unclench every muscle in my hands, tell the *look out!* voices to clam it. And now I feel the frozen air so I roll the window up, relax my jaw. I am a fine driver. This is okay, driving by myself—by myself with Elanor.

A car passes pointedly on the right. Good for them. I hope they get pulled over. I for one am going to obey the speed limit and traffic laws and have a lovely drive. I move to the slow lane.

Signs tell us our exit is a quarter mile ahead.

"You sure?" I ask.

Her hands are on the dash, determined. Excited. "Dario's waiting."

I brake slightly into the curve of the off-ramp, accelerate out of it, and we are south on Interstate 5 to Los Angeles: 184 miles to go.

಩ಠ

"Technically, he said Placentia," I tell her, tossing her a highlighter. "Not Los Angeles proper. Is that nearer or farther?"

She pulls the cap off with her teeth and highlights the route in purple. "Um . . ." She studies the lower section of

California's highway system. "It's like . . . half an hour farther. I think."

"Okay. No big whup." I rip open one of my Dario York bags.

She buries her face in her arm, sneezes a million times.

"Bless you."

"Ugh. Thank you. Sorry. My parents refuse to medicate when we're sick; they just brew gallons of tea with weird crap floating in it and make us take echinacea, which is a complete lie."

"What is?"

"Echinacea! Hippie herbal bullshit, excuse my French, but it does nothing! I'm dying here, coughing my brains out, and dried daisies are going to cure me? Please. I snuck to town yesterday and got some DayQuil." She shakes a box of Liqui-Caps. "It'll kick in soon." She wipes her hands with a bunch of wet wipes and unwraps a steady stream of Yorks for me so my hands can stay at DMV- and Dario-approved nine and three.

She unwraps a few for herself. "What's the deal with the truck? Your grandpa really just *gave* it to you?"

"I think so. The keys, anyway, which sort of imply the whole truck is what he meant; otherwise the warrant will be for grand theft auto *and* kidnapping."

She rolls her eyes. "I'm at your house, and you're at mine; if Balin and Kai can keep their stories straight, no one will ever know we're gone." She chews thoughtfully. "I'm counting on Kai."

"I don't know," I say. "Balin may do all right."

The sun is nearly up now, somewhere behind the clouds. No rain yet, Saturday and the traffic is light. Two hours in, which leaves—

"Four hours and change. Cake!" she says.

Her confidence makes me want to hug her. Which I will not do while driving, as it is unsafe and also I am seat-belted in.

"Is driving weird?"

I nod. "But not in an 'I don't know what I'm doing' way. Don't worry."

"Oh, I'm not. You're a total natural."

"I know *all* the rules. Items one is legally allowed to toss out the window of a moving car? Water. Feathers. End of story."

"Fantastic."

Traffic picks up just enough to be interesting: semis loaded with cattle, families in RVs. It does not slow us down.

"Are they okay?" she asks. "Is she?"

"He didn't say."

"I miss him."

"Me too."

We pass a semi, merge back into the slow lane.

She nods. "He must really be missing you."

I shrug.

"Leigh. Of course he is."

She's got this thing where she says what you wish so badly to hear and think you never will, and how could she ever know you wish it? But she does.

"Elanor."

"Yeah."

288

"Thank you."

She lets her head rest against the Last Supper, folded over the back of the bench seat, then turns her face to me.

"You're welcome."

⊗⊗

We stop for gas near Pea Soup Andersen's, a hilarious truck-stop restaurant all about pea soup that has giant plywood cut-outs of two chefs, one holding a pea, the other wielding some sort of sledgehammer to split it with, and holes you can put your face in, right there in the parking lot.

Elanor has a camera. We put our faces in the holes, and a nice waitress on a smoke break takes our picture.

At the pumps, I put the gas nozzle in the truck and push away the cash Elanor thrusts at me.

"Please," she begs, "let me help."

"You *are*," I insist. "I need to get rid of this." I reach in the open truck window and root around in my backpack to show her the manila Pre-Need paperwork envelope stuffed with all the surplus Cake Icing Money that wouldn't fit in the toiletry bag. "I don't want any of it. Just . . . please, help me get rid of it and then I can . . ." I don't know what.

"Start over?"

I nod.

She squeegees bugs off the windows.

"You could donate it."

"I will. I *am*. I am donating to the cause of Get Dario's Wife the Hell Out of Mexico and into the Romantic Love Grotto of a Graveyard, Quick."

289

"He's ridiculous," she says. "He can't bring her there to *live*, can he?"

I shrug.

"Do *you* like it?"

"It's . . . I wish it was near the ocean."

The tank is full. I hang up the nozzle. Elanor replaces the gas cap.

"But," I say, "I mean, it's not the way it was. At the start. I am warming to my patron sainthood."

Oh good Lord. Out loud, in the daylight . . . more ridiculous than hobbits.

"I'm sorry—your *what*?"

"Dario says," I sigh.

"Okay."

"I am a patron saint."

"Of what?"

"Death."

"*Dario* told you this?"

"Yeah," I say.

"*Why?*"

"I was born on the Day of the Dead. Same as the real one, the real saint. November first?"

"Yeah, we get people ordering gladiolas. Really?"

"Apparently."

"Oh, wait, *yesterday*—Dario was so insistent—God, now I feel even worse. I can't believe I missed it. I'm so sorry!"

"I'm glad you did."

She nods. "Happy late birthday."

"Thank you."

"What a perfect day to be born."

"You think?"

"Poetic."

We climb back up into the truck and find a spot near Pea Soup's entrance.

"You know," I say, "if you want, we could—would you want to maybe come over sometime? When we get back? To Sierrawood?"

She smiles.

"Because you could see, then. How it is."

"I'll bring yarn," she says. "I'll show you how to knit."

I haven't ruined it.

We go in for quick scrambled eggs and toast because out of the blue, I am *really* hungry. Not York hungry, actual-food hungry. We also get a side order of oatmeal and hot chocolate to go. Because I've got icing-on-the-cake cash to burn. Because we can. Because we are on a mission, yes, but also—we are on a road trip.

CB∞

"Buttonwillow," Elanor reports.

Two and a half hours and I'm starving again, but turns out, I-5? Not a culinary tour de force.

"Anything good?"

She checks the touristy AAA map against the Rand McNally.

"Nothing. Taco Bell. KFC?"

"*No.*"

But Dario is waiting, so Denny's it is. Pancakes, hash browns—apparently I'm carb-loading for a marathon. Elanor is giddy about the lack of bean sprouts in all this roadside junk and orders Moons Over My Hammy minus the ham. We get strawberry milk shakes to go, and we're back on the road.

"How much longer?"

She follows her highlighter path.

"Looks like . . . two hours? Little more?"

"That's it?"

"You're an excellent driver!"

The most boring scenery in America, endless black highway, great big trucks, flat, empty brown fields—and it's going by *so* fast.

"Will your parents be super mad?"

"I'm telling you," she says, "they'll never find out. I have nothing but faith in Kai. Will yours?"

"They won't notice I'm gone."

"No. Really?"

"Not in a bad way. They'll just figure I'll show up eventually. I always do."

She takes the lid off her shake, goes after it with a spoon. "I wish mine were like that."

"I wish mine were like *yours*."

"No, you don't. They pull dumb crap all the time. Echinacea. Babying Balin. They're so impressed with how clever they are. Like, my middle name is Danger."

"That's nice, though—you're brave. It's a term of endearment."

"No," she says, "it's my *actual* middle name."

"*No.*"

"Yes. They named an infant Elanor *Danger*. My dad thought it would give me 'extra strength of character in the patriarchal society of America' or some jazz, and I'm like, can we not be clever with *everything*, people?"

"Remind me to show you the walkway in our yard."

"The minute I'm eighteen, I'm going straight to the Social Security office, so start thinking of nice regular names I can use."

"I don't know," I say. "It's pretty badass."

I get an eye roll. "You still okay?" she asks.

I reevaluate my mirrors and stretch my hands. Drink my shake. "Think so."

We put the windows down a little, letting some air and road noise in.

"Elanor."

"Yeah."

"I really am so sorry."

"Oh, come on, it's okay!"

"I was awful to you—"

"Leigh."

"No, I was. I didn't know . . . how to be."

"*Leigh.*"

She pulls a pile of napkins from her backpack, preemptively offers me some.

"What do you think happens when you die?" I ask. Way to bring it down.

Her spoon hovers over her shake cup.

"Well," she says, "I kind of don't. My dad says it's all ever-lasting souls forever in the ether, metaphysical plinkity-plink, but then what about really awful people? Where is Hitler, right? Because I don't want to be floating in the same soup with that guy. *Or* the dude that made up Dungeons and Dragons."

I let myself smile.

"And then my mom is all, *Reincarnation!* which is why we don't eat meat, but I don't know if I can really get behind the idea of mastering some spiritual caste system by eating soy, even though karma makes sense, but . . . I don't know."

"So it's what? Nothing?"

"No, not *nothing*," she says. "But I think I've decided to be okay with sort of . . . not knowing, maybe *hoping* everything will be the way it's supposed to be."

"Huh."

"But the thing is, I've never known anyone who's died yet."

"How is that possible?"

"My mom's parents died before we were born. Dad's are still alive. They live in Oregon. Just no one yet."

"Wow."

She nods.

"Wade says there's nothing. Blackness and nothing for-ever, and that's why you can't be lazy because this is it, our one chance for everything. *Anything.* He gets so mad when we sleep in."

"Oh jeez," she sighs, rolls her eyes. "That's just stupid."

"But what if it's true?"

"Well, first of all, if it is, then we'll never know so it won't matter anyway. But second of all—no offense, but is he on glue?"

The road speeds beneath our feet. Trucks thunder by, passing us left and right.

"Elves are immortal," she says after a while. "Says the Dungeon Master. 'Their life span is that of the world,' unless they're killed by a human or dwarf or something. But sometimes they live so long, they get tired. Too worn out to go on anymore. Or they could be lonely, or one could have a broken heart. And then they go to where the spirits of the dead go, to the halls of Mandos in Valinor, which I'm not completely positive but I imagine is an island. In the ocean. They sail west to the Undying Lands."

"With the hobbits?"

"Well, no, it's for elves. They let a few hobbits in, I guess. Couple humans. A dwarf maybe. But it's for the elves to go to rest. Eventually you can't see them anymore, but they're there. I'm sure you could feel them if they were near. Peaceful spirits. Safe and content at sea."

My throat hurts. Her voice is Bob Ross soothing.

She hangs her arm out the window. Lets her hand ride the current.

"'And the ship went out into the High Sea and passed into the West . . . white shores and beyond them a far green country under a swift sunrise.' My parents made us memorize it like Bible verses."

"It's pretty."

"And fun at parties."

The road noise drones comfortably. Fills a long silence.

"Leigh," she says. "Emily is *not* nothing. She could never, ever be nothing. You know that."

I clutch the wad of Denny's napkins.

"And I'll tell you something else: if you *are* a patron saint of death, you really should have figured all this out by now."

"You'd think."

Cars pass us. I change lanes. Hay trucks barrel by, yellow flying everywhere.

She offers me a York, the very last in the bag.

twenty-two

THE SOUTHERN CALIFORNIA SUN has pushed the clouds aside. We roll the windows all the way down, the sky smog hazy but still so blue, air *so* warm. Muggy.

"What time is it?"

Elanor pushes her sleeve up past her watch. "Quarter to one."

My stomach is getting tighter with every mile. So far inland, not even an ocean breeze to lean into, all this unfamiliar urban sprawl.

Elanor wrestles out of her tights, her long-sleeved shirt, fans her face with the maps.

What have I dragged her into?

"Almost there," she says. "Have we talked about how much Placentia sounds like placenta?"

"Uh, no. But *gross.* You're staying in the truck, right?"

"Sure."

"Promise?"

She laughs. "Yeah, I promise, but I don't see what the big deal is. It's the middle of the day! We go in, we get them, we leave. Just some friend's house, right?"

"I guess."

"Here," she says. "Turn off here."

No more I-5. Street to street the neighborhoods all have a bland sameness: oil-change places, fast food, playgrounds, graffiti, nice houses, junky ones. Grown men riding children's bikes. Lots of chain-link fencing around postage-stamp-size scrubby yards and no trees other than a few sidewalk palms.

Dario would never put me in danger on purpose; there are people around, lots of cars. Traffic.

But the staticky phone connection. Voices in the background. How many people will be there, and who are they? I *think* he said it was a friend's house. I don't remember now. He spoke for all of thirty seconds, just the address, please come get him. Them.

My hands could not be sweatier.

The nearer to Placentia, the bigger the houses, the wider the streets. Sort of. I can't tell anymore.

Elanor studies the map.

We are quiet.

"Okay," she murmurs, and looks up. "Here. Here, turn here."

Another long street of low houses. A dog trots by unattended, no leash. No collar. More chain-link fencing. But people are walking by, there are sidewalks, and cars pass. Just a neighborhood.

Elanor narrates the house numbers under her breath until—

"Here. This one, this is it. This is it!"

I make a wide U-turn, stop in a tiny patch of shade provided by an inflatable bounce house across the street. No one in it. The party is over or has not yet begun. I shift into park, set the brake.

Silence after hours of highway. We unlatch our seat belts and close our eyes for a minute.

"Looks okay," she says, craning her neck around me to check out the house.

The house.

Small gray stucco. The front yard is full of sparkly white rocks, and cement frog and mushroom figurines guard the mailbox. A cactus here and there. Kind of run-down but not scary bad—sort of has the curb appeal of the mobile homes in Gold Country Villa.

"Yeah," I agree. "Looks good."

We sit. A car passes, booming bass so loud the truck windows rattle.

"Okay," Elanor says. "So let's . . . shall we?"

I frown at her.

"Fine," she says. "Shall *you*?"

I inhale as deeply as the grimy hot air will allow. Step down to the street. "Lock the doors."

She presses the knobs obediently.

"I'll be right back. Roll the windows up."

"No way!" she yelps. "It's a thousand degrees in here!"

"Just *some*."

She rolls them up halfway. Then a little more. "Go," she says. "Hurry."

I shake my tingly legs, pins and needles in my numb feet. Walk.

Just a house. Just a neighborhood in the middle of the day. I'm being totally ridiculous, just picking up a friend from his friend's place, that's what he said. I'm sure that's . . . probably what he said.

I turn back once more to Elanor. She waves. Smiles. Dying in the heat.

Through the chain-link gate, porch, my hand to the door. Knock.

Dogs bark inside. Men's voices.

The door opens.

A woman. Older. She wipes her hands on a dish towel and pushes three or four little yapping dogs off her and back. "*¿Sí?*"

I make myself smile. "Hello!"

She just stands there.

"Um. I'm here for . . . is Dario here?"

She turns back into the dark house. "Samuel!" she yells. "Someone here to see you!"

"Oh," I call to her retreating form, "sorry, no, I'm looking for Dario. . . ."

"Hello!" Another voice comes from the depths of the

house. The sun is so bright, my eyes cannot adjust, but he is in the doorway, a man, younger than the woman. "*¿Cómo puedo ayudarte?*" How can I help you?

"Hello," I say. "I've come for Dario."

He smiles. "*Sí,*" he says. "*¡Dario!*"

"Yes." I smile back.

"*¿Y Ana, también?*"

"Yes, Ana also. Dario and Ana."

We smile at each other.

"*Sí, está bien,*" he says. "*Dario y Ana.*"

More smiling.

"So," I say, "are they here?"

He frowns. "*Lo siento, no entiendo.*"

Oh Jesus.

No English.

I'm going to get us all killed.

Your Spanish is beautiful.

Sure, Dario. If I'm discussing interment options.

I don't think. Just speak.

"*Mi nombre es Leigh. Estoy aquí para recoger a Dario y Ana. ¿Están aquí? Tenemos un paseo largo por delante.*"

He laughs.

My face, already pink with heat, flushes.

What did I say wrong? *My name is Leigh. I'm here to get Dario and Ana, and by the way are they here because we've got a long drive ahead of us,* subtly moving toward a "Let's get this wrapped up" vibe. I know every word was right; what is this guy's problem?

"¡Adriel!" he calls over his shoulder. *"¡Ve la blanca!"*

My wrists pulse with the blood and adrenaline thundering through my veins. What the hell? I'm "the white girl" his pal needs to come see?

Adriel is younger still, Lakers jersey and basketball shorts; he pokes his head around the corner, steps in the doorway. Smiles. Which pisses me off even more. Except his eyes aren't smiling. At all. So now I'm mad *and* scared.

"¿Por Dario?" he says.

Samuel nods. *"¡Preguntale algo!"* he goads. *Ask her something.*

Adriel leans in the doorway. Looks me up and down. *"¿No estás caliente en esos jeans?"*

"¡Sólo piensas en una cosa, hermano!" Samuel laughs. *"¿Un poco flaca, pero no me importaría si podría ver las piernas, eh?"*

For a second—just half a moment—I am terrified.

This is a Dateline "Danger Is Everywhere!" reenactment where a voice-over says, "I should have listened to my instincts. I knew right then I should have turned and run, called the police, gotten out of there. Hindsight is twenty-twenty. . . ."

But the moment is eclipsed by both a startling, ill-timed joy and my fully bloomed, impatient fury. First of all, Elanor is right; it's the middle of the damned day! If they had guns, wouldn't they have shown them by now? I have driven eight hours. I have come here to do one simple thing. I am not leaving until Dario and Ana are in that truck.

Oh, and the joy.

I understand.

No effort, no need to turn their words inside out to English and back, because I understand the straight-up Spanish. Too bad it's *these* guys' Spanish, but still.

Yes, Adriel, if that is your name, I *am* hot in these jeans. I am very hot. I'm sweating to death. But it was cold in the place I left this morning, and who are you in your stupid basketball shorts to pass fashion judgment? You don't know me! Jeez! And *you*, creepy Samuel. Seriously? I'm kind of skinny but you'd like to see my legs anyway?

"All right," I say, done screwing around, infused with my new power. "*Escucha. Mis piernas no son un tema que vamos a discutir hoy. Estoy aquí por Dario y Ana. Por favor sacarlos aquí, porque tenemos un horario ajustado y necesitamos irnos. Ahora mismo.*"

Loosely translated? *Listen up. My legs are not an issue we're going to discuss today. I'm here for Dario and Ana, so please get them out here because we are on a tight schedule and we need to go, right now.*

Smile time is over.

Maybe flexing my bilingual guns with these fine gentlemen wasn't the smartest thing.

Adriel disappears into the dark house.

Samuel steps out onto the patio. Stands close to me. "*¿Cómo sabes Dario?*" *How do you know Dario?*

I swallow. Glance across the street. Elanor's face is pressed to the half-down window.

Please just stay in the truck, I think. *Don't be a hero.*

"*Trabajamos juntos. ¿Y tú?*" I answer. *I know Dario from work. And how do you know him?*

"*Amigo de un amigo.*"

Right. *I'm sure Dario is friends with tons of shifty guys like you, pal.* I think this but I don't say it, because now I am outnumbered by "friends." Adriel has dragged yet another guy out here with him, none of them much taller than me, but all three unhappy—owing, it seems, to my obvious grasp of both languages. Hard to tell how much English they know, and I'd have thought they'd appreciate the Spanish effort, but instead it's making them circle the wagons.

My heart is pummeling my ribs.

Not so many people walking by on the sidewalk. The sun is pulsing, everything too bright. I get the sick feeling something is definitely not right.

Maybe Dario isn't here.

"*Si Dario no está aquí, me voy,*" I say. Matter-of-fact. *If he's not here, I'm leaving!*

And I do. I turn and walk. A gamble.

"*¡Chica!*"

"*¡Señora!*" I shout back.

Peals of laughter. I keep walking, praying they don't call my bluff. *Oh God, what am I doing?* Elanor is hanging out the window like she's about to lose her mind.

"*Señora, espera. Vuelve. Él está aquí, lo juro a tú, ambos están aquí.*" Okay. *He is here. They are here.*

I turn back.

"Then go get him!" I call. *"No tengo tiempo para esto. Tenemos que irnos. Ahora."* I don't have time for this. We need to leave. Now.

Samuel walks out into the sun, through the gate, and stands with me at the curb.

"¿Dario te explicó cómo funciona?"

Did Dario explain how *what* works? I come, I pick him up, we go home. That's "how it works."

"Yes," I say. "I understand. I'm here to get him."

Samuel shakes his head. *"¿Te dijo acerca de la tarifa?"*

Tarifa? No, he did not tell me about a *tarifa.* I scroll through all the nouns I know.

A tax? A fee.

Irony doesn't translate well, and also I am back to being scared to death; otherwise I would congratulate this creep for doing such a great job of strengthening stereotypes.

"Quieres dinero." I sigh. Unbelievable. *You want money.*

People nearly die getting to America, and then this jerk pretends he'll help, but all he's doing is working with the stupid coyotes, one last chance to screw people over. He's a living cliché.

If I was furious before, I've got some rage happening now, luckily still cut with a healthy dose of fear to keep it in check. Just barely.

"It's a fee," he says, "for services. *Estamos aquí para ayudar."*

Yeah. He's here to help. The service of holding people for

petty ransom. I'm terrified, but I also want to punch him in the face—him and the jerks still standing on the patio guarding the dark doorway.

But what can I do? And where is Dario?

"*Verlos primero*," I demand. *"Ambos de ellos."*

Samuel shakes his head. "Money first," he says. *Then* I see Dario and Ana.

"We're done," I spit. English. "No way."

I walk blindly once more to the truck, pushing tears of frustration off my face. Elanor unlocks the door, shoves it open, and moves back so I can climb in.

"What was *that*?" she whispers. "Who are those guys, are you okay, where is Dario, do they have guns, do you think they have *guns*?"

"I don't know," I whisper back. "I don't think so. They're just acting like punks. Hold on a second. . . ."

"Lady!" Samuel runs to the truck. Right on cue.

"Lock the door!" Elanor screeches, full voice.

"*¡Señora!*" Samuel says through the open window. "*¿Tienes el dinero?*" Do you have the money?

"No," I growl. "No! Not until I see Dario and Ana. *No hasta que veo Dario y Ana.*"

He drops his head back, his arms in the air.

"Okay! Okay, *ambos. Ambos equipos al mismo tiempo, tú nos mostrarás el dinero, yo te mostraré Dario.*"

What the hell is this, showdown at the O.K. Corral? *I show him the money, he shows me Dario?*

"Dario *and* Ana," I bark.

"Yes, *sí, por supuesto, Ana también. Dario y Ana juntos.*"

"Fine," I say. "*Los trae afuera.*" *Bring them out.*

He nods, all smiley and amused, then pushes past the two "friends" still dicking around in the doorway, back inside the house.

Elanor looks really, really pale. "What's going on? What's he saying? What are we doing?"

I grab my bag, tucked behind the Last Supper. "Money," I whisper, grabbing the Pre-Need envelope of surplus icing-on-the-cake cash.

"How much?"

"I don't— Oh God, I don't know, he didn't say!"

"You didn't *ask*?"

"I've never paid a ransom before!"

"*Ransom?* What is going on?"

"I don't *know*!"

"What are they going to do if you don't—if it's not enough?" Elanor looks toward the house. "This isn't good. All those guys. What about Ana?"

Oh God.

"No," she says. "No, I'm sure it's okay. Dario's with her. It's . . . just don't show them all of it, in case they want more. Start with— Here." She pulls out some fives, a wad of twenties. "Got anything bigger? Put it on top."

"*What?*"

"Just do it!"

There are fifties. Some hundreds. We stack a bunch, roll it all into a cash sausage, and snap a pink rubber band around it.

"Feels good," she says. "It's got heft. Right?"

"I don't know!"

"No," she says. "It's good. It is."

"How do you know how to do this?"

"Movies. It's homeschool, not solitary confinement. Cripes!"

"You think?"

"Yeah," she says. "Yes. Put it in your sleeve." Some color is flooding back to her face. "Let's go." She opens the passenger door.

"No! No way."

But she's out. Fearless.

"Elanor," I beg, "get back in the truck. Please!"

"I'll just stand there and say nothing; they don't know how much I understand. I'm another pair of eyes, a witness. Let's *go*."

"No."

"Let me help you."

"*No!*"

"Leigh, it's the middle of the day next to a bounce house; it's not like we're skulking around the seedy underbelly of Tijuana hiding from the border patrol. Let's *go!*"

True. *Still.*

"Also," she says, "Danger is my middle name."

She swings the door shut and marches through the chain-link gate. I run to catch up and pull her back to the curb.

"We'll stay on the sidewalk," I pant. "Out in the open. Yeah?"

She nods. Firmly astride in the boots, arms crossed. Pissed. Glaring at the doorway lackeys. All four feet, ten inches of her.

I stand beside her in my jeans, both of us boiling in the sun, trying to look intimidating. Or at least not terrified.

The doorway jerks laugh.

We wait.

Kids arrive for the bounce house party. Music starts up. Madonna.

Elanor stifles nervous laughter. "This is ridiculous," she murmurs. "If we get ourselves and Dario out of this alive . . . I don't know what."

"We'll do something fun," I say. "I promise. Anything you want. Okay?"

"Okay."

Samuel is on the porch. "Well?" he yells over Madonna. "*¿Tienes el dinero?*" He narrows his gaze at Elanor. "*¿Quién es este?*"

"*This is my sister,*" I say in Spanish. "*Our father is a police officer, so keep your hands where I can see them. You'll get the money when we see Dario.*"

He and the Jerks exchange bemused looks. They laugh, raise their hands. "*Los padres de todo el mundo son policías.*" Samuel smiles.

Yeah, I'm sure everyone he knows does claim their dad is a police officer, probably because he's always trying to pull illegal crap on people. I am so sick of this guy.

"*¿Dónde están Dario y Ana?*" I yell back. "*¡Vamos a*

conseguir este programa en la carretera!" Let's get this show on the road!

In the periphery, Elanor's mouth drops open.

"What?" I hiss.

"Your Spanish is amazing!"

"Están adentro," Samuel calls. He beckons us into the house. *"Entra y vamos a hacer esto."*

Inside the house? With you, Samuel?

Elanor clutches my arm.

"No," I say, everything in me desperately straining to be calm. *"Absolutamente no. Lo hacemos afuera, aquí, que los sacó, te mostraré el dinero, lo hacemos todo juntos. Como dijiste."* *Everything outside, both at once, just like you said.*

Adriel leans from the doorway, whispers to Samuel.

"Hey!" Elanor shouts. She grabs my sleeve, pulls the cash out. "Look!" she says, holding it above her head. "We've got it. There's a lot here. It's legit!"

"Legit?" I am light-headed.

But all three guys look up. Elanor nudges me, eyes wide.

"Yes!" I yell. *"¡Los trae afuera!* It's yours if you want it. Just bring them out."

And then Elanor peels off one of the hundreds from the rubber-banded bundle, wads it up, and throws it at the men. Like tossing a stick to a fetching dog.

My heart stops.

Samuel strolls casually to where the bill has landed on the white rocks. Picks it up. Uncrumples it. Passes it to the Jerks.

He stays rooted in the shade of the porch. Considers us for several very long seconds. He and the Jerks whisper to one another. Madonna is yammering about having a holiday, and kids are laughing, shouting in the bounce house.

Samuel folds the hundred into his shirt pocket, then disappears once more inside the house.

We barely breathe.

And then Dario is here. They are here.

They come blinking from the dark recesses of the house. Samuel's hand is on Dario's shoulder. *Don't touch him,* I want to snarl, but I wait. Elanor and I wait.

Ana—who must be Ana—is holding Dario's hand.

My chest clenches tight, then floods with unbelievable relief, so like the surreal moment the doctors said at last Kai would not die.

He is here. They are here. They are not dead.

Elanor's hands are clutched over her chest, but her face is carefully blank.

Ana is only slightly taller than Elanor. More beautiful than I'd dreaded. Delicate, lovely face, long hair twisted up in a messy bun. She looks so tired; they both do.

Samuel stops at the chain link.

"*¡Aquí está,*" he says, falsely cheerful, "*tal como prometí!*"

I don't remember him "promising" anything, but "*Sí,*" I tell him. "*Gracias.*"

Dario sees Elanor. He is clearly startled. His eyes find my face.

What? I want to say. *What should I do?*

"*Así.*" Samuel smiles. "*¿Vamos a cambiar?*"

"What?" Dario says. "What are you exchanging?"

Oh, I've missed his voice.

Elanor gives him one firm shake of her head.

Ana closes her eyes. She holds Dario's hand tighter, her hands that made my skeletons. My Emily.

One last wave of adrenaline swells.

"Dario," I say evenly. In English. "Is Ana okay? Are you?"

He nods.

"Because we can call my dad. You know—the *police officer.*"

"No," he says. "Nothing."

All right, then.

This is what I'm doing about it.

"Samuel," I say, "*así es como bajará. Quédate donde estás. Dario y Ana van a venir aquí a la acera, y te daré este dinero encima de la valla. Vamos y nunca volveremos. ¿Lo tienes?*"

The words just come. Every grave we've ever dug, every word of every conversation, every part of speech and grammar point Dario has painstakingly taught me have led to this one ballsy monologue. Sarcasm, slang, maybe none of it translates, or maybe some makes it through because Dario and Ana look stunned, but most important, Samuel clearly understands I've decided, I am *telling* him, how it's all going down.

And amazingly, it does. Every word. Just as I say.

Dario and Ana step through the gate to the sidewalk, I

swing it shut behind them, and Elanor immediately puts her small self between Dario and Ana and the fence. Samuel stays where he is.

Over the chain-link fence I hand him the icing-on-the-cake cash. Most of a year's worth of hands held, tissues offered, Yorks eaten, graves sold, dug, tended, and buried.

Samuel lifts a few edges of the bills. Smiles. Nods.

I toss the truck keys to Elanor.

"Elanor," I say, eyes still on Samuel. "Let's go." She ushers Dario and Ana across the street and into the truck. Madonna serenades us appropriately with "Like a Prayer."

I back slowly toward the getaway truck, watch Samuel count the money, watch him watch me watching him.

He laughs.

"Oh, wait!" he suddenly calls. *"¡Señora, espera un minuto!"* He yells to the Jerks. Adriel steps back in, then out the door, and hands something to Samuel, who goes to the gate.

"Aquí," he says, tossing the thing to me. *"Es la bolsa Ana."*

A bag. Ana's bag.

"Gracias."

I run. Climb up into the truck and give the bag to a grateful Ana wedged beside Dario, who is smooshed in next to Elanor. I yank my seat belt on and pull away from the curb.

"Hey!" Samuel shouts from the white rocks. *"¡Señora! ¿Quién te enseñó hablar español tan bien?"*

I roll the window all the way down, right foot poised over the gas pedal, the truck idling quietly.

Who taught me to speak Spanish so well?

"*¡Tu madre!*" I shout, slam the pedal down, and we are gone, a trail of dust and "Like a Virgin" in our wake.

"Leigh," Dario says. "Really?"

I am so punch-drunk with relief that I maybe shouldn't be driving. "Oh, come on!" I say. "You love it!"

twenty-three

WE ARE LOST.

I miss the Highway 91 entrance, blow past the I-5, surface streets now. Why does everything look so maddeningly the same?

"Elanor," I yell, "you're the world's worst navigator! What are you *doing*? Where are we?"

The map is whipping around in the loud wind because the truck is equipped only with what Grandpa calls "Dual 65" air-conditioning: both windows down, at sixty-five mph you'll get some air. Nice.

Dario and Ana are just sitting here silent, eyes forward.

"Um . . ." Elanor fumbles with the giant folded sheets of roadway. "Anaheim? And I could be wrong, but—" She peers out her window. "Isn't that the Matterhorn?"

"You are high on DayQuil." I sigh. But I squint into the pale violet haze of smog hanging low over the ever-increasing traffic.

A snowcapped peak reaches up, high above the concrete all around us.

"What time is it?"

"Almost half past," she says.

"Past what?"

"One."

"One what?"

She eyeballs me over Dario's lap. "Are *you* high? One, one o'clock!"

Twenty minutes. We were doing hostage negotiations with minimum-wage cash in broad daylight in the middle of a residential street for only twenty minutes.

I could have sworn it was hours. I've aged years in that twenty minutes. Wait, *twenty minutes*?

"Elanor."

"Yes."

"I need to get out of this truck. We need to park. I think I'm having some kind of . . ."

Dario snaps out of his daze.

"Leigh," Ana says. "Are you okay?"

Wow. Perfect English. Of course.

"I don't know," I admit. The adrenaline is draining fast. My head hurts, there's nowhere to park on these stupid streets, so many red curbs, a million honking cars, billboards and freeway overpass signs directing me too many ways, the sun pulses into the windshield.

"Take a breath," Elanor says, very calm, face down in the map. "Listen to me. There's a parking lot coming up. A really, really big parking lot, very easy, we're almost there, can you make it?"

I nod.

"Okay," she says, "so wait just a second and . . . turn. No, here. Okay, left . . . and here, left again here and . . . right here, we're here, just go, go forward, go straight."

Straight into Disneyland.

"Sixteen dollars!" Elanor yelps. "Holy crap, are you kidding me? To *park*?"

Happiest Place on Earth. Seems like a bargain.

I pass a crisp fifty to the attendant from the dwindling stack in the envelope, take the change, and slide the ticket on the dash.

Elanor hangs her head out the window.

"Our whole lives, Balin and I have cut out magazine pictures of the rides to make hint collages for my parents. They never gave in, and I know it's so awful and commercial and plastic and bad for the environment and the princesses are sexist, gender-normative hookers with daddy issues, but I can't help it, I can't believe we're here! Even just the parking lot. I never thought I'd get this close."

We circle the rows again and again until—

"Oh," Elanor chirps. "Hooray, those people are leaving, do you see? Go, hurry, go, get that one!"

It's even near a tree. Shade. Thank God.

I turn the engine off.

Quiet.

We all close our eyes. Lean our heads back against the Last Supper.

We are safe.

They are here.

They are alive.

"Feel better?" Ana asks.

I turn to her.

Even tired, oh my God, is she beautiful.

"Do *you*?" I ask.

She nods.

"It was mostly waiting," Dario says. "But they wouldn't let us leave. How much did you give him?"

"Some."

"How much?"

"I don't know, and it doesn't matter."

"I'm so sorry," he says. "Our guy in Mexico said it was his friend's house. I'll pay you back, I promise—"

"No," I groan. "Please, the money's not . . . It isn't mine. It wasn't mine."

Dario frowns. "Whose was it?"

"No one's. It was for this. Meant for this."

"Leigh."

"*Dario.*"

"You'll get it back."

"It wasn't mine. Get over it."

And now my brain has held it together as long as it is able, because apparently it is time for me to cry. Again.

Dario stares.

"Yeah, you like that?" I choke. "It's all I do now. It's awesome. Hey, El—"

Elanor passes me the last of the Denny's napkins. "Don't worry," she tells them. "It'll be over in a minute."

"Sorry," I sob. "I'm sorry . . ."

Ana puts her arms around me. *"Pobrecita,"* she murmurs, "you're just tired."

Humiliating. She and Dario have been dodging death for days, weeks, traversing the desert on foot, hiding from the border patrol, dealing with stupid Samuel and God knows what else, and *I'm* crying? Ugh.

"All right, we need to stretch our legs before Leigh drives anymore," Dario announces. "Fresh air, we need water, let's find a fountain."

"A what?" Elanor says.

"Fountain, a drinking—faucet?"

"Gross," I moan. "Let's just go eat somewhere. I need lemonade. Root beer, something."

Dario sighs.

"What?"

Ana squeezes my hand. "They took everything. My bag they let me keep, but all the money, anything worth selling, everything else . . ."

"Except the rings," Dario says. "We hid those. I won't say where."

Ana shoots him a look. *"Dario."*

"The rings!" Elanor squeals. "You're *married!* Let me see!"

Wide silver bands Ana made, then sewed into a panel in

the bottom of the bag. She rips the seam, pulls them out. A matched pair.

"They're beautiful," I say. Truthfully.

"My parents are sending the wedding money everyone gave us," she says. "It will come soon, but not right away. I'm sorry. . . ."

"People!" I pull the rest of the icing-on-the-cake cash from the Pre-Need envelope, from Meredith's seashell bag, still hundreds left. "Will everyone pay attention to the words I am saying. This money is not mine; it is ours. And I am begging you, please, help me help myself. We've got to get rid of it. Seriously. Please."

"That makes no sense," Dario says.

"Who is in charge here?" I say. "Who is driving?"

"Who *taught* you?"

"Someone annoying."

"Kids," Ana says, "enough!"

Elanor raises her hand. "I have an idea."

"Fantastic," I say. "What?"

"Well," she says, "I mean, we're at a place that sells drinks. And other things. *Expensive* things that use up lots of cash, and also it's a good place to walk. For leg-stretching. You know."

"Interesting," I say. "That is a very interesting idea."

"Yeah." She nods.

"Okay," I say, "who here has *not* been to Disneyland?"

"Leigh," Dario says.

"I'm just asking."

"I have not," Ana volunteers, "and I understand that is something to be pitied."

"It *is* to be pitied," Elanor confirms. "It really is."

"Well," I say, "I have. But only once. And I was two years old and it was with my gramma, so I don't think it counts."

"Leigh," Dario says again.

"*What?*"

"We're going home."

"I know. Of course we are. Just one more quick survey: Who here is really tired?"

Elanor's eyes are saucers.

Dario's hand goes up. He looks ready to pass out in the perfect Disney parking lot landscaping.

Still, I am in charge.

"Three hours," I decide, "not a minute more, I swear! We can do Pirates and Space Mountain and the teacups and we'll *still* be home around eleven."

"*Leigh.*"

"Dario," Elanor says, so happy she is on the verge of flight, "this is American democracy in action, and sadly for you, you have been outvoted."

"*Querido,*" Ana says, and pulls Dario's face to hers. I look away. "You can sleep the whole ride home."

He demonstrates being married and gives in.

We buy four one-day passes, giant bottles of water, four Mickey-shaped chocolate-dipped ice-cream-on-a-sticks, three mouse-ear hats with our names embroidered on the back, hooded Disneyland sweatshirts, and a gender-normative rhinestone princess tiara for Elanor. And we walk across the drawbridge into Sleeping Beauty Castle to make the best use of three hours and the last of the Cake Icing Money any of us could ever have imagined.

twenty-four

MAYBE THE GREATEST FEATURE of the Death Mobile (I have *got* to stop calling it that) is the heater. It is powerful, and when we hit the cold of Northern California, it keeps us warm. And sedated.

"I'll stay up with you, Leigh," Elanor yawns. "I swear!" And she's gone. Dario puts a sweatshirt between her head and the passenger-side window.

Ana is beside me on the bench seat, her long hair down, and it brushes my shoulder. Her left hand on my knee, her right holds tight to Dario's. I have to stop myself from waking her to remind her not to touch the gearshift.

I cannot think about the desert anymore—the coyote, the border patrol, guns. Her head drops to Dario's shoulder. He closes his eyes. We ride in silence. I forget to be scared of driving. The heater hums. Ana and Elanor sleep.

I am not sleepy. Tired, but wide awake.

"Dario," I whisper.

"Mmm."

"Are you okay? Really?"

"Yes."

"Is Ana?"

"Ask her yourself."

"I can't *ask* her that. I feel dumb. I'm a dumb gringo."

"Okay, John Wayne, let's be a little more dramatic. Ask her to make you a burrito."

"Oh my God," I sigh, "just tell me."

He opens his eyes, turns to me.

"She is. She's okay; we were very lucky. She's really brave."

I nod.

"Leigh."

"What?"

"I didn't understand the pirate ride."

"Which part?"

"All of it. It's not really a ride, is it? It's so slow."

"It's not about speed, dummy; it's about seeing the stuff. Like you're in their world; you're a pirate. You didn't get that?"

"I don't know."

"They make it pretty clear."

"I guess. I did like being in the boat."

"Well. Sure."

Almost midnight. All around us dark farmland, no other headlights. We could be the only people in the world.

Dario closes his eyes. Smiles.

"You and Elanor," he says. "Not to be messed with."

I smile.

"I didn't want to call you, because I knew you would come. But I did. Because I knew you would come."

I nod.

"Don't cry," he says.

"I'm *not!*"

"Okay."

We're almost home.

CR⁊

Snow. It is snowing.

A mile from the turnoff to Sierrawood and flakes are zooming around, flying at the windshield. I panic, can't find the wiper switch. I turn on emergency lights, switch headlights off and on. The windshield is nearly covered. I step heavily on the brake and pull off to the shoulder. Ana wakes up.

"What is it?"

I mess with buttons, turn knobs.

"Oh," I whisper casually, "nothing." I nearly break the turn signal forcing it up farther than it can go.

"Here." She reaches over the wheel, pulls the headlight switch forward. The blades come to life, sweep the wet snow aside in graceful arcs.

Elanor shifts, keeps sleeping.

"Thank you," I say.

"Thank *you.*"

Dario snores. Loud.

"Good luck with *that.*"

325

She sends her eyes skyward.

I might love her.

"Hey . . . was the wedding—how was it?"

"Oh, Leigh." She lays her head on Dario's shoulder. "I wish you were there. All his friends."

"I wish we were, too. Lots of pictures?"

"A million," she whispers. "My mother will send them. But oh, wait . . ." She finds her bag at her feet, pulls out a Polaroid. "Look how handsome!"

Dario smiling, blurry, in a suit. Red poppy in his lapel, dark curls combed off his face.

"Will you be okay?" I ask. "Without your family?"

"Dario is my family."

I nod.

"Also," she whispers, confidential, "my family's a little . . ."

"*Really?*"

She nods. "I love them. But I think . . . maybe some distance is a good thing."

Now I *know* I love her.

I signal, ease back onto the road. The snow swirls, gets drier. Stickier. Ana pushes Dario's arm.

"*Mira.*" Look.

He sits up, leans forward, face tilted toward the clouds. "*Leigh!*" he whispers.

"I *know!*"

"So slow down!"

"If I go any slower, we'll be parked. Don't worry about it."

Secretly I am sweating and scared, Gramma and the driver's ed films shouting, *No chains! Black ice! Oil and water mixed makes for deadly roads! Driving at night in a storm is certain death! Ahhhh!*

Elanor is awake.

"Leigh!" she says.

"I know!"

We are here. Home.

Dario jumps out, unlocks the frozen Manderleys, and leans back in the open door to say, "Hey. Park a minute?" He directs me airport-tarmac-style to the pond.

You'd think the guy would want to rush his bride off to her new home first, but apparently it is more exciting and romantic to spend some time with cemetery ducks in the freezing middle of the night. God, Wade has ruined him.

Inside the Manderleys, the trees, the lawn, the graves, the office, all white.

"Everyone bundle up," he says.

We pull on our matching Disneyland sweatshirts, climb from the warm truck, and quietly close the doors.

Silence. The close, cottony silence of snow. The wind moves, and out of complete darkness comes a sudden swing of blue light. Our faces move up in unison to see thinning clouds float coolly past a full, glowing moon. And still the snow falls.

We huddle together beside the pond. Heavy black clouds bring darkness again; then wispy ribbons and the silver-blue moonbeams set the snow glowing. We pull our hoods back to watch the sky glow, then go dark, glow, dark, glow, dark. Unreal blue light, unnatural blackness.

Still more snow. The power lines along the road droop listlessly, bearing the unfamiliar weight. Electricity is probably out all over town. We are silent in the silence. Around us the graves are more still than ever, cozy beneath their thick white blanket, fragile flower blossoms peeking out, marking headstones. The weeping willow bends, limber, dips into the black glass of the pond beneath the soft weight of snow.

Dario has Ana's bag. He goes to the pond's edge and crouches there. The water is alive, each snowflake sending a million concentric circles spreading, joining, moving. He stands and steps back.

A little light pierces the black water. It floats, burns fiercely in the dark, sheltered by wings. Bright red wax-paper butterfly wings on a tiny balsa-wood boat. Somehow they kept it safe all the way here, the whole way home. Butterfly boat. It bobs and sails in the falling snow, glides to the center of the pond, fragile wings protecting precious flames.

We breathe the clean, frozen air and we are not cold.

"Sorry I missed your birthday," Dario says. "How was it?"

Emily's grave, bright with candlelight just last night, warms me. *"Habrías estado orgulloso,"* I say, and it is true. He would have been proud.

He hugs me, practically collapses my lungs.

Ana and Elanor pile on, all amazed we're here. We are weepy. We are a mess.

"Ana," I say, "I love my pony. My Emily."

Still strange to say her name out loud.

She kisses my cold cheek. "I've told Dario enough with the skeletons." She reaches once more into her Mary Poppins bag of magicalness and presses another familiar twine-bound tissue package into my hand. "I made this for you. We hid it with the rings—don't ask. . . ."

"Yeah, okay."

"With the cocaine," Dario whispers.

She gives him another look. Squeezes my hand. "Happy late birthday."

It is a butterfly, shiny silver on a sparkly chain. In the moonlight I barely see but can feel tiny indented dots outlining the edge of each wing. Mourning cloak. She turns me around, pulls my Disneyland hood aside, secures the clasp at the nape of my neck. The butterfly rests cool against my throat. Which swells, of course, now that I'm the World's Biggest Crier, so instead of actually saying thank you, I hug her and hug her.

The snow falls on us.

On Dario, on Elanor.

On Emily.

Clouds float, cold, ethereal, past the moon. I turn to Emily on Poppy Hill.

Sierrawood is all glittering white hills glowing silver in reflected moonlight. They could be hills in any park, in any forest. Except beneath them sleep the peaceful, quiet graves. They are still here. Emily is here. I do not pretend otherwise. It can never be otherwise.

Ovid knew the truth; there is beauty in this impermanence. In this metamorphosis.

Dario holds Ana to him.

Elanor beside me. My friend.

The butterfly boat burns bright.

It's kind of too much. But mostly it is perfect.

epilogue

AT THE WILLOW GATES of Rivendell, Balin and Elanor wait. It's early Friday morning one week later. They're in their pajamas. Kai jumps out so Elanor can sit beside me, and Balin climbs in last to snuggle up to Kai.

"You guys," Elanor whines. "Ick! Too early!"

"Hey, Leigh." Balin nods.

"Good day, sir. Got your dice?"

"Always."

"Excellent."

"I have your birthday present," Elanor says. "Sorry so late. Close your eyes."

Over the rearview mirror she slips a crystal sea star, silver thread strung with blue sea glass. It swings rainbows across our faces.

"Oh jeez," Balin says. "You guys and the crystals."

"Dario loves them," Kai says.

"No, he definitely does not. He's a dude."

"He said he does!"

"He's just being nice."

But I think Balin is wrong. I think Dario loves the crystals because Ana does. Like the Christmas lights we made sure were lit, so she saw them, bright through the falling snow. So she would feel welcome. So she would stay.

Elanor reaches up, sets my crystal spinning.

"I love it," I tell her. "Thank you."

She sits back, smiles.

"Happy driving!"

∞

Sea grass waves tall and slender on the bluffs. We stand at the precipice, so close to the jagged cliff edge we taste the salt spray of waves crashing against the rocks below.

The warm winter Mendocino sun.

"Ahhhh, the sea. *The Sea!*" Kai yells into the wind.

"Okay now, Meredith," I sigh.

She laughs.

Balin reaches around my shoulders, a strong one-armed hug. "Not bad," he says.

"Yeah," I agree. "It's pretty good."

I'm getting used to all the hugging going on lately.

Ship bells ring.

"Oh my gosh," Elanor breathes. "This is— I cannot believe we're here. I love the ocean. I love a road trip. I love you having your license. Do you hear me? *Love! It!*" She sits in the warm grass, and I do, too; the wind whips our violet cotton skirts around our knees.

"Okay," I call out. "Dinner?"

"Cap'n Flint's," Kai votes.

"And tomorrow?"

"Glass Beach. Bay View for lunch and ice cream."

"*Glass* Beach?" Elanor says. "Like *sea* glass?"

"It's where the mermaids live," Kai says.

Two nights, all of us in sleeping bags in one room at a bed-and-breakfast, and I've finally got what I've wanted. Empty Pre-Need folder. Empty nautilus toiletry bag. Empty shoe boxes beneath my bed.

I can start again.

The mourning cloak butterfly shines silver at my throat.

Waves fill my ears, my head, my heart. The sea-salty wind pulls the tops of the waves to us.

"Teach me when we get back?" Elanor says.

"To drive?"

"Yeah."

A gull floats past, tips its wings to glide low over the water.

"You'll love it," I promise.

Dario and Ana are home, tending Emily for me until we get back, even though I know the truth, because I believe Ovid.

Those things, he says, *that nature denied to human sight, she revealed to the eyes of the soul.*

She is here, home beside the ocean. She is with me. With us.

We stay until the sun is only a glow at the horizon, tall

ships sailing west to the Undying Lands, waves singing the evening in. We lie back in the grass, beneath a pink sky in this impossible beauty, and my heart is warm and fast, full of love for the waves. For the warm sun. For being here, together. For it all.

author's note

I WAS IN EIGHTH GRADE when my dad and one of his running club pals bought our town cemetery, partly as a financial investment but also so he could say "I bought a graveyard!" at parties.

My sisters and I picked up rocks in the grass among the headstones for the sake of the mower blades, weeded flower beds, and planted bulbs, and now and then we took off our muddy gloves to file papers or answer the office phone. One summer the regular receptionist/grave salesperson took an extended vacation, so I filled in and—I am not making this up—the first customer on my first day was At Need, there to bury his son. That guy cried. *A lot.*

At Need is commerce mixed with grief, an odd cocktail from the same bartender who brought us *Commerce + Love = Huge Expensive Weddings. Commerce + Death = Pre-Need* means carefully planned caskets and flowers and headstones and a new black dress because apparently navy blue is insincere and I'll never make *that* mistake again.

But oh, *Commerce + Grief.*

This is sitting across from people so heartsick they can't breathe for crying, and your instinct as a normal person is to comfort them, but instead you've got to keep asking them questions about money. And sure, they came to you expecting this, and yes, this is your job, so you keep it together, but *God.* Eventually they take a cue from you and pull themselves together long enough to get the money part over with, when what they really want to say is "Just do whatever, I don't care, it doesn't matter." Because it doesn't. Still, someone has to prepare the body, and someone has to dig the grave or fill the urn. Someone in the mourning family must be voted to take the checkbook and keep it together while someone else sells them a grave and keeps it together.

I wasn't in the office for long, and never under duress. But at the desk and out in the graves, the whole "grief as commodity" thing really started to get to me, which led me down the rabbit hole of the unequal distribution of who gets to fall apart and who has to keep it together. When do the keep-it-together-ers get to be the fall-apart-ers, or do they never have a turn? It made me want to yell at everyone standing over the open graves, *This is not a contest!* I watched people bogart grief (and the attention it got them) like you wouldn't believe, while someone else just as sad had to provide ballast in the storm with silent calm. Keeping it together.

Six Feet Over It is a story about a girl keeping it together. Maybe she shouldn't have to, but she's good at it and someone has to do it, so she does it until she just—can't. And then what happens?

If she's lucky, maybe what happens is she finds people who take her hand and help her raise it. So she can ask for her turn.

acknowledgments

HEARTFELT GRATITUDE TO:

Melissa Sarver. A saintly patient magician of an agent is gift enough, but one willing to stick to her author's various guns and who is also a whip-smart editor with a refreshing lack of tolerance for foolishness? Words cannot adequately express my gratitude to her, for her.

Chelsea Eberly, who found the real story hidden among a few hundred thousand superfluous words and showed me how to tell it. How I got so lucky to have her for an editor is one more mystery, like all the best in life, that will never be solved. So I'm content to just be endlessly thankful.

Mallory Loehr and her team at Random House Children's Books for rescuing this book from limbo; her New York number on my caller ID nearly gave me a stroke. Still not over it.

Amazing. And Jenna Lettice for her tireless efforts and remarkable patience.

Alison Kolani and the copyediting staff at Random House for ridiculously meticulous, sharp minds—and pencils.

Sarah McCarry; first to read, first to give me reason to keep writing. Elizabeth Kaplan and Suzy Capozzi for loving the story. Margaret Kelso, Charlie Meyers, and Bernadette Cheyne at Humboldt State University. The Belt and Hermann families for an apparently bottomless well of detail and memory. Daniel Lazar, Jenni Holm, Lisa Brown, Jessie Sholl, Jen Nadol, Sangu Mandana, Cheryl Klein, Chris Baty and the staff of NaNoWriMo, and Beth Lisick and Arlene Klatte of San Francisco's Porchlight Storytelling Series for writing guidance and inspiration.

Brett Douville, John and Coe Leta Stafford, Stephen McManus and Renee Diascenti, Julia Thollaug, Julia "J. K. Rizzle" Neal, the Wallach-Neal family, Jean and Ruby Fife, Carmel Adams, Erin Wright, Brad Comito, Lida Jones, Karen Corby, and Amy Wagner for early reads and immeasurable kindness. Sarah Nelson for a place to write in Seattle. Ellen Harding and Christine Falletti for friendship, comfort, and rallying when revisions made me cry. And always.

My family: Joe Hart; Daniel Slauson; Patrick Clark; the Temmermans; the Kiekhaefers; James, Henri, and June Longo;

and Tim and Vickie Longo for unfathomable love and encouragement. Robert Irvin for more than I can say. Sarah and Alex Neuse for open hearts, willing shoulders, steadfast love. Analise Langford, inspiration incarnate, whose own metamorphosis was a wonder to behold. My sister, Christine Kiekhaefer. Writer, reader, editor. There from the start, there for it all. My heart. I could not do without you.

Cordelia Longo: A reader to write for, a writer to learn from, you are the reason for it all. Fearless heart, best person I've ever known. Thank you.

Timothy Longo Jr.: This one is not for you but because of you.

about the author

JENNIFER LONGO holds an MFA in Writing for Theater from Humboldt State University. She credits her lifelong flair for drama to parents who did things like buy the town graveyard and put their kids to work in it—because how hilarious would that be? Turns out, pretty hilarious. Jennifer lives in Seattle with her husband and daughter and writes about writing at taotejen.com.